"I'd like to m said.

He took her raise
continue. "I like you, Beck. You like me. And you want more sex in your life."

"Yeah, but not willy-nilly."

"Nothing I'm proposing is willy-nilly. I'd like to offer you companionship, conversation and sex while you look for the man you want to marry. Or until our relationship has burned its course."

"A little man on the side."

"Little? Come on." He tried to act insulted, but the way her hand came up to her mouth in embarrassment was too cute not to laugh.

"But the on-the-side part is right?"

"I guess, yes. You are free to date other people. I'm free to date other people."

"So why would we be dating each other?"

"Because we like each other. *And* because you probably need time to kiss a few frogs before you settle on your prince."

Dear Reader,

Like *Dating by Numbers*, this book emerged out of my own forays into online dating. I... well, I wasn't good at it. I met the Viking, fell in love and got married, so I was successful, but "good at it" seemed to mean I went on a lot of dates (I didn't) and knew what I wanted out of the experience (I didn't). You think, *Everyone is telling me to do X, so I'm going to do it.* But X isn't you, and you can't fight you. Enter Beck. Happily married when you first meet her in *Dating by Numbers* and on her way to divorce at the end. Confused, frustrated and scared by the entire experience—but determined.

From stage left comes Caleb, who claims to know what he wants and what he's doing.

The truth, of course, is that dating *is* scary. There are those who admit it to themselves and those who don't. But we're all fumbling our way through until we meet the person with whom our muddy waters suddenly clear.

Oh, and for those curious, the pictures of my dog got more likes than any of the pictures of me.

Happy reading,

Jennifer

JENNIFER LOHMANN

Her Rebound Guy

 HARLEQUIN® SUPERROMANCE®

Recycling programs
for this product may
not exist in your area.

ISBN-13: 978-1-335-44927-6

Her Rebound Guy

Printed in U.S.A.

www.Harlequin.com

Jennifer Lohmann is a Rocky Mountain girl at heart, having grown up in southern Idaho and Salt Lake City. When she's not writing or talking with librarians around the country about reading, she cooks and laughs with her own personal Viking. Together, they wrangle three cats. (The boa constrictor is better behaved.) She currently lives in Durham, North Carolina.

Books by Jennifer Lohmann

HARLEQUIN SUPERROMANCE

Dating by Numbers
Love on Her Terms
A Southern Promise
Winning Ruby Heart
Weekends in Carolina
A Promise for the Baby
The First Move
Reservations for Two

Visit the Author Profile page at Harlequin.com for more titles.

In memory of Tweedy, who was always there for me when I needed her. I'll miss you, dear friend. Take Seamus for a walk for me.

CHAPTER ONE

IT'S A BIT like shopping the J.Crew catalog back in high school, Beck Macgruder thought as she finished posting information about who she was and then took a look at the men on the online-dating site she'd picked to try first. Some of the men were, well, she hated to be uncharitable, but they weren't attractive at all.

Or, at least, she corrected in her own head as she scrolled past picture after picture, they hadn't posted a flattering picture of themselves. Perhaps they didn't have a flattering picture. Maybe they hadn't known better. Maybe they didn't have a friend to look at the pictures they posted and suggest something nicer.

There. That was a more charitable version of the story that had resulted in such a terrible picture posted on a dating website. It wasn't that they were unattractive; it was that they hadn't known it was a bad picture.

Picking a photo for a dating website was hard. Hard, of course, because there wasn't a soul on earth who could look at a picture of themselves with anything like an objective eye. At least Beck had been able to get the opinion of her friend Marsie, who had found a man through online dating. Or, not exactly *through* online dating. Marsie's fellow is a coworker of hers. They'd challenged each other to see who could find a partner first through an online-dating site, and then ended up deciding they were perfect for each other.

Right, Beck thought as she scrolled past another guy. Online dating wasn't a guarantee of finding the perfect guy. As Beck figured it, online dating opened your mind to the possibility that there was someone out there for you, so long as you were looking for them. It was like tempting fate, but in a good way.

And it's not like she was looking for one guy; she was looking for a lot of them. As she figured it, online dating was also a way to sample the merchandise before even deciding if she wanted to buy. Again.

Marriages weren't returnable and you never got back what you'd paid out.

She clicked on a guy with potential and scanned the information he'd included about himself. Ah, yes, just like catalog shopping. This one looked good, but he wasn't for her. This one was the male equivalent of spaghetti straps. Bandeau tops. He'd probably make someone else's arms look good, but not hers.

Dampness bumped against her knee and she absently reached down to scratch the head of the boxer-pit-hound-and-probably-something-else dog she'd picked up at the animal shelter several months before. Seamus was a good-looking dog. All the pictures she'd taken of him in the months since he'd joined her household included a big grin, ears that could flop or perk depending on mood and a tail that looked more like the handle of a delicate teacup than anything that should belong on an animal with a room-clearing fart.

Of course, he was adorable in all of those pictures, so she'd included one of him by himself and one of them together in the photos she'd posted to the online-dating site. Best for men to know that she had a "manly" dog. He didn't even eat vegetables, for God's sake. Especially since the other information she put on the site included that she was a coordinator of events, mostly weddings. And she had wicker furniture on her porch.

With her dog's chin resting on her knee, she hit the back button and scanned over her options again.

There. That guy would fit her like the perfect shoe. At least from his picture. Dark, messy, romantic hair and light green eyes. A man who would sit in her wicker rocking chair and read Byron's poetry to her. Romantic—at least that's what she assumed Byron's poetry would be like.

All swoony.

And, after a nasty divorce where she'd felt every last second of North Carolina's required year-long separation, Beck needed swoony.

She clicked.

Her disappointment must have rippled through her body, because Seamus huffed a little on her leg. Mr. Swoony wasn't an English professor. Or a poet. Or a playwright—a pale imitation of a poet, but it would match the curls in his hair.

Mr. Swoony did say he was a journalist, though. That was a *type* of writer and some-what swoony. And he liked biking. That was interesting. Long bike rides down some of the trails in The Research Triangle area. Maybe they would plan a complete Rails-to-Trails ride from the mountains of North Carolina to the coast. She could picture his hair curling out from under the rim of his helmet along his neck. And, oh yes, there would be picnics.

Beck could make a mean picnic. After years of working events and in restaurants, she knew how to choose food that would be easy to eat no matter the circumstances. Bride wearing a dress with long bell sleeves that brush across the table? No problem. Bride with a healthy décolletage who doesn't want to fish food out from between her breasts before the honeymoon starts? No problem. Food that packs nicely, is good at room temperature and easy to eat with your hands? No problem.

She put her hand on Seamus's head while she considered her next move. Mr. Swoony looked like he would enjoy a nice picnic. *And* the kind of guy she would like to make a nice picnic for.

And Beck missed making a picnic for people. Neil hadn't been interested in picnics. Of course, she hadn't thought she'd be interested in picnics, either, until she'd clicked on Mr. Swoony's picture. It didn't matter what he called himself on his profile. She was going to think of him as Mr. Swoony. And she was going to click.

A wink, to start. Messages on the first night of exploration seemed a little forward. She still didn't know the rules of the online-dating world. She didn't even know if there *were* rules. Heavens, despite all this data and Marsie's insistence that online dating could be hacked with the perfect algorithm, online dating still seemed like the Wild West of meeting men. Which was why she was starting small, with one site, even when there were newer, flashier dating sites available.

Though, Beck considered as she evaluated the next picture on the screen, online dating couldn't be any more Wild West than going to a bar and trying to look pretty.

Not that she would admit doing either to anyone right now. Everyone from her mom to Marsie to the servers at Buono Come Il Pane said she should wait a little longer before dating again.

"Get that husband of yours out of your head." That bit of advice she rejected out of hand. Neil had been her college boyfriend and the only man she'd ever seriously dated. How could she get him out of her head if she didn't have an idea of the kind of man who could replace him? Or even if a man should replace him? Seamus might fit in that companion spot nicely. And then there was the option of empty—empty could be good.

"Find yourself." Which was stupid, because Beck knew where she was and she had a dog who snored in her bedroom to ground her to the fact that she was here, in her house, and Neil—the dog hater—wasn't.

"You're young. Take your time." She paused a little every time that objection came up. Not because it was one hundred percent valid, but because it wasn't a hundred percent *invalid*. She was thirty-two. Not *young*, unless she was being compared to her parents, but not old, either.

Maybe the biological clock existed. Maybe it didn't. But something in her head had been ticking nonstop since Neil moved out—and before then, if she was going to be honest with herself, here in the privacy of her own home. She wouldn't let the annoying noise of others run her life, but she wouldn't *ignore* it, either. *Enough*.

Marsie's single piece of advice had been not to let online dating be the way she measured *anything* about her life, and it was the one piece of advice Beck had listened to. Getting responses wouldn't determine her self-esteem level. She wouldn't only look for dates. And, while she generally rejected Marsie's insistence on all things scheduled, she would at least set up a schedule for checking her profile responses. No reason to have online dating become another Facebook that she trolled because she was bored.

On the other hand, she thought while Seamus sighed for his dinner and a walk, winking at *one* guy felt like a tacit admission that the men online weren't all that interesting. Or that she felt over her head. Or that all those people were right and it was too early for her to be here.

With only a quick glance at the pictures and a more cursory look at the profile information, Beck winked at a few other guys. Then she logged out, snapped her laptop shut and put the thing someplace inconvenient while it charged, just to lessen the incentive to obsessively check if any of the men had responded to her wink.

When she stood, Seamus hopped on his hind legs. He didn't jump *on* her—they'd been working on that—but he bounced. When she reached for the leash, he bowed and barked once, sharply, before running to the door and trying his doggy-darnedest to sit at the door through his excitement and get his leash attached to his collar.

Once she and Seamus stepped into the fading winter sunlight, online dating was forgotten. Mr. Swoony included.

THE PROBLEM, CALEB Taggert thought, with scheduling dates anytime during when the General Assembly was in session was that you couldn't control when the men—and it was mostly men talking—would shut up. In theory, everything and everyone had a time limit. In reality, the battles of the General Assembly waged on and on and on. And had for years now.

The guy talking now had been talking for hours. Okay, so maybe it wasn't hours, but Caleb had stopped taking detailed notes and was letting his recorder do most of the work. The representative had stopped saying anything new or interesting at least ten minutes ago. The bill under discussion was this man's pet project and he was going to say what he wanted to say. For reasons Caleb didn't know, but probably had to do with some backend deal he *wanted* to know about, committee leadership wasn't cutting this guy off. Of course, half of what he said was bullshit. Caleb's copy for the Sunday paper would include a lot of fact-checking and reminding the people of North Carolina about the rules regarding voter registration, IDs and the history of poll taxes.

The Civil Rights Era had a long tail, with battles like gerrymandering and voting rights seeming to stick to his beloved home state like dog shit to a shoe. The only bright spot—if one could call it that—was that debates like this one reminded Caleb why he'd become a reporter and who he was responsible to. The representative blathering on would be an entertaining guy to have a beer with, but there wasn't much else good Caleb could say about him. But the constituents whom the man shook hands with when he was home deserved to know what he did with the faith they put in him.

Caleb's article would also include some nice details regarding the recent polling about gerrymandering and one-voter-one-vote done in his home district. Stark comparisons like that made good copy.

Finally, the guy stopped talking about voters counting twice, voting in districts where they weren't registered and—the money shot of scare tactics—undocumented immigrants voting. The session was about to be wrapped up and then all the people crowded into the committee room would spill out onto the lawn for a rally in favor of election-map reform. He'd need to stay for that, too, and talk with some of the protestors. The paper was sending a photographer over—there were bound to be some good signs and probably an arrest or two.

Politics in North Carolina hadn't been boring...well, they'd never been *boring*, but they'd certainly gotten more interesting in the past ten years. Power grabs tend to do that, no matter which party has its grasping hands out.

Caleb had a date in thirty minutes and a twenty-minute drive looming before he could hope to park. Of course, the representative who had driveled on about voter fraud had no knowledge of Caleb's personal life and wouldn't care if he did. The paper didn't care about his personal life, either. He had other reps to interview, copy to write and deadlines to meet. None of which was conducive to his evening plans.

Caleb gave in and pulled out his phone.

Diatribe about made-up voter fraud or not, he tried to adhere to the current research about phones, distraction and meetings, and he usually kept his phone hidden when he should be paying attention to someone else. Especially on a day like today, when the rumor was that a bill limiting the people's right to protest was going to be snuck onto the end of this bill—not quite in the dead of night, but they would certainly try to do it when no reporters were watching.

Besides, the research said loud and clear that "people can't multitask." It's just that researchers never established whether boredom to the point of drool counted as multitasking.

Plus, he had his recorder going. If the guy slipped and mentioned that he had just bought a house outside of his district—well, Caleb would have that shit on tape. And the rumor about the rider with limits to protesting had come from an excellent source, one who would get Caleb the rider as soon as she saw it.

Power grabs also made for strange bedfellows. Swiping down on his phone screen brought a list of notifications, most of which weren't a surprise. Twenty work emails, three of which promised information in exchange for keeping the sender's identity a secret. Ten personal emails. And a text from his dad.

Whoa-hoe… What was this? A notification from one of the dating apps he used. A wink—so a passive sign of interest from someone, rather than anything active.

Before he clicked to see who the wink was from, he texted his current date with information that he'd be late because of a work meeting and that he would bow to her wishes whether she wanted to wait, reschedule or call him an ass and kiss him goodbye.

After a quick glance up to make sure he wasn't missing anything, Caleb flicked the notification open. Dogfan20895 was cute. Square jaw, but a big, toothy smile that more than made up for it. Dark brown eyes. A wicked way of lifting her eyebrows—wouldn't that be fun to see her do in real life. Given that she had one photo of her with a brindle hound and one picture of the hound itself, she wasn't kidding about being a dog fan.

But…she had a nice set of breasts and he couldn't get over how arched those brows looked, so he winked back. Then he looked at her pictures again. Her smile was nice. The way she was laughing in that picture of her with her dog was even better. Caleb clicked the message button and typed out something quick.

Hey. Cute smile. Cute dog, too. What's his name?

It wasn't his best opening line, but he was working, supposed to be meeting another woman for a date and hadn't read her profile yet. She'd either bite or she wouldn't.

The world—especially the online-dating world—was full of women. If she didn't at least nibble, well, there'd be another woman along with a smile that suggested she knew what he was up to.

CHAPTER TWO

"I DON'T LIKE the wall color," the statuesque blonde with her hair up in a neat French roll said as she swept her arm around at the creamy, peachy beige that made up the walls of Buono Come Il Pane. "It's too…bland. My wedding won't be bland. It will be *different*," the prospective bride said with the same finality she'd used for every proclamation she'd made about her wedding.

Different. Special. Unique. Memorable. All a lot of requests for something special out of a woman named Jennifer. Not that there was anything wrong with the name, but…

But the name was on every tenth woman, or so it seemed. Being one of a hundred Jennifers in any given square mile probably contributed to her desire for a unique wedding. Beck could be more forgiving.

Maybe.

Buono Come Il Pane hosted events of all kinds. Graduations. Retirement parties. Anniversaries. Birthdays. And weddings. Beck loved weddings the most—she really did. Her divorce hadn't changed the fact that she loved happily-ever-afters and romances and engagement stories. But there were particular brides she didn't love, and this woman seemed likely to walk down the aisle as one of them.

"Buono Come Il Pane's decoration evokes the warmth of Tuscany," Beck said. *Buono Come Il Pane* translated to "good as bread" and it meant something like "good as gold." They served a small menu of finely crafted Tuscan food. They didn't boast of the size of their wine list, letting the quality of their selections speak for themselves instead. The interior design was much the same—not spare so much as elegant.

"Its simplicity isn't for everyone, of course. That's a decision you and your fiancé have to make." Beck glanced at the groom, Tanner, who'd come to the appointment with his future bride. He'd come—Beck would give him that. But that seemed to be the only nod he'd make to participating in planning the event that would cement his life to another's.

Maybe he had a stressful job, she thought. Or perhaps he was worried about a friend of his. Or had something else on his mind, other than the wedding. There, Beck thought, satisfied that she'd turned her irritation with his silence around. The prospective groom was here to support the love of his life, but they both knew he had a lot on his mind because…work. Work was a nicer reason than a sick friend he might be worried about.

Beck smiled charitably at the man before turning back to the woman, who was standing with her hands on her hips, looking thoughtfully at the walls.

"I don't suppose you could paint the walls…" Jennifer said, trailing off.

"No. It is important to us that we make our brides happy and that their wedding day is special, but we can't repaint the walls."

"Well, rats," the woman said. Beck tried not to laugh. The woman was high-maintenance and, despite all her talk about special, unique and different, had no idea what she wanted her wedding to look like. But she had said "rats" with such honest disappointment that Beck couldn't help but try to like the woman.

"Buono Come Il Pane has a specific look and a specific feel. Might I ask why, if we're not what you wanted, did you make an appointment? And why are you still considering us? We'd love to be the right place for you, of course," Beck hastened to add, "but we know we're not the right place for every bride and it's important that you're comfortable with the location you choose."

"This is my dad's favorite restaurant," the future groom chimed in from his spot against the wall. "If we pick here, he'll chip in half of the wedding costs and her parents will give us the difference for a honeymoon."

"Our house down payment," the bride said. "That's a better long-term decision."

See, Beck's inner nice chided. *It's good that you decided to like the woman. She's like all the other brides, trying to plan her future in the best way she knows how.*

Even if she wants you to repaint and will probably want different linens. And different silverware. And won't like the wine options. Or the food.

But she was a woman who was trying to figure out what she wanted and was determined to make it happen. That was worth a nod of respect, if nothing else.

"Money is important to consider when deciding on wedding venues. It's easy to spend more money than you'd planned on and then be strapped later. I can't tell you what to do, but we offer a basic set of options for brides, things that we think best show off our restaurant and the beauty of the occasion. If those aren't what would make your wedding day the party you've always wanted, then perhaps we're not the best place for you."

It was easy enough for Beck to turn down one bride. Buono Come Il Pane was booked for June over a year in advance and the rest of the year's availability was usually gone eight months in advance. When she was done with this appointment, she had a bridal event to plan for and she usually came out of those events with a couple more bookings.

Plus, a happy bride was the best possible advertising. An *unhappy* bride was the worst. If the woman was going to be unhappy with her wedding at Buono Come Il Pane, it was worth the money to pay her to go away.

"We might be willing to accept this restaurant's style," Tanner said, interested in the conversation now that money was on the line. "Right, honey? It could be worth our time."

Jennifer smiled indulgently at him. "We want to honeymoon in Belize, and we have our eye on those private suites on stilts out in the water. Right now, it's a *wee* bit out of our price range. Though, a down payment for a house would still be a better investment."

"Well," Beck said with a clap of her hands and quick glance at her watch. "You both have a lot of thinking to do before you decide on anything. Personal opinion, spend a lot of time— separately—thinking about what you each want. Then come together and make sure you overlap on the big stuff. That you're not giving up anything that's important to you. That's really life advice—" the kind Beck wished she had taken "—and a wedding is a good place to start. It is the beginning of your life together."

"Huh," the groom said as he turned to stare back at the walls and art, clearly no longer interested in the conversation.

But his bride evaluated Beck more closely before asking, "Are you married?"

For most of her career, she'd loved to answer "Yes" and tell the bride that she'd had the most beautiful wedding under the sun. To say that they were blissfully happy. That she wasn't always a bridal and events planner, but a bride. That she had been the magical bride, happy enough to walk on water, and had known what it was to come home to a loved one, share a glass of wine and chat about your day.

But those days were over. "I'm not," she said, not willing to go into any details with a customer and a stranger.

"Divorced?"

"Well, yes. So I know of what I speak when I say you need to think about what's important to you and make sure your fiancé feels the same." She and Neil had always felt perfect for each other, until they weren't.

The bride leaned in close to Beck, like they

were teen girls sharing a confidence. "Tanner and I met through online dating. It's possible, you know. The trick is to make sure you pick the right dating site. Some are for people looking for easy…" She paused, words rolling through her eyes before she settled on, "Companionship. The good sites attract men looking for marriage and commitment. Pick one of those."

"Thank you," Beck said surprised. The woman wasn't giving her new advice, and she was a stranger, but she meant her advice honestly. Sincere, much like Beck had been when telling this couple to think about what they want before settling on a wedding venue.

"I'm looking," she said, hesitant to confide too much to a stranger and prospective—though unlikely—customer. "I'll admit it's hard."

Though, there was that message waiting for her when she'd come home from the walk yesterday.

She'd thought about that message all through making her dinner of roasted beets, blue cheese and pita bread—all things her ex-husband hadn't liked. Eating her dinner, she'd still been thinking about that message. At that point, the amount of time she had been putting into thinking about the message had seemed excessive. And a little scary.

So much portent put into a little message by someone she didn't know and might not even like. So much power in that little notification at the top of her cell phone.

She understood now why people said that you couldn't take online dating personally. She hadn't even been twenty-four hours in and already that message felt like life or death.

So, she'd made a deal with herself. No checking the message until she hadn't given it a thought for *at least* five hours. By her count, when the bride had mentioned online dating, it had been four hours and fifty-seven minutes, not counting the hours she'd spent sleeping.

Close enough.

Jennifer patted her on the back. "You'll get there. It's hard, but it will happen. You'll get your Prince Charming," she said with a loving glance at her fiancé, who was looking too closely at the art on the walls to really be looking at them at all.

"Thanks. I hope you're right." Beck had only been separated for a year and divorced for twelve days, but she knew she wanted to get married again eventually, even if she occasionally pretended otherwise. The saying about fishes and bicycles was all well and good, but what if the fish *wanted* a bicycle? What if coming home to a bicycle had been better than coming home to nothing?

Take your time. Learn to love yourself alone. Spend time looking at all those couples you work with. Then *you will know what you want out of your next husband. Get right into that dating pool or all the good ones will get away. Make sure to use a good moisturizer. Once you start getting wrinkles, it will only get harder.*

All the advice was well-meant and none of it helpful. The fact that one piece of advice often contradicted every other piece of advice, sometimes out of the mouth of the same person, only muddled her already muddy mind more.

"You seem like a good person," the woman said, giving her another long look. "So, I'll give you a little more advice. Stay away from the handsome men."

It was rude, but Beck couldn't help glancing at the woman's fiancé. He was good-looking enough—on the cusp between someone she thought would look good on someone else's arm and who would look good on her arm.

"Tanner's good-looking, but not handsome," Jennifer said under her voice. "And as my grandmother used to say, handsome is as handsome does."

Beck wasn't entirely sure how to take this

piece of advice, so she said, "I'll keep that in mind," and decided to leave it at that.

If his picture was anything to judge, Mr. Swoony was handsome. She smiled to cover up the desire to beat her head against the wall. The message might not even be from Mr. Swoony. It could be from someone else altogether. Mr. Less-than Swoony, for example, or Mr. Rotten Eggs.

"Thank you, to the both of you, for coming in today," she said, her hand outstretched for the prospective bride to take. "Even if you decide that Buono Come Il Pane isn't for you, I'm glad to have chatted with you and we appreciate you thinking of us."

"Oh, of course. Tanner's father insisted. And this does look like a nice place."

Nice place, hah, Beck thought, the advice and comments about the wall colors and thinking about handsome men getting to her.

If only getting remarried didn't have to involve *dating,* this process would be much easier. Meet a nice guy. Fall in love. Get married. That's what she'd done in college, with Neil.

And here she was, newly evaluating what she wanted out of her future. *That,* at least, was a lot like college.

Once the happy couple left, holding hands and whispering to each other as they walked out the door, Beck went back to the tiny room they called her office and sat in front of her computer. Before she got back to her planning document for the bridal event she was working on, she pulled her phone out of her purse and checked the message.

Hey. Cute smile. Cute dog, too. What's his name?

Mr. Swoony had written back. Her shoulders fell with a relief that she would be embarrassed to admit to anyone. Whether or not she should need validation from a stranger on an online-dating service, getting it felt better than *not* getting it and that was the darn truth.

Before writing back, she checked her other notifications. No other messages, just a couple of winks and a couple of likes for the pictures she'd posted. She held the phone up a little closer to her face to see those likes of her pictures.

Well, she thought as she sat back in her chair. *There's a fine how-do-you-do.* All three likes on her photos were on pictures of Seamus.

At least men seemed to like her dog. She hoped he appreciated how popular he was among the men online. Mr. Swoony had even taken some of the precious real estate in his short message to say he was cute.

For a brief second, Beck thought about changing her profile picture to one with her and Seamus, but then decided she was over-thinking the whole thing and needed to stop before she drove herself crazy.

Instead, she did what she thought was the reasonable thing and replied to Mr. Swoony's message.

Thanks! Seamus, my dog, is a sweetheart. Stinky breath, but really, what dog doesn't have stinky breath? You said in your profile that you like to hang out in downtown Raleigh. What's your favorite place? I loved Busy Bee and was enormously sad that it closed.

What will I do without those tots?!

Her finger hovered over how to sign the message. With her name? Mr. Swoony hadn't signed with his name. Maybe names just weren't done at this stage in online dating. Maybe they were supposed to get to know each other a little better.

Maybe he's not an online-dating veteran, either, and everyone in this room knows you're overthinking this, Beck. Self-chiding done, she sent the message and called herself done with online dating for the day.

She had work to do and better things to think about than a romantic-looking guy who, if she were to believe today's bride, was too handsome for his own good.

WELL, HELLO, CALEB thought as he read the message on his phone from Ms. Dogfan while he waited for his takeout, sitting in one of the plastic chairs in his favorite Chinese restaurant. Like the tables, the chairs were mostly for decoration. No one ate here—they ordered off the sign above the counter and got their food to go. The food was good and the restaurant catered to the busy professional who didn't have the time or energy to figure out how to use the kitchen.

Or, as in Caleb's case, only swept the crap off the kitchen counters when company was due over.

He'd shove everything into his office and shut the door for Ms. Dogfan. She hadn't written very much, but it was cute. Short. Succinct. Charming enough to make him want to know more. That and her smile was enough to write back.

Ah, yes. Busy Bee had the best tater tots. And huevos rancheros. You could never go wrong with their brunch. It's not a bar and it's not tots, but have you had the fries at Chuck's? I'm partial to those. And the milkshakes don't hurt.

Seamus, huh? That seems like a good name for your dog. Does he have a green collar? And do you buy him a little green bow tie on St. Patrick's Day?

—Caleb

There. That was enough to keep the conversation going. After all, these emails were really about deciding if they wanted to meet in person. Best not to give too much away and either not live up to the email charm or say something so phenomenally stupid that the woman wouldn't be interested in meeting at all.

Not exchanging lots of emails was part of the trick, too. Emails gave you time to think about what you wanted to say, to edit your words and your tone. To rethink. He'd been on a couple of dates with women who'd been absolutely enthralling over email but flat in person.

Likely, a few women had thought the same about him before he'd learned to offer a date early—like three quick exchanges in.

"Thirty-five," the man barked from behind the counter. Abby, his daughter, must be at soccer practice tonight, because she wasn't working the register. She was a bubbly girl who chatted with the customers as she rang up their orders; she even shared little details of her life with her favorites. Caleb knew how to ask questions, so he knew what college she wanted to apply to—North Carolina State University. What she wanted to study—Fashion and Textile Design. And what her parents thought about her dreams—nothing good.

Caleb felt for the girl. He'd disappointed his parents, too, despite trying to do the opposite when he'd started writing for his college paper and discovered that he loved it. Whenever Abby complained, Caleb gave her the same advice that every young adult needed to hear—life was long and your life almost never turns out as planned, but it usually turns out okay if you let it.

Much like online dating, Caleb thought as he accepted the plastic bag of food Mr. Lin shoved across the cracked laminate.

His phone rang as he approached his car. Only after he'd opened the passenger door and shoved enough papers out of the way to have a place to put his food was he able to reach into his pocket. A missed call from his sister, Candice. After he got settled, he called her back.

"Caleb, you have to get me out of this date." Her voice echoed against the hard surfaces of whatever room she was in—probably the bathroom.

The hairs on the back of his head stood at attention. "Do I need to come get you, get you out of this date?"

"No. It's not that bad. Just, I said yes to a date with a coworker and I shouldn't have, because, awkward if it doesn't work out."

"Just tell the guy that you're not that into him." He was backing out of the parking spot, which is why he didn't notice the silence on the other end of the line. "You've slept with him already, haven't you?"

"Is it better if there wasn't any sleeping?" He groaned and she tsked. "Not like you have any room to judge."

"Dating is a game and it's not an even playing field." Like life and all the best sports, there was a strategy to dating, and Caleb had studied it. Not that he *abused* the tricks he knew—he wasn't out to prey on women or trick them into a date they didn't want. But he wasn't going to sabotage himself, either, and he fully expected the women on the other end of the computer to be using the same tricks—or be in the process of learning them.

But he knew the rules were stacked in his favor. Candice *generously* shared with him all the dick pics she'd gotten, even though he assured her that one was enough. But he'd rather look at "the log," as she called them, than any of the screenshots she'd sent him of men calling her a bitch when she wouldn't show them hers.

"You say that…" He didn't need her to finish her sentence. They'd had this argument many times, usually when she called him because she'd gotten herself into a sticky situation.

"You've got to think about," he started to say, stopping when he heard her voice finish the admonition, "what your desired outcome is."

Candice said her desired outcome was a steady job, steady housing and a steady boyfriend. Then she would do something like have sex with her coworker before she knew if she liked him, put her job at risk and—this was his baby sister, after all—then she'd likely find out the guy was also her new roommate's favorite cousin.

"You sleep around." A familiar argument for a familiar ride home.

"I like women. I'm looking for company for a night or two. Nothing else."

He liked how soft a woman's skin was and all their laughs and the variety of their bodies and their smells. Whenever his coworkers said he was a lady's man—almost always with a raised eyebrow and a twinge of jealousy in their voices, even the married ones—he told them they could be, too, if they started liking *all* women and approaching them with metaphorical open arms. Women knew when a man was listening to them just because he wanted to get some. And make no mistake, Caleb liked sex and usually wanted some with the woman he was on a date with, but he'd enjoy the conversation and the company whether sex was on or off the table.

He'd watched a few of his coworkers approach women at bars during happy hour. Some women they wanted to listen to. Some they just wanted to bang. And in other cases, it only seemed to matter that they had two X chromosomes. Women could *feel* the difference in the way a man approached them, and they responded accordingly. And men couldn't fake it. They were either genuine or creeps.

The car in front of him stopped suddenly and Caleb had to slam on his brakes, holding out his arm to stop his dinner from flying forward into his dash. The phone, sitting in the center console, nearly spilled out onto the floor. If his sister landed in the pile of papers covering the floor mat, he'd never find her. And he'd never hear the end of it. He might have embraced the idea that all journalists are pack rats, but his sister still called him a slob and wondered what the appeal of the unkempt writer was.

When this special series on election maps was over, he'd bundle all this paper up in a box, nicely labeled, and pack it in his attic, until the next story buried him.

He recovered enough from the near accident to pay attention to the phone call and hear his sister's voice fill his car with, "Maybe all I want is a man's company for a night or two."

"Then walk out of the stall you're in, head to the guy's table and tell him the one night was fabulous—"

"It wasn't."

"You're about to dump him. You can lie about the fabulousness of the night."

"Do you lie to your dates?"

"We're talking about you and how you're going to tell him that the one night was all you wanted. And you're going to stop telling men how you need to find a nice guy. That's what gets you into these situations."

"I *do* want a nice guy."

"No, you don't. Like me, you want a good time and a disappointed father."

Candice's giggle carried Caleb down the street to the entrance of his own neighborhood. "Did you get a text from him today, too?"

"The one about the Kerrs having their fourth grandchild? Yup."

"What if this guy gets mad?"

As he turned into the small road leading to his townhome, he repeated the same thing he always told her. "If he gets mad, then you made the right decision. If he doesn't get mad, he might be worth another night of a good time."

Then he remembered what his sister had said about her one-night stand. "Only not this one, since the first night wasn't that good of a time."

As he put his car in Park, he thought about the book he joked about writing. *Dating Advice by Caleb.* Something to compete with those creepy pickup artists who advocated cornering women and never taking no for an answer.

His goal was good company, great sex and no long-term commitments, in that order. He was also just fine with the idea that a woman had sovereignty over the decisions she made about her time and her body.

"I just got home. We good?" He turned the car off.

"Yeah. He probably suspects something is up. Mad or not, he won't be surprised."

"Uh, no," he agreed with a laugh.

"You have a hot date you need to get ready for?"

"Hot date with a continuing-education class on writing narrative nonfiction." Tonight, his relationship included not alienating his computer by spilling fried rice on it while he finished his copy. He needed the keyboard to still like him enough that he could pursue his own passions after meeting his deadline.

"I didn't know you were interested in writing nonfiction."

"I'm a man of surprises."

She laughed hard enough to practically bray. "No, you're not. You just think you are."

"Go out and break a man's heart. Send me a text and let me know how it goes when you're done."

"Bye, bro."

"Bye, sis."

Once they'd hung up, Caleb tossed his phone in the bag with his food and prepared for the usual night of a single man, rather than the nights all his coworkers imagined he lived. If he were feeling especially frisky, maybe he'd ask the cute dog lover to meet him for drinks. That was all the action he could handle tonight.

CHAPTER THREE

BECK STOOD ON the sidewalk outside a cocktail bar in Durham's small downtown, trying not to look stood up. It wasn't easy. With all the people out and about early on a spring evening, there wasn't much space to stand with anything approaching nonchalance.

Caleb, aka Mr. Swoony, was late. She looked quickly at her phone. Okay, calling him late wasn't entirely fair, since she had been fifteen minutes early. She'd rushed *everything* today, starting from the moment she'd sat bolt upright this morning, an hour before her alarm had gone off. She'd had three cups of coffee, two more than she usually had when she woke up. But she'd tried to waste some of her extra hour over coffee and a magazine. It had been that or stare at her closet and rethink what she'd planned to wear today, which was guaranteed to be a bad idea. Of course, too much coffee had given her the shakes, which meant her homework assignments for her art class were a mess.

And then she'd stared at herself in the mirror, trying to figure out what first date hair and makeup should look like. And she'd changed her mind about what to wear before settling back on the ruffled cream-colored dress with a peachy cardigan, seafoam green scarf and matching bangles. Later, when she'd called her friend Marsie—who had been dating *forever* before meeting the man she was set to marry—her unhelpful friend had told her not to worry about what she was wearing and instead think about what she would talk about with a stranger.

Knowing what to say to a stranger had never been a problem for Beck, but finally she had decided Marsie was right about the first part. She pulled out the outfit she'd planned to wear originally, got dressed and then left for her date.

Of course, she'd driven too fast and there hadn't been any traffic, so her plan to sail casually through the door of the bar at exactly six in the evening wouldn't work. Now she had to try to make it look as though this wasn't her first date since...college.

And, as it had for the entirety of the day, trying was failing her. As she shifted from foot to foot to foot and wondered where to rest her hands, she probably looked like a woman who'd already had too much to drink and was about to have more.

"Beck?"

She started at the smooth, deep voice that said her name from the left. "Caleb?" she asked as she turned. All this time she'd been staring out to the parking garage to the right, not expecting him to come from the left.

His shoes were nice. Casual black loafers, well-worn, but not scuffed, like he both wore them a lot, but also took care of them. Dark jeans with trim hips and the hem of a light purple button-down.

And an outstretched hand, which she took before meeting his eyes. But when she did meet his eyes... God, they were as light green in person as they had been in his pictures. Not only were they an unreal light green, but they were smiling, and his entire face was surrounded by pitch-black hair that made it look as though he'd just gotten out of bed in the best possible way.

He might be the most handsome man she'd ever seen in real life, and if it wasn't for the slight crook in his nose where he'd probably broken it, she'd think he stepped out of a photoshopped magazine spread.

He was slender and tall, too. Willowy, without being weak-looking. Frankly, it was all a bit unreal.

She smiled back at him as she took his hand. Well, if this was going to be her first date in over twelve years, at least she was starting on a high note.

"Nice to meet you," she said. God, his hand was warm, even on a cool late-spring night when he wasn't wearing a jacket. He was probably perfect and did things like keep the woman in bed next to him warm, even if she always had ice-block feet.

"Likewise. Shall we?" He swept one hand onto the glass of the bar's front door.

"Yes."

He opened the door for her and she took one step into what felt eerily like her new future.

BECK WAS NERVOUS enough that her hand shook as he had gripped it in his. She even walked like she was nervous, with her shoulders up near her ears and quick, rabbit-like steps that made the ruffled bits at the bottom of her dress bounce about her fine legs. And her square jaw had tightened as she'd smiled, rather than opening in the bright grin he remembered from her profile picture. Her rich brown hair was shoulder-length and feathery around her chin and collarbone.

She was just as cute as she'd been in her profile pictures, with intelligent eyes and an open face. In fact, her nerves were endearing. Caleb couldn't remember the last time he'd been nervous on a date, nor could he remember the last time he could recognize that one of his dates was nervous.

Her profile said that she was divorced. If he had to guess, she hadn't been divorced long. Once inside, he stood back to watch her move as she approached the bar.

"Hi," she said to the young woman wiping a glass dry. Then, to his surprise, she stood on her toes and her legs looked almost a mile long sticking out of the bottom of her dress. The hem of her cardigan lifted, though not enough for him to see if she had a nice ass.

He was trying to figure out what she was all about when she said, "That's a nice dress," to the younger woman behind the bar, who beamed wide with pleasure. "That's a Marauder's Map on your dress, isn't it?"

"Yes, ma'am," the girl says. "You like *Harry Potter*?"

"Doesn't everyone? Or everyone who knows anything." Beck sank back on her heels and Caleb could see that she was smiling.

Well, isn't this different. Caleb had been on hundreds of dates and planned to go on hundreds more before he died. Many of those women he'd gone out with had been nice.

They'd been friendly to waitstaff and kind to the person who helped them in the shop. But Beck struck him as different. She was one of those rare people who was kind to people because she saw each and every person in front of her as a unique and interesting individual who was worthy of getting to know.

That was different from someone being polite because they were supposed to or because they were a cheerful introvert. Even through her nerves, Beck exuded a warmth that even the bored-with-life hipster behind the bar responded to. Caleb had been to this bar what felt like a thousand times, both on his own and with dates. The bartender had never looked back at him with a real, honest-to-God smile, no matter how polite he was.

Beck was different, alright. If Caleb had to guess, he'd say Beck was one of those people who hugged strangers and they didn't mind.

He was so lost in his own thought and evaluation of her that he didn't notice she'd ordered and paid for her drink until the girl was handing over a martini glass with a purplish liquid in it and Beck was agreeing to start a tab.

"Anywhere you want to sit?" she asked, turning to face him.

There weren't a lot of seats in this bar to begin with, and his favorite date table was taken. "How about that one?" he asked, gesturing to a booth away from the door.

"Sounds good," she said and then stepped away. He stayed put but continued watching her make her way through the people until she was at the table he had gestured to. Then she got out her phone, typed something quickly, and then seemed to turn the volume down and put the phone into her purse.

He'd turned the ringer of his phone off back when he'd parked his car. And it was a point in her favor that she'd done the same and tucked it away where it couldn't be a distraction. He turned back to the bar and ordered his gin and tonic and some bar snacks. He ignored the little voice in his head that told him his life was changing today. His life had the possibility of changing every day, with every breath.

Beck was sweet and he dug the intelligent sweep of her eyebrows, but she wasn't going to change his life any more than any of the other women before her had. Even if the smile she greeted him with held a hint of mischief.

CHAPTER FOUR

"SO, TELL ME about your dog. Why is he named Seamus?" Mr. Swoony—she supposed she should be calling him Caleb now—asked as he lounged in the bar's booth. *Lounge* was a quiet word for the sprawl of all his limbs across the fabric. Only a man at ease with his body from tip to toe could so easily extend his extremities without worrying about whacking over the large vase of flowers next to his right hand.

He was probably good in bed. A man that comfortable with himself had to be good in bed, right? Or, maybe, it meant that he only thought of himself. What did she know? Neil was the last man she might have looked at and evaluated how good he'd be in bed, and yet she couldn't remember if she'd ever done that. Since it had been college, probably not.

She took a sip from her Aviation cocktail, smiling a little. At her thoughts. At her lack of experience. At the big leap she felt like she was taking into life. She wasn't smiling at Caleb, exactly, until she caught his gaze and a shiver of pleasure ran down her spine.

Definitely good in bed. More certainly, it had been over a year since she'd had sex and that was long enough to make a woman imagine orgasms in every man's gaze.

"Seamus?" She looked away quickly before she actually imagined what the sex would be like. That sounded too much like committing herself to a roll in the hay, and she wasn't sure she was ready to do that. Over a year might be a long time, but she could wait longer. She wasn't looking for an open barn door.

"The shelter said he was found muddy, in a swamp. The woman who found him and cleaned him up said he looked like a half-dead beast dragged out of the bogs." She shrugged, a little self-conscious. "It made me think of Seamus Heaney."

He raised a black brow, which made her more self-conscious. "Poetry, huh?" Then he smiled and her self-consciousness disappeared with his casual acceptance.

"I'm proof that English majors get jobs."

He barked a laugh. "So am I."

They shared another quick glance that made her toes tingle. It was harder to look away this time.

Friends told her that she needed to know

what she wanted with this whole dating thing, but they hadn't told her how to know what the person she had a drink with wanted out of the experience. Well, except for the bride, Jennifer. But Jennifer's advice had only been to pick the right dating site and avoid handsome men. Caleb was in direct violation of at least one of those pieces of advice.

What did Caleb want?

Unable to bring herself to ask that question, she asked, "What do you do?" instead, spinning her martini glass on the table. His profile had said he was a reporter, but that was vague.

"I write for the Raleigh paper. Politics. I cover the General Assembly."

That set her back a little in her seat. "Not a simple job. And always something to report on." Anything happening in national politics had to have a run in the state first, sometimes including the out-and-out battles.

"All those bills made in the dead of night. I have trouble keeping track," she confessed. "And the laws they pass don't seem to relate to anything. What does women's health have to do with motorcycle safety laws?" She'd been against that one on principle. And Leslie was one of her favorite people to work with, so she'd been against the bill that banned people from bathrooms and even called her representatives about that one. She was prouder of her stance when she learned later that the bill had included a bunch of other stuff about restricting local government. Frankly, she was generally against bills coming out of her state capital on principle. Maybe she would be for them under different, more open circumstances, but she didn't know what was in them because they were presented and passed within hours.

Secrecy was bad, and being against secrecy was easy. That was a political stance she could get behind. But having to admit that she struggled to keep track made her feel like she was out of her league, especially when the only other thing she could think to add was, "Your job sounds hard."

He smiled, like he heard it all the time. But also like he enjoyed his job and was not-so-secretly pleased every time someone said, "Oohh."

"It uses my writing skills, which is good. And I like talking to people, and being a reporter gives me an excuse to ask people questions. And," he shrugged like he was humble about his job, even though she could tell he wasn't, "I think freedom of the press is important. So, I'm glad to be a part of that."

"You said English major, not a journalism major. Do you have a wild tale of career changes? Some dark experience in your past that made you determined to expose evildoers and right wrongs?"

"Like a bite from a radioactive spider?" He had the most delightful shrug. Comfortable and agreeable, like he'd seemed to be all night. She tried to imagine him tracking down sources—if they even called them sources—or badgering someone he was interviewing until they gave away their secrets. Tried and couldn't. He seemed too slippery to be hard, and she didn't even mean slippery in a bad way. More like water, flowing around obstacles and making its own path.

And, like water, he could settle into a comfortable stillness, which he did as he answered her question. "I liked to write as a kid, tell stories and make up lives of the neighbors' pets. I'd sit them down and ask them questions about their day, then report the gossip to my parents."

His face froze for a moment, so clear that she thought she could see all the way to the bottom of his soul and some inner hurt he was trying to hide, but then he smiled and the secrets he might be keeping were obscured by the mask he wore.

A reflecting pool she would be tempted to sit and think next to suddenly revealing the soul of the water sprite inside.

"My dad didn't like me telling those stories," he said. "Especially after Mom died. She'd been the person who liked to hear them most. 'Kids' nonsense,' he used to say, and he would tell me I was too old to be playing make-believe."

His cheeks were smooth, his eyes were wide and clear, and anyone glancing over at their table wouldn't think he might be saying anything upsetting. For all Beck could tell, he didn't consider this to be an upsetting story.

Still pretending, she thought. Only he doesn't realize he's pretending anymore.

"That's the kind of guy my dad is, you know. Old-fashioned. Men are men and that means stoic faces and no talking to pets. So, I would tell the stories to my younger sister and we would play television. Game shows and TV news, with me reporting on the pets. For some reason, my sister always reported on weather and sports." His voice softened when he spoke about his sister, and that was cute. And, if she were honest, made her a bit jealous as an only child.

"Anyway," he said with a shake of his head that cleared the emotion out of his voice, "Once I got to college, I thought I should be a writer, because I liked to tell those stories. My room-mate worked for the college paper and I tagged along, writing stories for them. I covered town politics and how it affected the college."

He snorted. "I used to joke that college town politics were a lot like the politics of the pets— all that emotion sharing a tight space. One Christmas, I was watching the nightly news with my dad and sister. I don't even remember what the reporter was talking about, but I remember my dad complaining about politicians and 'the man' and the cheats. It's not like he did bad. He was a car salesman at a nice dealership and he made a good living, but he seemed to always think the world was keeping secrets from him and those secrets were why he wasn't doing better."

Beck nodded in sympathy. "I grew up in DC. I really should know and understand politics better than I do, but it always seemed too... *opaque* is the word I want, I think. And getting older hasn't made it any easier to understand." She hadn't paid that much attention, either. Both because North Carolina politics were dead-of-night things and because politics, like her parents, had always seemed cold.

"Yeah. That's how most people feel, I think. My dad is my audience, even though he thinks I'm as crooked as the people I report on."

She winced at that admission.

"*I* understood what the reporter was talking

about. The local politics I was reporting on for the school paper are almost as far from national politics as a cat is from a dog, but they're still pets and I understood pets. My dad didn't and still doesn't."

"Reporting seems like a manly job. Smoke-filled backrooms. Secret committees." She knew what it was to have parents who didn't approve of your work. Her parents had been remote and never deigned to talk with her about their jobs, but they were still shocked when she didn't follow in their footsteps.

Her parents thought she was a glorified waitress. They didn't see how she made memories for people or why that might be a worthwhile job.

"Some of it is contamination by proximity." This shrug was less effortless. "Politicians are all crooks and, since I count some politicians as my friends, then I must be a crook, too."

"And are you? That seems like the sort of thing I should know, even if this is a first date."

She meant it as a joke and he laughed, both of them pretending that what she'd said had actually been funny. For all the momentary glimpses she'd gotten of his soul, his surface might as well be a thick sheet of ice. Short of some thaw, she couldn't see in.

And he can't see out. Or in, either. There was

a little boy in there still hurt by his father's disapproval, and that little boy didn't talk to the man sitting across the table from her.

"I don't think my dad *wants* to know more about the rules that govern his life. If he knew, he might have to do something about the things that make him unhappy. And some of it is that he doesn't like his son knowing more than he does. To him, I'm still telling stories and by stories, he means lies. Holidays at my house are a barrel of laughs."

He snorted again, a wry noise offset by his embarrassed half smile. "I don't know why I'm telling you any of this, especially after one drink on a first date. Normally, I just tell people that my sister and I played television news as kids, but I like writing more than I like television news, so here I am. That's the sanitized version."

It was her turn to shrug and she tried to make it the easy, careless movement he'd seemed to perfect. "I'm easy to talk to?"

"Yes, Ms. Dogfan, yes, you are. In fact, you are so easy to talk to that I'm going to get another drink. Want one?"

"Yes, please." She liked being thought of as easy to talk to. Nothing he'd confessed had been scandalous, but she knew why it felt personal. And she didn't think it was that she was easy to talk to so much as it was the dark bar, with soft music and bench seats that cocooned around them. A little bubble, where nothing they confessed to each other would escape.

Safe, she thought. He had felt safe talking with her, which she understood, since she felt safe sitting here with him, too. Which surprised her. Standing outside the bar, shifting back and forth on her feet, she'd felt like her nerves were radiating out through Durham's small downtown, forcing walkers to push through it like it was a heavy wind.

Those nerves had stayed with her as she'd ordered her drink and as she'd silenced her phone. Then Caleb had sat down, asked about Seamus and poof—all those nerves were gone. If he asked, she might lay out all her secrets on the table for him to pick through.

Might. She was determined to be smart about this whole dating thing and laying her baggage on the table for Caleb to examine was not even in the same time zone as smart.

Though, she considered as she watched the way he laughed with the bartender and chatted up other people at the bar, smart didn't seem like much fun when his lanky body was part of the equation. In the abstract, all the contradicting advice left her at sea in her own life, each life preserver she was being tossed leading her to an unknown shore.

She could land on Caleb. She'd probably be back adrift again, but kissing those shoulders might be worth it. And then she could say she tried. One less choice available to her.

She was still watching him as he returned with two drinks and a report of snacks. Carefree as he was—or as he was pretending to be, considering the story he'd told her about how he got into journalism—her staring didn't seem to bother him. "It's not dinner," he said as he sat down and told her what he ordered. "But we could go get dinner, if you want."

She cocked her head. "You just ordered us another drink."

"Well, yes." He looked amused and she wasn't sure what he was smiling about until he said, "Am I just a two-drink dude, or might you want dinner even after that second drink?"

"Oh!" He'd told her that personal and revealing story, which was sweet, but that he liked her well enough to think even an hour into the future hadn't occurred to her. *She'd* been thinking well over an hour into the future, but she'd been thinking about how good his black hair would look against her white sheets. Dinner hadn't played a part in any of those thoughts.

"Let's see how we feel after this second

drink and round of snacks. Maybe we won't need dinner," she said.

For a moment, she thought she saw the hurt of rejection flitter over his face, but then he seemed to consider what else she might mean. He put his hand on the table, palm up. "No dinner, huh?"

Emboldened by the soft lighting and a little alcohol, Beck put her hand on top of his. "*Maybe* no dinner. Depends on how hungry we are."

He raised an eyebrow. They were holding hands, or not quite. When he curled his fingers, the tips brushed her palm and she could feel his touch in her toes. "Does it also depend on what we're hungry for?"

"Yes."

"Your lead, Beck." Their hands were still touching, hers on top, both with the ability and acknowledgment that she could pull away at any moment. That he wanted her to be touching him, but wouldn't argue if she felt otherwise. She relaxed her arm, letting her palm fall onto his and curled her fingers around the side of his hand.

His recognition that she could say no made her want to say yes. It made her want to scream "yes" as he was on top of her, maybe kissing her neck.

Sex with a near-deadly handsome near stranger was an option to her now. She could take this man home with her. She could go home with him. The realization made her feel almost two feet taller. And she certainly felt stronger. There had been moments during her separation when she had realized that she could make her own choices, but for the first time, she felt like she was in control.

The second feeling was different and it was heady.

She didn't lift her hand when their snacks were brought over. He didn't move his hand, either, and they both switched off drinking and eating with the other hand. She didn't want to let him go.

Over their second round of drinks, he asked her about her job. Her second cocktail buzzed through her head. The room was dim. So, when he asked her what she liked about her job, she felt comfortable enough to confess the truth. "Honestly, it's been hard. I'm not a wedding planner and people come to my restaurant for other types of celebrations, but mostly it's weddings. I talk to a lot of excited brides who are certain that this is forever and, well, that's hard right now."

She looked at the bar for a moment, studying the bartender's movements and the way the woman leaned into customers she liked and leaned away from the ones she didn't. Once she felt less immersed in her own pain, she turned her attention back to Caleb. "It's a little easier now than it was. I'm no longer angry at my ex, at the world and especially at the happy couples."

She paused to take a sip of her cocktail. "Work is easier when I can celebrate *with* my customers, instead of pretending."

"Newly divorced, then?" he asked.

"My divorce went through..." She paused, pleased the date didn't pop into her head immediately. "A couple weeks ago."

She pressed her lips together, but the words slipped out anyway. "You're my first date since Neil left. God, which makes you my first date in over ten years."

He sat up straight, which amused her. He had looked so good when he was relaxed and easy in his chair. Sitting up straight, shoulders back, chin lifted didn't seem to fit his romantic, sensual lips. "Am I? Well, then, I shall be extra good tonight."

"You would treat me differently because I haven't had a date in forever?" For reasons she couldn't put her finger on, she found that offensive.

"I remember what it was like to be divorced. I felt like I was hunting around for the real

Caleb, who I was without my ex around. I didn't know what I wanted or why. The first woman I went on a date with gave me time to figure myself out. And she was patient when I freaked a little. It's a gift I would like to pass on to you."

She still eyed him suspiciously. "Should I worry that you're too perfect?"

"No pressure is the point. No one needs pressure, but you especially don't need it now."

"So, am I going to be disappointed by man number two that I date?"

He shrugged. "I can't speak for man number two. I hope not. But I understand men can be shits. I'm probably a shit more than I realize. Or would admit to."

She laughed. She couldn't help herself. He was open and disarming. It was almost an impossible combination to resist. She picked up the last olive and popped it in her mouth, and then took a sip of the last bit of her drink. "Let's go," she said, tightening her fingers so that she had a hold on his hand.

"Dinner?" he asked.

"I have food at my house." She could make her own choices and she was choosing him. At least for tonight.

"Are you okay to drive?"

She turned her head and knew the answer immediately. "No."

"Are you okay to invite me home?"

"Yes." She bit her bottom lip, but in for a penny, in for a pound. "I think I made the decision to bring you home when you put your hand out. I didn't need the second drink to loosen my inhibitions, but I did want to talk with you more."

"Give me a chance to mess up," he said, but he was smiling and there was no malice in his voice.

"I like to think I was giving you a chance to succeed beyond your wildest dreams."

"Tell you what. I'll go and close out our tabs. We can add your drinks to my bill. We'll get a takeout pizza from the place down the street so you don't have to make us dinner. Then we'll head to your place."

"Are you giving me a chance to change my mind?" For some reason, the idea that he might be doing that pissed her off. She appreciated the lack of pressure. She didn't need to be treated like a child.

"Hell, no." He caught her gaze and the air between them practically caught fire. "I'm hungry. I like pizza. And I plan on stripping your clothes off as soon as we step through your door." He hadn't needed to tell her his plans;

she could read them in his slow, sensual smile. "That won't leave you time to make us dinner."

"Okay," she said with a nod as she scooted out of the booth. She wanted this. She wanted him.

She waited by the door, watching while he paid for their food and drinks. His body was long and lean. He'd slouched and practically relaxed all through drinks, but he was also in control of each part from tip to toe. He lounged because he was completely comfortable in his body, not because he was lazy. He rolled with that confidence as he walked toward her. "Ready?"

"Yes," she answered as she slipped through the open door.

Out on the street, she took the elbow he offered and sank against him for the walk to the pizza place. She hadn't had so much to drink that she was unsteady on her feet, but she usually drank wine, not cocktails. And at home, not a bar. Plus, there had been all those months that she hadn't kept wine at home, for fear that it would become too quick a companion to her sorrow.

The Aviations were going straight to her head. The knowledge that she was going to have sex was going…well, it was going straight to the rest of her body, making her weak in the knees. Coming on her own wasn't the same as sharing the experience with someone. And Caleb was going to be a good person to share the experience with.

"Do you trust me to drive your car?" he asked, after they'd ordered their pizza and were back on the sidewalk, escaping the press of the crowded restaurant.

His question pulled her back, unhappily, to reality. She'd been happily imagining what his hand on her breast would be like and had to ask him to repeat himself.

"Do you trust me to drive your car?" When she looked up at him, the streetlight caught a twinkle in his eye that made her think he knew exactly what she had been thinking.

"Why?" She wasn't sure of the answer. Trust seemed a tricky thing in a situation like this. She had trusted his emails enough to say yes to the date. In the bar she trusted him enough to slip her hand into his and let him lead her wherever he wanted her to go.

Which just proved Marsie right. When Beck had wondered if she should invite a man back over to her house after a first date or go to a hotel or something, Marsie's advice had been to ask why she would be having sex with a man she didn't trust enough to see where she lived.

Beck hadn't had a good answer to that one.

She had read *The Gift of Fear*. She listened to her gut. And Caleb didn't ring any alarm bells with her. But that was sex and walking through her front door. She didn't know anything about his *driving*.

They were standing close to each other on the sidewalk. She felt his every movement and had to focus on what he was saying instead of letting her mind wander to how his body would feel, naked against hers.

"Well," he explained, "you don't feel comfortable driving. And driving won't be a problem for me. I could drive you to your house in my car and, tomorrow morning, drive you to come get your car. Or, I could drive you in your car to your house and I'm the one who has to come get my car in the morning. Me driving your car seems both the more gentlemanly thing to do and the most practical. If we were going to my house, I'd say we should take my car."

She looked up at him and bit her lip. *What if he wouldn't leave in the morning?* She'd been living alone in her house for over a year and, to be honest, quite liked it. The toilet seat was never up.

"Or," he said as he leaned against the building and she felt like she had space to breathe— to think, "we could take our pizza and eat it over on the tables at Five Points and we can go our separate ways for the night. And there are hotels. Nice ones. If you're looking for a night, but not another date."

He shrugged. "But I'd like to see you another time."

The shrug was the clincher, full of interest but no pressure that she raise that toilet seat because he expected it. "Drive me home. We'll have pizza and see where we go from there. That sounds good."

He peeled himself off the building and was back in her space again. She liked him in her space. Frankly, she wanted him to be in more of her space. For there to be no space. He probably had dark, curly chest chair and she wanted to run her hands over it.

"Great." God, even his smile was romantic, slow and full of promises. She was going to have sex. She was going to come. For the first time in months, she wouldn't be completely responsible for making it happen. And it was going to be awesome.

The woman at the hostess stand gestured to them from the other side of the restaurant's big windows. Beck stayed outside while Caleb went in and got the pizza. When he hit the sidewalk, a box of hot pizza in his hand, she fell into step beside him while they walked to her car.

She didn't say anything, wasn't even sure there was anything to say. It felt almost like losing her virginity for a second time—she could either babble out her nerves or let them keep her quiet company. She chose quiet company.

down a big hole to swallow him up. Adam's apple first.

That first night back in the game after his separation, he'd opened the door to the bar and his only thought had been to get from the door to an empty barstool without drawing anyone's attention to himself. When he'd walked up to the first woman who made eye contact with him, she'd said, "I'm—"

CHAPTER FIVE

BECK DIDN'T SAY a word the entire way from the pizza place to her car, three whole blocks. Caleb would have worried, but she didn't seem reluctant to be coming with him. Or to have him coming with her, since they were on their way to her house in her car.

Nerves, he figured. He remembered those days, right after his marriage had ended when he'd been at a bar for the first time, looking for company. He hadn't been very good at meeting women when he'd been younger. Memories from his early twenties bordered on painful. Whenever he looked at pictures of himself from those years, he couldn't take his eyes off the Adam's apple as big as his nose and the Ichabod Crane awkwardness, complete with trying to woo the beautiful Katrina with poetry. Caleb had kept his life, but there had been moments when he'd wondered if the poor schoolmaster had been relieved to have his humiliation disappear at the hands of the headless horseman. In those years, he certainly wouldn't have turned down a big hole to swallow him up, Adam's apple first.

That first night back in the game after his separation, he'd opened the door to the bar and his only thought had been, "Let me not be alone for an hour." Instead of poetry, he'd walked up to the first woman who made eye contact and said, "Hi, I'm Caleb," while sticking out his hand.

All his confidence about talking with random strangers after years of being a reporter puffed out in an embarrassing whimper when she'd said, "I'm taken," making her friends laugh. Except one of the women had come up to him at the bar a little later and introduced herself as "Sabrina, but my friends call me 'Not Taken.'" It was his turn to laugh. He'd stumbled through questions about her job and her interests and they'd ended up back at his house.

The nerves had only disappeared when Sabrina had left the next morning. And they'd shown up again and again and again for the first year as slowly the memories of shuffling his feet and bad poetry faded into the background. Sometimes he missed the nerves. He didn't miss being *nervous*, really, but that lack of nerves reminded him that he'd been dating for a long time.

That was not a thought he liked, though

he wasn't sure what the alternative was. And without dating, he wouldn't meet a woman like Beck. There was something about that square chin and big, round smile that did him in—reality was even better than her profile picture.

"Anything I should know about the car?" he asked after he'd put the pizza in the back and slid into the driver's seat.

"Nope. Drives like it's supposed to."

He turned the key. "Good. I like it when the *D* means *drive.*"

Unless she was giving him directions, Beck also was silent for the entire drive back to her house. Which was also fine, since Caleb wasn't certain he'd be able to hear her over the growl of his stomach as the smell of pizza permeated everything.

EVERYTHING WAS HAPPENING in slow motion, Beck realized as she stuck the key into her lock and turned it. Seamus was barking in the background. She could *feel* Caleb behind her, a large, mostly unknown presence that she welcomed, even if she wasn't sure what she was going to do with him. Or, she knew what she *wanted* to do with him, but she just worried that she was out of practice with the whole process, from pre-sex to post-sex. The last time she had taken a near stranger to her house was…well, it would have been her dorm room in college and they had both been drunk enough that she couldn't remember if she'd had a good time.

Since then, it had only been Neil. With a shock, she realized she was glad it wasn't Neil tonight.

As soon as the door opened and they both stepped in, her dog was there, bouncing up and down and making any need to talk to each other moot. Caleb actually got down on one knee, holding the pizza box up high. Seamus gave him one big lick before settling down for a solid ear scratch.

"This is the famous Seamus," he said, looking up at her. Seamus had a dopey grin on his face, his tongue lolling out to the side. The dog slobber added a shine to his nose, making Caleb even more perfect.

She nodded. "No green collar, though. Maybe for St. Patrick's Day."

He rocked back on his heels and then stood, still balancing the pizza box. "It'd look good on him. But the blue collar he has now looks good, too."

"Thanks."

They stood in her entryway, Seamus between them, looking back and forth, waiting for one of them to do something exciting. Give him a slice, probably. Lucky to be a dog and know both what he wanted *and* to not feel self-conscious about how to get it.

"What do we do now?" she asked.

"That depends on what you want out of the night." He held his arms out. It felt like an invitation, though she didn't step inside them. Not yet. "I'm here. If you changed your mind about what I'm here for, I'll take an Uber back to my car. No hard feelings. If you didn't…"

"I didn't," she interrupted. The last thing she wanted was for him to think she was changing her mind. "I'm just nervous. It's been…" She paused. "A long time since I've done this."

"Had sex?"

"Over a year for that. Divorce, you know."

"I know," he said with a slow nod and she felt that same instant connection she had in the bar, this sense that he understood her nerves and didn't judge her for them. That she was safe.

"And sex during marriage is different," she said.

"Well, sure. In the best case, you manage to be both experimental and steady about what gets the other person off. In the worst case…" He shrugged. She didn't need him to finish that statement. In the worst case, you didn't have sex and either your libido died a slow, lonely death or you relieved your frustrations else-where. Horrible cases, both.

"How about this? I need to wash the slob-ber off my face and Seamus probably wants a trip outside. Let's take care of the practicali-ties and come back to reassess. We can talk. Drink a little wine. There's pizza to eat. Calm the nerves a little."

"Am I the only one that's nervous?"

She must have caught him off guard, because his eyes went wide for a moment before return-ing to their regular, dreamy state. "I remember being nervous, but it's been a long time. Maybe it went away. Maybe I just learned to ignore it."

The other questions floating about her head settled into one decision. "The powder room is to the right. The kitchen is through there," she said with a gesture of her hand. "The wine should be pretty easy to spot, if you want to open a bottle. The glasses should be easy to spot, too."

"Okay," he said with a long stride in the di-rection she'd pointed. She thought about it for a moment, but then she decided to be amused by how easily he moved through someone else's house. If he was practiced, well, that would make the rest of the night, especially with her nerves, easier.

As soon as she heard the pizza box hit the

counter, she set her purse down and snagged the leash.

Seamus did his business and then wandered back inside and straight into the kitchen to check out the new person in the house and the pizza. Beck dashed upstairs for the condoms she'd bought after signing up for online dating. They might make it back to her bedroom for round two, but she had spent the car ride imagining the snap of his buttons as she undressed him, and she didn't plan to wait until after dinner. Nerves be damned.

Both Caleb and a glass of red waited for her when she walked into the kitchen. The wine glinted in the light above the center island. Caleb smiled at her and she had to take a deep breath before she was able to smile back. Tossing the strand of foil packets on the counter, she took the wine in her hand, tasted a sip just large enough to make her skin feel sensitive and then set the glass on the counter, next to the condoms.

He raised a brow at the string of condoms and then a corner of his lips rose as she took his glass from him and set that on the counter. But he didn't say anything. His eyes followed her every movement as she walked around to stand directly in front of him and then lowered as she stepped close to him. It was her turn to be in his space. He smelled a lot like pizza and a little like wine and Dove soap.

The tip of her nose touched the underside of his chin, nudging his face up to expose his neck. "So, do we kiss first?"

She could feel his smile as the muscles of his face changed against her nose. "Is this *Pretty Woman*? Kisses aren't part of the deal?"

He moved his chin a little and her nose bumped against his skin. "Which one of us are you implying is the prostitute?"

That question made her look up. His pupils had gotten big, making his eyes nearly a forest green with only the slight line of sea green around the edges. Angry? Aroused? Probably a little bit of both, given what she hadn't meant to imply. "I'm not sure what to do," she said.

"What do you want to do?" he asked, his voice deep and gravelly.

Beck pressed her two palms on either side of his face and pulled his head down to hers for a kiss. He had large, romantic lips and he knew how to use them. She sank into the kiss, sank into him and sank into the touch of another person.

She could disappear.

Their lips stayed connected as he sidestepped a couple feet to one of her barstools and hopped up on it. He opened up his knees and pulled her in between his legs, nibbling the edge of her lips and cradling her body in his. He was hard; she could feel that through his jeans and her thin skirt. Strong thigh muscles, too, probably from the biking he said he was into—her last conscious thought before he shifted forward in the stool, slipping his hands down her back to her butt and pushing her forward. The movement pressed the wetness of her panties against her and the evidence of her own desire aroused her more.

"This will be my first time in a long time," she said after she pulled her mouth away and was dropping kisses on his jawbone. He had a sharp jawline and the scruff of his beard was rough against her skin. A good kind of rough. A rough that she would remember tomorrow, long after he had left.

"I know." He leaned back in the chair, pressing harder against her. "You mentioned that."

Emboldened by his casual acceptance, she shifted so that she could kiss her way down his neck. As she worked her way down from his neck, the buttons on his shirt popped open with the same satisfying noise that she had hoped they would. He sucked in his breath when she took his nipple into her mouth, the mess of dark hair she'd expected tickling her nose.

She had never wanted to enjoy the male body

so much in her life. Never before wanted to explore its hard edges and soft lines, to match a kiss and a touch to a noise of pleasure. Like water, she'd thought of him before, only now he was water in a desert and she was thirsting. His fingers slipping beneath her underwear to her pussy hinted at the relief of a deep drink, though pressing her forehead against his chest wasn't enough to quench her ache. His fingers stroked and twirled and played. If she didn't think, she wouldn't remember to breathe. Then there were no thoughts left to be had, no breath left to be had and she came in a glorious, light-filled rush.

"My turn," he said.

She was too empty to pay much attention as he shifted her around a bit to undo his jeans and slip a condom on. His hands were back on her butt, lifting her and moving her, and suddenly she was straddling him on her tiptoes and he was inside her.

"Oh, God," she said in a hot breath. "I have missed this."

"Yeah," he said, moving her on him in long strokes. His palms gripped her tightly, his fingers prodding into her flesh and guiding her where he wanted her to be. "Like it?"

"Yes," she said, throwing her head back and pushing herself forward, pushing him deeper.

Sex was great. She hadn't forgotten, just hadn't wanted to remember, so that she didn't feel lonelier. With Caleb inside her, there was no reason to feel empty. Plenty of reason to look at him, though. She snapped her head back forward so she could see the way the muscles of his face tightened with his pleasure, enjoying the tensing of the ligaments of his neck and feeling the hot burst of breath against her cheek as he grunted with his efforts. Her first sex in well over a year and she was going to memorize the details, hold them out and examine them when she was lonely.

His hands stayed on her butt while his nose bumped up against her face. A handsome, kind, interesting man buried deep inside her. He'd given her pleasure and she was giving him pleasure. This—this man and this moment—was what she had been looking for when she'd signed up for online dating.

Especially *this man.* When she turned, his lips caught hers, and with one gentle bite, he held her mouth against his. Then his muscles stilled and he grunted with a couple last hard pushes inside her.

He lay his forehead against her and they stayed still, connected and intimate. Then he shifted, pushing her gently away. "I've got to go take care of the condom."

"Of course." She pulled herself off him, feeling empty as he slid out of her and headed to the powder room. She had missed sex. But she had especially missed married sex, where sex didn't have to end because of a condom, but you could stay joined until the man's cock softened enough that he slipped out. She missed a man's softened cock between her legs in their shared dampness.

Well, that wasn't going to happen while she was dating. That was a committed, monogamous relationship feeling only.

She shimmied a little and adjusted her panties so they were back in a comfortable position. Married sex was a thing to miss, but this non-married sex had been wonderful and she'd take advantage of it for as long as she could.

She swiped the empty foil packet off the counter and tossed it into the trash. After Caleb was out of the bathroom, she slipped in and she washed her hands. To her pleasant surprise, Caleb was already getting out plates for dinner.

"I hope you don't mind," he said as he rested two plates on his forearm. "I figured we were both hungry, so I should get everything as ready as I could."

"I don't mind at all," she said, enjoying the truth of that statement. He stood in her kitchen like he belonged there.

CHAPTER SIX

CALEB TOOK THE plates to the dining room while Beck grabbed flatware and wineglasses. They both came back for the pizza box and wine bottle. Which had come first, she wondered, his ability to move through another person's space with no self-consciousness or his reporting? He'd said he started reporting with his college paper, and it was fun to imagine him busting into the dean's office, some hot question on his mind and his reporter's notebook in hand.

For some reason, she didn't picture him as a hot college student with his romantic hair and intense green eyes. He'd probably had the eyes, but she imagined him more awkward, with a buzz cut, maybe, and needing time to grow into his limbs. It fit better with how at ease he could make her feel—like he knew what it was to be out of place and ensured those he cared about didn't feel that way.

Cared about. Silly turn of phrase after one

date. If she wasn't careful, she'd get ahead of herself.

"The pizza's gotten cold," he said, pulling her out of her imaginings as the box slid out of his hands to the table.

"It'll be good anyway. And it was a good trade-off," she said, with a shy smile, the idea of caring about someone after one date lingering in the back of her head. What did it even mean to care about someone? And how much did letting a man inside you change that? How much did being inside a woman change that?

Did sex have to change it at all?

"Absolutely," he agreed. "This is a nice room, by the way."

"Thanks." She hesitated, with more she wanted to say on her tongue and too much on her mind to remain light and funny. Of course, he'd not remained light and funny with her— not with that story over drinks. If he could share something so personal, so could she.

She was at least that brave. And he was at least that safe. "One night, not long after Neil moved out, I was sitting on one of the barstools, eating a frozen dinner, when I realized that I had this huge house and was only using one bathroom, one bedroom and the kitchen. So I've been eating in the dining room ever since."

"Making the space your own. I remember

that feeling," he said with a nod, and she knew she'd made the right choice—the right choice about everything tonight.

Caleb reached out and opened the pizza box. To Beck's surprise, he first grabbed her plate. "How many pieces do you want?"

The pizza smelled amazing. It had lamb meatballs and kale, and she could eat every slice, if she put her mind to it. Back when Neil had first moved out, she'd been afraid to allow herself any indulgence, for fear that she wouldn't be able to stop. Like with the dining room, she'd been letting her fear ruin her enjoyment of her house, of food and of her life.

"Two, please." They were small pieces, and she had come a long way since Neil had moved out.

He placed two pieces on her plate and then set it in front of her and filled up her wineglass. "Mind if I take the rest?"

"No. Help yourself."

"Thanks." He took the other two pieces and then sat back in his chair.

They each ate a couple bites in silence until Caleb took a sip of wine and cleared his throat. Beck looked up from her own food. "I was the one who moved out. I moved into this random town house. It was the first thing

I could find after we decided to separate. I still live in it, actually."

He took another drink of wine and she realized that, for the first time tonight, he *was* nervous—though he probably didn't realize it. "I spent the first three months thinking, 'this is where Leah would put...' whatever it was I was holding in my hand. She was particular about where she put stuff, more so than I am. I think it took longer for me to get used to putting pictures up where *I* wanted them to go than it took me to get used to sleeping in a bed alone."

"I'm still not used to that," she admitted before she took another bite of her pizza, which was salty and rich and delicious. After she swallowed, she said, "It's one of the reasons I got a dog, actually."

"Seamus sleeps on your bed?" he asked, with a raise of one eyebrow as he looked around the room for the dog. "Will I fit, too?"

Her forty-five-pound hound mix sat patiently by the edge of the table, waiting for handouts. Begging was on the list of things to work on, after he stopped jumping up on people.

Beck shook her head and chuckled. "A dog on the bed seemed like a good idea at the time, but Seamus doesn't like sharing a bed with me any more than I like sharing a bed with him. He likes his personal space. I don't like to be kicked. I got him an expensive dog bed for the bedroom and now we're both happy."

"Good. I was hoping to stay the night. And I don't share."

Warmth from the pizza, the wine and the heated look in his eyes spread through her body. "I was hoping you would, too." He would wrap around her body quite nicely in a bed, her butt tucked against his crotch and his arm draped across her shoulder. Both naked, because they'd just had sex and she was the satisfied kind of sleepy that only came post-orgasm.

Yes, quite nicely indeed.

The thought was as delicious as the pizza.

"Like you, I miss sharing a bed." He put his wineglass on the table and picked up the last slice of pizza on his plate. "It's not enough for me to want to get remarried, though."

And—like God had snapped Her fingers— all her warmth was gone. "Not get married again?"

"No. Divorce was horrible." There was pain in his voice and his eyes, though when he blinked, it seemed to go away and he was back to being a charming man who seemed to have no problems. Did the mask fit so well that he'd forgotten he wore it?

"Fifty percent of marriages end in divorce." He recited the words with the flat expertise of a man who dealt in facts for a living. "The odds aren't good, especially given how *bad* the bad can be."

"But…" She took a deep breath to control the sinking feeling in her chest. "The good can be really good. I remember being happily married." She remembered the fighting *more*, but the good memories were in her head. Somewhere.

He shook his head. "I'm not sure I had anything good enough to make the bad worth it. Leah isn't a bad person—we just suffered the difficulty of two people making a life together and not picking that right person to do that with."

"Why date?" She wanted to get to know the world of men, sure. Have some sex and have a good time. But getting married had always been at the back of her mind, even if she hadn't agreed to this date thinking that Caleb would be *the one*.

"For the same reason you are. Companionship. Conversation. Sex."

"But not marriage."

"Not long-term, no."

Beck was silent for a long time while she processed what he meant, what that meant for their night and what the rolling of her stomach was trying to tell her, especially when she still wanted to curl up in his arms and feel the soft puff of his breath on her neck.

Her silence didn't go unnoticed. He put his pizza down and assessed her. "Have I said something to upset you?"

Yes. "I'm surprised is all."

"I didn't think you would be looking for marriage. Not now, right after your divorce has gone through."

I didn't think so, either. If asked, she would have said she wanted to get married, but that first she wanted to date around a bit. Learn about men in their thirties, instead of in their late teens and twenties. She would have said exactly what Caleb had assumed.

But hearing it said back to her… No, that wasn't what she wanted. Not that she had assumed she would stay with the first man she met, but she didn't know how to have sex without thinking about something long-term. Not that it had to lead to marriage, necessarily, but that marriage had to be a possibility. It couldn't be so far off the table as to be on another continent.

To buy herself some time, she reached for her wineglass and took a sip. Then another. Then another. Once some of the warmth was back, she experimented with a white lie. "I can't say I'd thought about it one way or the other."

Mostly true. Hardly counted as a lie at all.

"I didn't send you a message or arrange this date expecting a wedding ring in a year."

Completely true.

He let out a long breath. "Okay. Good. You're interesting. You're incredibly sexy and we've got enough of a connection that I didn't want to be sent home." He gave her a look bordering on naughty and said, "The sex was good."

"The sex was good." She wanted more of it. With Caleb. And she wanted to fall asleep with their limbs all in a tangle and the possibility of morning sex between them. Marriage was still a long-term goal. This night, with him, was her short-term goal and she was going to meet it.

If nothing else, she was going to prove to herself that she could do it. What *it* was, she wasn't exactly certain. One-night stand, maybe. Let herself be comfortable with a stranger. Not pin her hopes on talking him into something she believed in, but he might not want. Not try to convince him of the rightness of her ways.

That was a short-term goal that matched up with her long-term ones.

Her mind made up, Beck popped the last bite of pizza in her mouth. "In fact, I'm done eating. I say we take this wine bottle up to the bedroom and see just how good more sex can be."

His smile was wide and romantic, back to the

Mr. Swoony that she'd called him in her mind. "I'm game for that."

Beck wasn't quite on her game as they joked and laughed while cleaning up their dinner. But she wanted sex again, and so she pretended, knowing she wouldn't have to fake the orgasm. And, right now, that last part was more important.

CHAPTER SEVEN

BECK HAD BEEN right about not needing to fake her orgasm. The force of it—brought on by Caleb's magical tongue—should have put her right to sleep. Should have, but it didn't. Instead, she lay in bed all night—Caleb breathing softly next to her and Seamus snoring softly on the floor—wondering what she was going to do in the morning.

Was this a one-night stand?

I've never had a one-night stand. But I've got nothing against them and I'm supposed to be trying new things. No reason a one-night stand can't be a new thing. I've never had one, though. You've never been divorced before, either. The goal is not to figure out your future based on one night. You don't even have to know now what you're going to do come morning.

You don't have to decide anything now.

And so it went. All night, in an exhausting bout of self-doubt and confusion.

Though not exhausting enough to put her to sleep.

But by the time Caleb had woken up and his hand had reached out for her skin, she knew that she was going to end their relationship as soon as they got out of bed. Trying new things, not pinning her hopes on one stranger…all of those things were fine, but company, companionship and sex with no end goal in sight was not something she wanted.

The one thing she wasn't confused about was how much she had missed having sex. And an orgasm was definitely on the list of things she wanted, and Caleb was good at giving them, so she pushed herself into his exploring hands and reached out to do a little exploring of her own.

CALEB PRACTICALLY SLID out of Beck's bed, uncertain if his legs would hold him. Three orgasms in the span of twelve hours would do that to a man. "Mind if I clean up a bit?" he asked over his shoulder.

"You can take a shower, if you like. There are extra towels in the cabinet. I'll make coffee."

Beck's voice had an edge that cut through his fog of sex and morning and had him turning around to face her, suddenly conscious of how naked he was. "Is everything okay?"

She was resting against the headboard, the

sheets pulled up to her neck, hiding a magnificent pair of breasts. Clearly, he wasn't going to have those nipples in his mouth again this morning, but he hoped for the next weekend. Maybe another night this week, if they could both swing it with work schedules.

"I didn't sleep well," was all she said. The vague sentence didn't answer his question, but he didn't push. Mornings after were weird. Being divorced for a couple years hadn't made them any less weird, though it had made him more forgiving of how other people reacted when they woke up to find a stranger in their bed.

"Odd to share a bed with someone again?" he asked.

"Something like that."

He gave her a long look, waiting several seconds to see if she would elaborate, but she didn't and he didn't press. Sex didn't make them buddies. The two intimacies weren't the same and he had no right to her interior thoughts. "Well, I appreciate the shower and coffee."

"Do you take cream? Or milk? I might only have almond milk."

"Nope. Black's fine for me. No sugar, either. I used to drink it with both, but I kept forgetting to buy some and then it wasn't worth it anymore."

"Black it is." She didn't hurry to get out of bed, as if she was nervous about showing him the body that he'd had his hands all over last night.

Again, mornings after were strange. Instead of asking any more probing questions, he headed for her bathroom and the shower. Giving them both a little privacy.

WHEN CALEB ENTERED the kitchen, there was a dog sprawled on the tile and a cup of coffee sitting on the counter for him, a small cap of tinfoil over the top. "I didn't know how long you were going to be," she said, when he commented how thoughtful it was.

She wore a menswear-style pajama set with light and dark blue stripes and a slick pair of navy blue slippers. Her brown eyes were still heavy with sleep and her hair was mussed. Perfect bedhead. Her cute pajamas enhanced the "straight out of a magazine" look she had going. He would expect to find a picture of her while flipping through a travel magazine with ads for hotels he couldn't afford, especially with the way she leaned against her counter and sipped from a steaming white mug.

You want to be me, or be part of my life, the ad would imply. Or would, if she had her smile back. And if she wasn't looking past him, to the door. Even Seamus had raised his head and was eyeing him like it was time for him to make his exit.

Between the lack of a smile and the sharp tone in bed this morning, he knew he'd overstayed his welcome, cup of coffee with a tinfoil hat or no. In the best-case scenario, she had something she needed to be doing. In the worst, this was an example of morning-after regret and he was sorry to be the cause of it. He set his half-drunk cup on the counter. "I should go. Let you get started with your day." Optimism never killed anyone, so he added, "I'd like to see you again."

A Hail Mary, especially since her face was as close to a scowl as it probably ever got. But, if you didn't ask for something, then you never got anything. The sex had been good. He'd enjoyed himself and he was pretty sure she had, too. If she'd been faking, she'd done a damn good job.

Plus, she was interesting. She was open about her nerves and her feelings and…

"I don't think we should see each other again."

And…smash. Apparently, her being open about her feelings didn't bode well for him. He was a decent guy and she had every right to kick him out, so he wouldn't argue. "Okay."

But he was going to clarify. "Why?"

Her mouth twitched and, for a moment, he wondered if she was going to say, "I don't have to tell you," like they were siblings in the middle of a spat. Then she sighed and set her cup on the counter. "I like the *idea* of dating to date. Of finding a guy to hang out with and fuck…"

He winced. A couple messages online and one night had already taught him that language like that wasn't natural on her.

"…but I realized last night that I can't do it. I can't find someone I like and want to spend time with and not leave myself open to wanting more. You were clear that you're not interested in more, which means we're done," she said, with a decisive nod of her head.

Before we even started. Her tone of voice carried those words to his ears, but he felt them deep in his gut, too.

She'd mentioned that she was taking an art class and had a list of things she wanted to try, now that she was single and discovering herself as single. Once he walked out those doors, he would never find out what else was on that list.

And he wanted to know.

But did he want to be just another bullet point on her list? A box she'd checked off and knew she didn't need again. Morning-after regrets were one thing, but being the to-do list disappointment hurt.

"When did you decide this?" he asked, still a little stunned. While he'd been in the shower? Looking at him in the kitchen and deciding she didn't like how he drank coffee?

"Last night." Her cold tone reverberated through the kitchen and must have spooked Seamus, because the dog hauled himself off the floor and walked over to her for reassuring pets.

Caleb sat on one of her barstools. They were hard, wooden stools with a short backrest that caused more pain than it could possibly provide in relief. No comfort or pets for him. He was on his own. "Before or…"

She pressed her lips together and then reached back for her coffee. She cupped the mug in her hands without drinking it, Seamus at her feet, staring up in adoration and concern. "After. I think."

"You think?" He wasn't trying to argue with her, just… To be honest, he was surprised and he'd thought women had stopped surprising him a while ago. He'd certainly been on enough first dates and had enough one-night stands to feel like he'd seen everything and knew the various routines people went through.

Beck was recently divorced. She was interested in dating. His experience had told him that she was his perfect type—interested in playing the field before committing. And he was happy to be her field.

Life was full of surprises. Beck was a big one.

"Well, it didn't occur to me that I couldn't do sex without some hope of commitment until you said you were never getting married again and my heart stopped. But it took me the entire night to decide what to do about it." She put her cup up to her lips. He doubted that she was drinking anything, more communicating that she was done talking.

"Why didn't you kick me out last night?" Surprise number seventeen to come from the pretty, smart woman standing across the kitchen from him.

"I missed sex," she said frankly. "Once you leave, I don't know when I'm going to get any next."

Surprise number eighteen. If she wasn't kicking him out, if he'd had a chance to keep counting, he might possibly run out of numbers. But with wishes and horses and flying pigs being what they were, he wouldn't have to test himself.

"Okay," he said slowly, still not sure if he could get out of the chair yet. Between the sex and being dumped, his balance might be off for the rest of the day and well into tomorrow.

"You can finish your coffee, though. If you want. I don't mean to kick you out."

"You do mean to kick me out," he said, her veneer of kindness pissing him off more than being discarded did. Plus, he *liked* her, dammit. "That's what this entire conversation is about. Out of your house and out of your life."

"We want different things." Straightforward and straight through the gut.

Not just the gut, he realized as he gulped half of his coffee, but several inches higher and a little to the left. He was sad that he wouldn't see her again. For twelve hours, she'd brought a spark into his life that he didn't remember feeling with any other of his dates. Saying goodbye would leave a hole.

Better to leave, while the hole is small, before the wanting of different things leads to fighting and silences and sleeping in separate rooms before someone can move out.

Rationally, that made sense. Irrationally, he asked, "But you like me?"

"What does that matter?"

"I like you." This should be simple, right? Relationships that lasted a week *were* simple. Two people who like each other enough to hang out. Easy decision.

"You like me enough to dump me sometime in the future. I like me enough to dump you now," she responded, complicating the easy decision with both truth and the future.

"You don't know me well enough to know what you want out of a relationship with me."

She raised an eyebrow at him. "You don't know me well enough to know if you'd want to marry me or not. And yet, you're certain you won't. Ever."

"I guess..." Grasping at straws would be easier. At least then he'd be able to hold on to something while drowning.

She waited, but he didn't finish his sentence. Frankly, he didn't know how to. He'd *never* pushed before. If a woman said, "Get out," he said, "Okay. You're the boss."

There were always more women. Not interchangeable so much as a never-ending variety.

But he'd never told a woman about his relationship with his father... Dating rules he'd assumed were set in stone were turning to quicksand and he was sinking.

"What are you getting at?" she asked. "What do you want?"

You. But he didn't want her. Or, not in the way that she—possibly, in the future, if this went well, if the stars aligned—wanted him to want her. The future was nebulous. She couldn't know if they would make it past two weeks still liking each other and yet she was ending this because he didn't want to get married.

Her rationale was frustrating as hell. *She liked him.* This should be easy.

"I like you," he said, slowing his frustration down to give himself the chance to remember she could say no and then he would leave. That those were the rules a decent guy operated under. But, if she could be frank, so could he. "I wish I had the chance to get to know you better. I'm sad that I won't."

"Oh." She made a near perfect moue with her lips, but then shook her head and her lips were straight again. "I didn't expect you to be sad."

"That makes two of us." With another woman, he would have walked out and felt like he'd been saved from an awkward moment three weeks down the road. With Beck, it felt as though that awkward moment would be worth it, if only for the three more weeks.

They stood in her kitchen, staring at each other, her gigantic granite island between them. A strange standoff, to be with a woman who wants to be with you and whom you want to be with, but who was telling you to leave and never come back.

Timelines mattered. And her possible timeline included forever. His didn't.

"I'd like to make a proposal," he said, realizing that another chance to admire her toothy grin was higher on his list of priorities than the great sex.

He took her raised eyebrow as an invitation to continue. "I like you. You like me. We like sex with each other and you want more sex in your life."

"Yeah, but not willy-nilly."

"Who said I'm proposing willy-nilly? I'm offering you companionship, conversation and sex while you look for the man you want to marry. Or until our relationship has burned its course."

"A little man on the side."

"Little? Come on." He tried to act insulted, but the way her hand came up to her mouth in embarrassment at what she accidentally intended was too cute not to laugh.

"But the *on the side* part was right," she clarified, her fingers muffling her voice.

"I guess, yes. You are free to date other people. I'm free to date other people."

The spot between her eyebrows wrinkled. "So, why would we be dating each other?"

"Because we like each other. Because you probably need time to kiss a few frogs before you settle on your prince, and I can ribbit with the best of them."

Her giggle encouraged him. "Also, knowing you have a steady diet of companionships, conversation and sex might help you not jump into a relationship that's not good for you."

"Are you telling me that having regular sex with you means I won't be so quick to have sex with some other dude and that's a good thing?" She had been scratching Seamus behind his ears and her sudden stop made the dog bark once.

"It's not my best argument ever," he said with a shrug.

"At least you admit it." Her laugh this time was full-bodied and deep. Then her face smoothed out and she considered him. "You're proposing we be fuck buddies."

"Yeah."

"Shouldn't we be buddies first?"

For all his dating around, for all his quick, one- or two-week so-called relationships, he'd never had a fuck buddy. It...well, more than implying that they were buddies before the sex, it implied they would be buddies once the sex was over. He was friendly with most of the women he'd been on dates with, but not *buddies*.

He could imagine wanting to be buddies with

Beck, though. Sharing even that little bit of his family history had been easy with her. She was the kind of person you shared things with and, if they played their cards right, they could close out their relationship with him better able to share bits and pieces of himself in the future and with her having solid knowledge tucked in her back pocket—not just that she wanted to get married again, but what kind of man she wanted to marry.

This could be a win-win. And those were the best kinds of wins.

"Give yourself some time to enjoy being single," he said, pressing his case. "To go out and have a good time. To enjoy the company of men. Maybe what you want now is different than what you wanted back when you got married. Maybe *you're* different. I know I am not the man I was when I got married." He was less starry-eyed about the future—that much was true. And he knew himself better, which included knowing that he wasn't good for the long term.

You're not reliable enough, his ex had said— enough times and with enough examples that she was probably right.

But he wasn't in the room with his ex. He was here with Beck and he wanted to keep being here with Beck. "I'll be the pause you need, without stopping your life completely."

She set her coffee back on the counter and folded her arms over her chest. The movement caught the hem of her pajama top and he could see a thin line of skin. Skin that he'd kissed last night. Skin that he wanted to kiss again.

"Are you the dog who doesn't want to give up his bone?"

"I don't know."

It clearly wasn't the answer she wanted. "At least you're honest."

"I thought about it, that maybe I'm just upset because I'm being dumped and not the dumper. But I don't think that's it. I *hope*, at least, that I'm a better person than that." He was *pretty* sure he was. "I've been dumped before and not put up an argument. A woman's got a right to dump a dude without him badgering her."

A horrible thought occurred to him. "I'm not badgering you, am I? I wanted to know why you say no more and to state my case for at least one more date, but I can leave now if I'm badgering you."

He understood her headshake to be a sign that he wasn't harassing her, especially because she asked, "Why then?"

"For a thousand reasons." All those surprises she would bring to his life during the short tenure of their relationship. "And for one simple reason. I like you. Plain and simple as that. I want the chance to get to know you."

"For our relationship to end later. Which is a certainty, because you don't believe in marriage."

"I don't think marriage is for me. That's different. And our relationship doesn't have to end in marriage or disaster. We could end up being great friends."

He could not explain why he was arguing with her. She wanted this to be over. He should stop and just let it be over. But he had to try. He wasn't so stupid not to know that she was a good thing. He didn't have to want to hold on to her forever to want her in his life longer than twelve hours.

"I'll give you dating advice," he said, though that argument wasn't any better than his last one. "Help you sort the creeps from the good ones."

She laughed, which was a fair response to his last-ditch effort. "I didn't expect you to put that in your pros column."

He pushed his empty coffee mug closer to the sink, pulled his phone close to him and clicked open the Uber app. Fabulous. Cars nearby. "I'm going to head out. I've made my case. Think about it, okay. Let me know either way."

She nodded. Didn't even respond with "okay," so Caleb knew he was doomed. He walked out of her house an emptier man than he'd been yesterday.

CHAPTER EIGHT

"HEY," BECK SAID as she walked into Marsie's house and gave her best friend a quick hug. "How are you?"

"Good. Busy. Hectic." Marsie stepped back, holding Beck's arms open and clearly giving her the once-over. "How are you?" she asked, almost impatiently, like she had expected a ticker across Beck's forehead and was disappointed not to find one.

"I went on a date last night." Beck tried to say the words casually, but Marsie's raised eyebrow made it clear she wasn't fooled into thinking anything other than *first date in over ten years*.

But all she asked as they walked together into her kitchen was, "Oh? How'd that go?" Her friend's kitchen was full-on Marsie. Everything was organized within an inch of its life, with labeled jars of flour, beans and sugar in open shelving for the world to enjoy, and for Beck to be jealous of Marsie's dedication to cleanliness.

It was full-on Marsie, but it was also a little

different since her boyfriend, Jason, had moved in. There was a box of Cheerios on the counter, next to the container of granola, and Beck was willing to bet there was milk in the fridge. And the changes in the kitchen didn't take into account the changes to the rest of the house. The last time Beck had been here, she'd noticed a book on woodworking on the dining room table and one of Marsie's bookshelves had been removed. "For Jason's desk," her friend had said, like it wasn't a big deal to completely rearrange her office to fit the needs of her boyfriend.

Marsie bought this house years ago when she'd first gotten her job in North Carolina and Beck had been a waitress at the only restaurant Marsie seemed to eat at. For years, Beck had listened to Marsie talk about her house and how she was setting it up exactly as she wanted, no men needed. Even when Marsie's former boyfriend had moved in, she had been unwilling to adjust from what she found comfortable and thought was right.

Then came Jason. And her sharp-elbowed friend was softer. Not kinder, because Marsie had always been kind, but more willing to let other people see that she was kind. Jason's box of cereal sitting on the counter only scratched the surface of the small—but good—changes in her.

How will I get better when I find the man I want to marry?

Only that wasn't the question Beck needed to answer for herself and it wasn't the question Marsie had asked.

"My date was…" Beck paused, not knowing what to say. "The date was good. Mr. Swoony—Caleb—is everything I could have hoped my first date would be. He's super cute. Nice. Interesting. Good in bed."

"Are you going to see him again?" Marsie asked, reaching for the wineglasses. Red wine sat in a decanter, waiting for them to be ready to drink it.

"I don't know." Caleb's offer was absurd. Date, have sex, go out to dinner—but not expect anything other than maybe to be friends when it was over. What kind of agreement was that?

An appealing one. One that would get her regular sex and someone to hang out with. And, like being relaxed with a stranger, taking a risk on a date and inviting him into her home, it was an agreement she wanted to know if she was capable of, to be honest. She didn't think she could have sex and not think of a long-term possibility, but there was long-term potential. As friends, sure, but it was there. And while he'd made the point of sex with him keeping her from having sex with someone unsavory at a moment of desperation, there had been truth to that benefit.

She'd been nervous with Caleb, but she'd felt safe with him. Safe had been enough to override her nerves. Would she get lonely enough that the chance of company would be enough to turn a blind eye to warning signs?

Dislike of marriage or no, Caleb was a good guy. He'd challenged her, but at no point had he pressured her to give more of herself than she was willing. Neither had he whined about her leading him on or being unfair. He'd stated his case, confident enough in himself to walk out the door.

It would be nice to have a good guy in her life, if only for a little while.

These rationales were all fine and good. But could she accept that part and not risk falling for him? Or, could she go on dates with Caleb and also find someone else to date?

Wouldn't she get stuck in thinking that she *should* be monogamous, even if that wasn't part of the agreement?

Can I do it? The question was both a challenge to accept and to hide from.

"He sounds dreamy," her friend said, pouring wine into their glasses. "What about him don't you like?"

"He doesn't want to get married again."

Marsie stopped mid-pour and looked across the counter, one brow raised. "Like he's been married before and sworn off the experience based on an n of one?"

Beck shook her head. "N of one" was one of Marsie's favorite retorts, but in this case it didn't really fit. "Should a man or woman really have to be married more than once to know if it's not for them?"

"Yes," Marsie said with as much authority as she put into every declaration she ever made. "Marriage is the one place where I think an n of two is sufficient, but if one has been married once, one shouldn't dismiss it out of hand without therapy and another try."

Therapy. Trust her friend to expect a form of self-education to be involved, no matter the topic at hand.

Beck reached for her glass of wine. She would need it for this. "What about those people who say they never want to marry?"

Marsie stared up at the ceiling, pensive as she took a sip of her wine. "Well, they're making their declaration based on ideology, rather than experience. Presumably, their ideology is grounded in a broad understanding of modern marriage growing out of a patriarchal institution and need to solidify property arrangements. I'm okay with an ideological rejection. It's rejecting a centuries-old institution based on a shared experience with one other person that I'm against."

Her friend cocked her head and seemed to think a little longer before saying, "Gives that other person a rather lot of power, don't you think?"

When Marsie put it that way, Beck felt like her decision to eventually remarry was as revolutionary as it was sound. Reject the power! Reject Neil's power! She could put those slogans on a sign and march in front of her house, if only to remind herself that she was more than a man's wife and one man shouldn't have control over her feelings and her future.

Only, it still didn't help her decide if she was going to take Caleb up on his offer.

"As I was kicking him out of my house this morning, he offered to be my good time on the side."

Conversation halted as Marsie coughed. "Like a fuck buddy?"

"Exactly that," Beck said. "Only we've not been buddies first, so less buddy."

"What was his reasoning?"

"For not wanting to get married again?" Beck realized that she hadn't specifically asked and he'd only said, "I'm not the type," vaguely. That fifty percent of marriages end in divorce wasn't really a reason, so much as it was an excuse to cling to. Maybe he had a good reason. Maybe his reason was one she could sympathize with. Maybe she should ask first and judge second.

Before she did any asking, she needed to figure out if she was going to see him again.

But the way Marsie was shaking her head told Beck that she was answering the wrong question. "No, silly. For being your piece on the side."

Silly? Love had done funny things to Marsie. "Give me a frog to kiss on the regular, so I don't kiss a toad by mistake."

Marsie put down her glass of wine. "Did you tell him that you wanted to marry him?"

Beck shook her head. "No. But I told him that I wanted to marry again, sometime. And that I didn't think I could casually date—and sleep with—someone who didn't have the same long-term goals in mind, even if he didn't turn out to be the one."

"That's not a surprise, really. You like weddings."

"Weddings pay my salary. But it's not the wedding I want. I'd elope or have a courthouse wedding. I want someone to share my life with again. Despite how Neil and I worked out, I miss that sharing."

Sharing a life had been part of the reason she'd married Neil. Her parents had always had this cold marriage based on—as far as she could tell—common financial goals and ambitions more than love. They'd been so busy working and pursuing a career in the rushed pace of politics in DC that they'd never sat around the family table and shared a meal. The beautiful, gleaming table that had once been Beck's great-grandmother's sat unused unless her parents were hosting a dinner party, in which case Beck had been banished to her room, even as a teenager. Dinners were usually at a restaurant or takeout or what the babysitter made.

The first time she'd met Neil's parents, they had all sat around the kitchen table—not even the dining room one—and shared a noisy meal, passing serving dishes and salt and jokes. Beck had wanted *that*, with a couple of kids sitting at the table, and maybe her kids' friends staying for dinner after playing basketball in the driveway, too.

Since that had been how Neil had grown up, she'd assumed he wanted it, too, even after he'd specifically told her he didn't want kids. Stupid on both their parts, when she looked back at it. She had assumed he wanted the loving, engaged family he had grown up with. He had assumed she would be happy with the silence of a devoted companionship and shared goals.

Of course, he'd assumed that because she'd never contradicted him. She'd silently and idiotically waited for him to change his mind.

"Yeah. I love sharing my life," her friend said with a quick glance to the garage, from where Beck assumed Jason could appear at any moment.

"Mr. Swoony thought I should see what kind of person I am, have a little fun, before I think about marriage. That the men who are available in your thirties are different than the ones who were out there in your twenties. That I'm different, too." She'd thought that, as well, before she'd been faced with the reality of what it meant.

"I should start dinner," Marsie said, turning away from their conversation to the cookbook open on the counter. Beck knew she wasn't being ignored; her friend needed to think.

Beck stood at the counter, wallowing in the wine and her thoughts, while Marsie got vegetables out of the fridge and set a wok on the stove.

"What are we having?" Beck asked, gesturing with her wineglass to the wok.

"Chinese food. I was complaining about the lack of delivery options available near us, so Jason got me this." She nodded to the cookbook open on the counter. "He said the author was the first Westerner to graduate from some well-known cooking school in Sichuan. So, I'm trying all the recipes to see what we might like."

Beck reached over the counter and flipped the cookbook over so she could see the cover. *Every Grain of Rice.* "It says she's the author of other cookbooks."

"Yeah. Apparently this one is the home-cooking-style one. Seemed worth a try. I took a trip to Grand Asia to buy everything we needed for tonight."

"Need help?" Beck asked, abandoning her wineglass and coming around the island to where she might be of use.

"Yes," Marsie said, relief evident in her voice. "I've made two other dinners out of this cookbook. Good, but a lot of chopping. There are notecards on the table, each labeled with a recipe and the things that need to go in each dish, broken out by the order they go in. Here, let me get you some bowls."

A cabinet opened and closed, and then a stack of small glass bowls appeared in front of Beck.

"Start with a card, chop all the things on that

card and put them in the prep bowls as indicated. I'll work on the measuring."

They worked side by side, Beck's knife hitting the cutting board and Marsie's measuring spoons bumping against glass providing comfortable sounds to settle in to. More than needing to talk, Beck needed to be around her steady, thoughtful friend.

After the counter was filled with bowls and Marsie had turned the heat on under the wok, Beck went back to her wine. The smell of garlic and ginger sizzling in oil filled the kitchen, and the bowls of chopped vegetables and sauces turned into bowls of chicken and mushrooms, stir-fried celery, broccoli with garlic and peppers, and fried tofu with some sort of brown sauce. Considering the ease with which Marsie was swirling food around the sizzling wok, a stranger might think she had been cooking Chinese food all her life. Beck knew better. Marsie had probably memorized the recipes and plotted out the best order for cooking everything, including what would be good room temperature and what should be served piping hot.

At her friend's direction, Beck put small bowls out on the kitchen table and spooned rice into a serving dish. "No Jason?" she asked, when she grabbed three sets of chopsticks and Marsie shook her off.

"No Jason. His mom is having some health problems, so he's having dinner with them tonight," Marsie said as she set the selection of dishes out on the kitchen table.

"I'm glad you didn't cancel our dinner plans." She needed Marsie's straightforwardness and reasonability now more than she needed the dreams and hopes some of her other friends would provide.

Her friend sat, shook out her napkin and then set it on her lap. "While cooking, I've been thinking about your dilemma."

Beck halted, her napkin hanging down from her hands as she looked at her friend. "You think there's another choice than saying no?"

"There's always another choice. Inaction is a choice. Action is a choice. Yes is a choice and no is a choice."

One of these days, Marsie would make a great mom. And, years after she became a great mom, her kids would appreciate gems of wisdom like that one. Until that moment, her friend's kids would probably be like Beck was now and wish she would just give straight advice.

"Okay. So, what's my other choice?" Beck asked as she spooned some of the chicken into her bowl. "This looks great, by the way." The chicken looked amazing and smelled even better.

"Take Mr. Swoony up on his offer, of course. And I think you should."

"What?" Beck stopped, chicken and chopsticks midway to her mouth. Her friend was blithely putting a piece of tofu in her mouth like she hadn't just said the most un-Marsie-like thing ever. "Are you serious? Of course, you're serious. You're always serious."

"I am serious," Marsie confirmed, as though there had been any doubt. She rested her chopsticks on the edge of her bowl and lifted her hand. "One, I've never known you without Neil. I might be surprised by what kind of man you're interested in. You might be surprised, too."

Marsie ticked off another finger. "Two, I think you need a little joy in your life."

"Mr. Swoony isn't guaranteed to bring me joy. I might fall desperately in love with him and this might end in heartbreak."

"If we're examining possibilities, he might fall desperately in love with you and have his heart broken when you dump him because he can't commit. Frankly, you're my friend and I love you. I don't know Swoony from the next guy. All *my* evidence points to you being the heartbreaker here."

"Cute," Beck said, catching her friend's gaze across the table and enjoying how amused Marsie was by her own statistics joke.

"Do you want to marry this Mr. Swoony?" Marsie asked.

"I don't know him enough to answer that."

"Do you want to get dinner with him and have good sex? The sex was good, right?"

"The sex was good," Beck confirmed. Just thinking about the previous night had Beck missing Caleb's hands on her body.

"We're not talking long-term. If you feel yourself falling for him, we'll reassess this conversation. In the meantime, eat out at nice restaurants with a swoony man who gives you orgasms, and keep your online-dating profiles open. Let other nice men take you out. Take them out. Buy lots of condoms. Then see where you are."

Marsie's advice made Beck's heart and stomach flutter, one with excitement and one with fear. She could do this. She could give herself time and see who she was, as Beck, solo. She could have fun. And she could put off worrying about when she would get married again for at least a couple of months.

She could just not think about it.

"I'm going to do it," she said, punching into the air with both her fists. "It'll be great." Though Beck wasn't so certain about that last part. But she was certain that she wanted to push her boundaries, and now was a good time to do it.

CHAPTER NINE

CALEB FELT THE presence behind him before the person cleared their throat so that he knew someone was there. The throat clearing told him who it was. Bernetta McClarin, representative from the great city of Durham, stood behind his desk at the legislative building with a stack of papers in her hand. She tossed the pages onto his desk, the binder clip clinking as it hit the metal.

"In case you haven't already seen this," she said, irritation crowding her voice while he stared at the pages on his desk.

"H372 Judiciary Reform," the title of the bill said. Innocuous titles made Caleb suspicious—always have, and the current state of politics in North Carolina hadn't changed his impressions. An experienced reporter could understand how deep the conflict of interests in a bill went based purely on how innocent the bill's title was. The bill Bernetta had tossed on his desk had to be a doozy.

"When did this show up?" he asked, wondering how he hadn't heard about something big enough to inspire Bernetta to take a special trip past his desk.

"I learned about it this morning," she said, her voice still clamped in frustration. "The bill's sponsor and I..." She paused. "Aren't friendly."

Caleb looked back down to see who the sponsor was. Representative Ross. "Oh, yeah," he said, as understanding began to dawn. "We're not friendly, either."

Ross wasn't a fan of either Caleb or Bernetta, and they weren't a fan of him. He'd made a comment about lynching as a solution to... well, Caleb couldn't even remember *why* Ross had spoken in favor of lynching, only that he had. Ross didn't like that Caleb had reported on the offensive statement, including in his story facts about the numbers of African Americans lynched in US history and some context about the role of lynching as a method of domestic terror.

Ross didn't like Bernetta for the same reason he didn't like three of the six elected officials from Durham. And Ross didn't like the white reps so much, either—he was just more subtle about it.

"Is this bill going to be as bad as I think it is?" he asked Bernetta. They'd come up in politics together, him as a reporter on Durham city politics and she as a city councilwoman. They'd moved to new positions in the legislative building at the same time and the friendship they'd developed back in city politics had followed them.

Which is why she didn't call him an idiot, but only looked like she thought he was one. "Right," he said. "They've been talking about changing judicial districts since they proposed their previous electoral maps. I just assumed that the sheer unpopularity of those maps and repeated court challenges would stay their hand."

"You thought wrong," the representative said drily. She pressed her index finger and its short nail on the page. They were bright pink this week. Bernetta's nails were a different color almost every week, a nod to creativity in the otherwise buttoned-down woman. She wore her black hair in a tight bun, slacks, silk blouses and pumps. As far as Caleb could tell, she never put any makeup on her dark skin and wore almost no jewelry.

But there were always those colorful nails. If she'd been on vacation or they'd had a couple days off, her nails had more than just color. They had painted-on flowers or small jewels, which she usually kept on for a couple of weeks. One July, she'd come back from the beach with little American flags. He'd never asked why the nails but no jewelry. Bernetta was a private woman in a public job and he tried to respect that distinction as much as possible.

She tapped the pages. "Always nice when my distinguished colleagues across the aisle can keep my journalist friends in business."

It was enough to make him rap his fingers together with evil glee. "Not to put too fine a point on it, but they aren't the only party who keeps me in business."

Her huff was the only acknowledgment she would give to the truth of his statement. Two-party politics in North Carolina had been steady until the party now in the minority had gotten a little too confident in its power. The pendulum had swung and the party who had claimed corruption was taking its turn proving the adage of power corrupting and absolute power corrupting absolutely.

"I won't claim innocence," Bernetta said finally. "But I don't think we did anything *this* egregious."

"When does it go to committee?"

"It was read in the house today. Nothing's on the committee dockets yet."

"So, might die there."

"Maybe. They've been talking about pulling a trick like this for a while. Whatever I think of the bill, it's politically premature. Might get yanked."

Caleb sighed. He definitely needed more sleep for something like this. The night he'd spent at Beck's had been great, the kind of heavy sleep a man gets after sex and orgasms. But he hadn't slept the next night. Or the next. The present weight of his eyelids did nothing to promise that tonight's sleep would be any better.

Work provided some relief, but at home, his mind rolled over all the reasons Beck hadn't sent him an email yet. Usually, his mind settled on the fact that he'd probably been an ass and should have left when she told him they wouldn't be seeing each other again. In theory, his mind settling should help. If he didn't get a good night's sleep soon, he would buy a box of over-the-counter sleeping aids and hope for the best. Otherwise, he was liable to make stupid decisions at work and miss the fine back-and-forth of politics at work in this building.

Not to mention the effect stupid, sleep-deprived decisions in his life would have.

He picked up the papers on his desk and scanned through the bill. He was going to owe Bernetta big for this story. And he already owed her big for being his source for the universally hated House Bill Two. She'd collect on her own terms, of course, but he couldn't worry about what that would look like until she showed up behind his desk, clearing her throat again—this time with her palm out.

A problem for another day, especially since she'd deserve every bit of assistance he could give her. And more.

"Thank you," he said, putting as much force of meaning into those two words as was possible. "Do you need it back?"

"Nah. I made this copy just for you."

"Thanks," he said, turning back to his desk to read the bill, but Bernetta didn't leave. He glanced back up.

"I saw you out on Friday night."

Friday night. With Beck. The night that ended Saturday morning and was still ruining his sleep. "I didn't see you," was all he could think to say in response.

"I know," she said, with as close to a smirk as he'd ever seen on her regal face. "That's the best part. You looked mighty sweet on her."

"She was my date. I always pay attention to my dates."

She waved that comment away with five pink-tipped fingers. "Don't doubt that you do. I know your reputation."

"What?" He had a reputation?

Worse. He had a reputation, and a member

of the General Assembly knew about it? Especially such a well-respected political figure as Bernetta McClarin. Her husband was a retired preacher, for Pete's sake.

"Sure. I'm old, but I know things. I heard they call you 'the most popular man online.' My assistant said one of her friends has been on a date with you."

Caleb grabbed at his head, hoping he might pull some understanding of who his date had been who was friends with someone who worked at the legislative building. He came up empty. Honestly, it could have been any number of hundreds of women. Except Beck. Probably. She worked at a popular downtown restaurant. But for all he knew, she was friends with a host of people who worked in this building who stopped in at her restaurant for a regular lunch of Italian food.

"Oh, God." One of the reasons he respected Bernetta's privacy so much was that he valued his own. Since his divorce, he'd worked hard to keep work at work and fun everywhere else. Apparently, he hadn't worked hard enough.

Or he'd had too much fun.

"Are you surprised?" She seemed almost as surprised to learn he didn't know about the moniker as he was to learn that he had one.

"Yes. I guess I shouldn't be." He did go on a

lot of dates, with a lot of different women. All shapes, sizes and ages. All income and education levels. He didn't sleep with all of them. Hell, he didn't sleep with most of them. While it was fair to say that many of the dates ended with him having enjoyed the woman's company but not interested in more, it was also fair to say that many of the dates ended with his date not interested in more from *him*.

News about both was sure to get around.

"You're a modern-day Lothario."

He winced. "If you're going to compare me to womanizers of yore, at least pick Casanova."

Bernetta cocked her head. "I don't see the difference."

Caleb would enjoy the rare occurrence of catching the well-educated and influential woman on something she didn't know, except that she'd compared him to a loathsome man, and the taint of that would be difficult to shower off. "Lothario seduces and betrays women. Casanova woos them, entertains them and leaves them better off than he found them."

She raised an eyebrow at him. "Really? Didn't Casanova also like women who were too young for him."

He'd really stepped in it. After Bernetta went back to her office, he was going to go back to never talking about his private life at work, even if someone else brought it up. But he'd said something stupid and he had to clean the shit off his shoe. "It's not a perfect comparison. I don't date women who are too young, and you'll have to ask them if I leave them better off. I'm just saying that I'm more interested in conversation than in conquest."

He could feel her assessing every line of his face and he stared right back, almost daring her to prove him wrong. Finally, she grinned and his shoulders fell in relief. "I've worked with you long enough to believe that. And, not only do *I* like you, but my husband likes you. His approval is harder to win."

He dropped his head into his hands and closed his eyes, taking a deep breath. When he had recovered from learning all that everyone seemed to know about his private life, he looked up and said, "Well, that's good at least. But why in God's name are we talking about this?"

"Because I saw you. And you didn't see me."

"I was paying attention to my date. As I should have been."

Her eyes were laughing and he was pretty sure they were laughing at him. "There's paying attention to your date and then there's life-changing adoration. You were the latter."

"I couldn't have been. It was our first date."

That was only one of the problems. "Plus, I don't believe in love at first sight. And I'm not interested in marriage."

"Who said anything about marriage?" she asked, one brow raised. Not the answer he'd expected from a preacher's wife.

"What else would life-changing adoration be?"

There wasn't malice in Bernetta's laugh, but she was clearly finding joy in this conversation. "She could break your heart. From what I understand, that would be life-changing."

"Can we pretend you don't know any of this?"

The representative raised her eyebrows, the glee still clear in her face. "I'll tell you something about my personal life, if it will make you feel better."

He shook his head. "That wouldn't make this any better. How about we go back to pretending neither of us have lives outside of this building?"

"Hah." Then her face softened. "I only met her once, but your ex-wife never struck me as a particularly nice person. And no one from the paper ever had anything good to say about her. Did she really hate your job?"

Banging his head against his desk wouldn't make him feel any better, though a concussion would give him something else to worry about. "Does anyone in this building *not* gossip?"

"When you gossip, you put it in a newspaper and call it reporting." She folded her arms across her chest. "And don't go blaming the women for the fact that I know your ex never had anything nice to say. The men are worse than the women."

"Oh, I know. I use the urinal."

"What?" Her face scrunched up, disgusted, and Caleb felt a small burst of pleasure that he'd caught her off guard for once in this conversation. Then her face turned thoughtful. "I knew those men were trying to ban people from using the bathroom for a reason. I just didn't realize it was so they could make deals in secret."

Caleb shook his head at Bernetta's reference to a bill that had complicated North Carolina politics further. The bill's several parts had so enraged people that several large companies had cancelled planned expansions in North Carolina and prominent singers had canceled concerts. The backlash had been bad enough that, in the next election, the governor lost his job. Rules about bathroom use had only been one of the many unpopular regulations that bill had included.

"Can we pretend we've not talked about my dating or my divorce?"

"Well, I just wanted to say that I saw you. And that the woman you were with looked really nice. You looked really into her."

I was. At least Bernetta didn't know how often he was checking his email and phone to see if Beck had sent him a message.

"And I also wanted to say that not all women are like your ex-wife."

"I'm well aware of that."

"And not all marriages end in messy divorces." Bernetta had been married since the dawn of time and her eyes still softened when she talked about her husband.

"That's what I understand."

"That's all my advice for today."

"Then why don't you head back to your office to call around and see if this is really going to be killed in committee, and I'll figure out how to report on it. And how to pretend your assistant doesn't have a nickname for me."

She laughed. "I'll ignore your bossiness because you're upset about that nickname. Though you probably deserve it." She didn't say whether she meant he deserved the nickname or to be upset. Not that it mattered. He wanted her gone so he could stew without an audience.

"Thanks," he said drily.

Bernetta was the elected official he was closest to. Because he spent most of his days over in the legislative building instead of in the newsroom, he didn't often go out and drink and gossip with the rest of the reporters. He spent most of his workday with elected officials and the public servants who made democracy work. But they weren't coworkers so much as they were the people he reported on—and that made relationships tricky.

Hard to be friends with the guy who might write a story about how you'd messed up your facts at best and lied at worst. Since he and Bernetta had risen through the ranks together, they had an easier understanding. Plus, she was Bernetta. He had about as easy a time believing that print journalism would experience a renaissance and they'd go back to publishing a morning and evening paper as he could believe that Bernetta would do anything underhanded. It wasn't that she was a preacher's wife so much as she was one of those people for whom exposure to the dirty parts of human nature only made them more determined to hold to the straight and narrow.

Hell, as far as the people he saw on a daily basis were concerned, his job was more important than personal relationships. Pretty much exactly what Leah had accused him of each time she said it wasn't the right time for kids.

No ability to compromise. Unreliable in a crisis. Too focused on work—and work that didn't have a future and didn't provide a good enough income, either. All strikes against him.

For the past few years, he'd made a concerted effort to forget about his ex. Mostly, he'd been successful. Mostly, he got around in life without remembering all the reasons he wasn't a good partner.

Not that Leah had said such things all the time. Much of their marriage had been fun. They'd been in love. They shared intimacies and secrets and hopes and dreams. It had taken Caleb *years* to realize that any time he brought up the kids they'd both said they wanted, his ex had only berated him with his faults.

He didn't help enough around the house, she'd said, so how could she trust him to take on his share of the childcare duties? He forgot to pick up toilet paper on his way home from work, so he'd never remember to bring home diapers. He was never home from work on time, so he couldn't be relied on to pick up the kids from daycare. "Then," she said, fully into her speech about his failings, "we'll be charged a late-pickup fee and have to pay for it out of money we don't have because you don't get paid enough. And, God, I read those articles about how journalism is a dying profession and I wonder what you will do when the paper lays you off."

She'd softened her face, like she often had when listing out his shortcomings, and said, "We'll have kids when you can get a more reliable job, one that means you can be home when I need you and you're not so distracted you forget to pick up bread."

The end had come when they'd been walking through their neighborhood and stopped to watch the kids playing soccer. They'd leaned their arms against the fence. The kids were little, like third grade maybe, and they ranged in skill from kicking the ball with enthusiasm to clearly not wanting to be on the field and doing cartwheels instead. They'd been cute, he remembered, as he watched them run and stumble and play. At that moment, he'd wanted kids of his own so badly he could almost feel one of the ones on the field in his arms, excited for a hug after an hour of soccer.

Leah, however, had apparently been watching the parents. While he had been caught up in the rush of fatherly desire for a child of his own, she had been…well, he didn't know what she had been thinking, but he knew what she'd said. "I would never want to be one of those mothers. Giving up their Saturday morning to watch their kids get muddy."

It was as close to being struck by lightning as he thought possible without daring God by standing at the top of a bald mountain during a thunderstorm.

He and Leah didn't want the same future. While it was true that he didn't make much money and he didn't remember to pick things up at the store and he was never home when he thought he would be, he could have a job where he clocked in at eight thirty and clocked out at five and made one-hundred-thousand dollars a year and she *still* wouldn't want kids.

Looking back, his marriage seemed like one clear line to divorce. He'd known journalism was a risky career and he'd gone into it anyway. He'd heard Leah's arguments about why they couldn't have kids *now* and he'd stupidly never pressed her for the question of *later*. But that clear line to divorce had included at least six months of denying that he'd been struck by lightning. And then there had been the six months of marital counseling, during which Leah had said she was willing to try to get pregnant—if it mattered so much to him.

By that point, he'd never been in the mood for sex. He'd gone from being hot for his wife all the time to feeling cold the moment she touched him. To him, children seemed like a gift, not something his wife should have to sacrifice herself for. And she'd made it clear that her offer to get pregnant was tantamount to ruining her life.

"This is the last time I'll be able to…" she'd said over and over and over. Like after kids they'd never be able to go out to dinner and she'd never be able to go to the gym and they'd never see another special exhibit at the art museum.

He hadn't wanted that burden and, frankly, he hadn't wanted the kids who had to shoulder the burden of ruining her life. So, he'd moved out. And she'd blamed him for abandoning her. "I always knew you couldn't stick it out until the end," she said, cold and hard, during their last fight.

People said mean things when they were divorcing. God knows, he'd said his fair share of horrible things. He'd called her a liar. He'd called her cold and unfeeling. One time, when she'd told him that he couldn't even be counted on to stick through and get her pregnant, his itch to slap her had been strong enough that he'd had to leave the house and take a walk to cool down.

He'd walked for two hours.

The lingering question was whether or not she was right. Journalism was a hard job that made a lot of demands on his time and energy.

He'd said he wanted kids, but maybe Leah had been right. Maybe the type of man who would choose this career, especially knowing its tenuous hold on the future, shouldn't have kids. Leah's condemnations were heavy words for a man to carry. He'd prefer to put everything behind him, smile and never marry again.

BECK STOOD WITH LESLIE, Buono Come Il Pane's banquet captain, and scanned the layout of the room. They were expecting a large party for a rehearsal dinner in thirty minutes. To Beck's eyes, the room looked great. The bright white of the tablecloths made the black napkins pop. Small vases on each table held bright bouquets of multicolored roses and greenery. The chairs were evenly spaced from each other, tucked neatly under the tables, waiting for guests.

"Look good to you?" she asked her coworker. Leslie had recently been promoted to banquet captain, after proving to have an eagle eye for detail and a kind way with customers, even irate ones. The new captain seemed to be able to listen and understand when most people would throw up their hands in frustration and walk off.

Beck had asked Leslie about this skill once. "People are only able to understand when they feel understood," had been the wise response, far out of range for Leslie's young years, though maybe not for their experience.

When Leslie had been hired, straight out of high school, the staff had spent a good couple weeks trying to figure out the new employee. The freshly minted busser was always the first one to show up with a broom when plates were dropped and could whisk a plate away from a table while both asking if the person was done and not interrupting the guests' conversation. All the servers agreed that last part was magic.

Good employee had been an easy slot to fit the young staff member in. Staff had a harder time fitting Leslie into other categories. In the white button-down, black slacks and ugly non-skid shoes, the busser had looked neither male nor female. When leaving work for a club with a fedora and lipstick, earrings, blazer and tie, Leslie had looked both at the same time.

Three weeks into Leslie's employment, Beck had been back by the lockers as two employees had been speculating. "This guy told me that the busser had been so quick to clean up the food their kid had spilled, and I said that I would tell…then I got stuck. I didn't know whether to say him or her to the guest."

Not one of them standing by the lockers had noticed Leslie walk by until a voice had said, "You could have asked."

"That would be rude," the server had said.

"So's gossiping in a back hallway," Leslie had replied as the server's mouth had opened and shut, a fish struggling to find oxygen.

Beck had agreed with both the server and with Leslie, but Leslie had invited the question and it had felt *ruder* to wrongly call someone a him or her. So, she'd asked, "Which do you prefer?"

"I prefer *they*, actually," Leslie had said with a force of conviction that made them sound far older.

That moment had been the beginning of an education for the restaurant employees, starting with Beck and the two servers in the back room. They had learned what the term *genderqueer* meant and stumbled over using a gender-neutral pronoun like *they* or *them*. One line cook, an English PhD in a previous life, had taken great pleasure in informing everyone that Shakespeare had considered *they* to be an acceptable singular pronoun, and if it was good enough for Shakespeare...

A couple of months after mostly everyone had retrained their tongues to use Leslie's preferred pronoun, some employees were on their way to understanding why, and the employees who slipped their pronoun use had at least stopped bristling when being corrected. Beck had asked Leslie what had made them so willing to correct the older, more senior servers on their pronoun.

"I knew people were gossiping," they had said. "And it had hurt. I couldn't see why me being a he or a she was anyone's business so long as I did my work. I had seen a blogger I admire add 'they/them' to their Twitter profile. So I did it and it felt amazing. Like I was *me* in a way people could see and maybe begin to understand. I promised myself I would embrace *me* at the next opportunity."

They sighed. "Sadly, that next opportunity was work. I wish it had been among friends. That would have felt safer. I got beat up a lot as a kid."

Being understood at work—or at least identified with the right pronoun—had changed how Leslie had interacted with everyone. They were still quiet and conscientious, but with a knack for telling stories of their friends' antics that could leave anyone listening in stitches, but which never felt mean-spirited.

Beck had related to Leslie's attempts to understand and find the good in people, and the two of them had bonded, becoming fast work friends.

"Restaurant looks good," Leslie said. "I

double-checked all the flatware. Whatever was making it spot has been fixed."

"Good." People paid them a lot of money for a beautiful event and the restaurant delivered every time. For a while, that had meant polishing each piece of flatware before setting it on the table because something was funky with the dish machine in the back. Everyone was glad they didn't have to do that any longer.

A black-clad server speed walked in front of them. "Hey," Leslie said to the waiter. "You're late."

Frankie, the waiter, came to a full stop. "I know. I'm sorry."

"And you're wearing white socks." As captain, Leslie was in charge of everything front of house, from the table settings to the uniforms of the staff.

"I know," the man said with a sigh. "My last pair has a hole in the toe. I'm late because I stopped at the store. They were out."

"Out of black socks?" Beck and Leslie said at the same time.

The guy shook his head. "I even complained to the manager. Apparently, it's a long story, but he appreciated my dilemma."

Leslie sighed. "There are extra pairs of socks in my locker. Please bring them back washed."

And this was why they had been promoted

from busser to server to banquet captain in just five years, leaping over other employees who had been here longer, but wouldn't have thought to keep spare pairs of socks on hand.

"How's dating going?" they asked, still keeping a keen eye on the continuing last-minute checks to make sure everything was ready for their guests.

"Going. I went on a date with this guy." Beck pulled her phone out of her pocket and swiped it open to show Leslie Caleb's profile pic.

"He's cute," Leslie said, taking the phone to look a little closer. "Oh, and I know him."

"What?" God, this would be embarrassing. She and Leslie were friendly for boss and employee, but not friendly enough for Beck to feel comfortable with the captain knowing about "the arrangement," as Beck had taken to calling it in her head.

"Well," they said, a slight correction in their voice. "I don't know him personally, but I've heard about him from my cis-het friends."

Cis referring to cisgender and meaning a gender expression that matches the sex assigned at birth, and *het* meaning heterosexual. Beck had known the latter and learned the definition of the former from Leslie. Getting to know Leslie had taught Beck that God was more creative with creation than weekly church sermons had led Beck to believe. The world was both more interesting and beautiful than she had known.

"Apparently he's a popular date to get. Good-looking, charming, good taste in food. Good in bed."

"All that's true," Beck said, and then realized what she'd admitted to in front of her employee when Leslie gave her a cheeky smile. "The good-looking and charming parts, of course. And good taste in food."

"I'll assume the rest of it is true, too," Leslie said, still grinning.

"So, he's the most popular man online." That fit. She had dubbed him Mr. Swoony.

"It's even better," they said, pausing the conversation to gesture at the two people setting up the bar. "You know the character of Annie in the movie *Bull Durham*?"

"Sure."

"And how players who hook up with Annie have the best season of their careers?"

"Yeah," Beck said, still not sure how this related to online dating or Caleb.

"That's what this guy is. Women date him, have a great time and the next dude they meet is the guy they marry. It's like an *honor* to be dating him."

Beck snorted. "Please tell me that he never used words like that to describe himself to your friends." No orgasm was worth a guy who claimed it was an honor to date him.

"No, no, no." Leslie shook their head, and then looked pensive for a moment, before shaking their head again. "At least, not that I know. My friends have said it, with pride. He's legend."

How much of that legend was created in the gossip and chatter of young people having a good time, Beck didn't ask. It didn't really matter. Caleb wasn't permanent; he was a stepping-stone to permanent. "I want to get married again one day, and he's already said he's not the man to marry me. But if dating him is the catalyst I need, then this should turn out better than I thought."

Clearly Beck hadn't said that with as much casual cheer as she'd hoped, because Leslie looked at her with one brow raised. But all the captain said was, "Dating is hard."

"It sure is."

CHAPTER TEN

ONCE BECK GOT home and had time to think about it, she'd decided that Leslie's gossip on Caleb made his offer *more* attractive, rather than less. If, as Leslie claimed, women left Caleb and then immediately found the man they were going to marry, then it would be *irresponsible* of Beck not to date him. Good sex wrapped up in a good-luck charm. Mr. Swoony indeed.

She sat down at her laptop, clicked "compose" and then typed her acceptance of Caleb's deal.

THINKING ABOUT HIS ex-wife had ruined another chance of Caleb's getting a good night's sleep, so he was wide-awake and scrolling through Twitter when the notification appeared on his phone.

"I accept," the subject line said. Clickbait from Beck, so he clicked.

The rest of the email was both specific and rambling, a combination that made him laugh.

You gave terms for our agreement and I expect you to abide by them. Good conversation. Orgasms. Good company. Dating advice. Perhaps we can try something kinky. I don't know. We'll see how much I trust you if that subject comes up. That new hotel in downtown Durham has those funny bathroom stalls with the fogging doors. I've never had sex in a public place.

He'd used those bathrooms. The entire floor was bathroom stalls, all single seaters and all open to whoever needed to use them. The doors were glass. When you locked the door, the glass fogged over for privacy.

Though it never really felt private. It hadn't occurred to him to have sex in one of those stalls, but maybe. He also hadn't checked any of his online-dating profiles since leaving Beck's house, so she'd already created unexpected disturbances in his life. Why shouldn't sex in a public bathroom be added to that turbulence? Her email continued.

Honestly, I don't really know what you're getting out of this arrangement.

What he was getting out of the relationship was easy—and the same things Beck had listed as promises.

Except for dating advice. Maybe he needed some, but Beck didn't seem like the type of person who would want to give it. Life advice, though, sure. She seemed like a person he could learn from, by example more than by any lecture or comment about where he'd gone wrong in life. She seemed kind. He could use more kindness in his life, and starting with himself was a good place.

And I heard you leave women in a better place than you found them.

Well, now, that was nice to get outside confirmation of. He'd share that nugget with Bernetta, except that he didn't like to kiss and tell.

I'm counting on that from you.

But no pressure, right? He thought with a smile. Beck and the strictures she laid out were a welcome challenge.

I promise not to be jealous about you dating other women. Just please don't tell me about it. Though, that seems unfair, because I'll be telling you about my dates. Well, you're not interested in more ever, and I might be. Maybe. So, the imbalance is fair. I guess.

She must be nervous. Their communication through online dating had been succinct. Or, maybe succinct was her sign of nerves and this sprawling email was her regular style of communication. If so, he was looking forward to receiving more of it. And he hoped that she started talking this much during sex. He liked dirty talk in bed.

So, when are we going out? I mean, if you're still interested.

Caleb read through the email one more time to make sure that he hadn't misunderstood and that she was indeed looking for a casual relationship. Then he read it a third time because she amused him.

His response was short and sweet.

I'm still interested. How's Friday? I'll make reservations.

They were going to have fun.

BECK WAS WORKING Friday night, but she sent him a text asking about another night. Which meant at five on a Saturday, she was standing in front of her closet, trying to decide what to wear.

They were going out to dinner. Caleb was picking her up. A date, not an HR screening. Dinner—actual dinner, not drinks and *possible* dinner. A meal sounded serious. It sounded like commitment. Or, she corrected her own hopes before they landed somewhere in her heart and started having babies, as close to commitment as Caleb said he was capable of.

She tossed her phone on the bed with a sigh. Her hopes could be a problem. Not her hopes for Caleb, since she didn't really know him from Adam, but her hopes for a future in general. What a mess she'd gotten herself into.

In theory, *New Beck* wanted to date around. Even before Caleb, she had wanted to kiss a lot of frogs. She needed to know who this Beck who wasn't married to Neil was. A Beck who could do something crazy, like sign up for mountain biking lessons.

But did that Beck actually exist? And what would *that* Beck wear?

Old Beck had worn pastel colors, soft fabrics. Pretty, but not necessarily sexy and not designed to be eye-catching. New Beck was in a relationship that wasn't going anywhere. New Beck *had* to look the part. Red lipstick. Plunging neckline. High heels that took practice to walk in.

The memory of the dress fell on her head

like someone had dropped a hat. A couple years ago, when she and Neil had talked about making time for monthly dinner dates, she'd bought a black dress with a neckline practically down to her navel, a gathered skirt and a glistening gold metal belt. She'd tried the dress on at the advice of the saleswoman, who had also supplied the black drop earrings, black stilettos with gold trim, and cute clutch that fit a phone and credit card, but nothing else. Beck had bought the whole set, brought it home, excited to dress up for a sexy night out with her husband and…it had never come out of the closet. Their monthly dinner dates had never happened.

But she hadn't been willing to throw the dress away. It was waiting, shoved to the back of her closet, for a night like this, when she wanted to feel desirable to a man who desired her in return.

Seamus came into her bedroom to lie on his bed while she got dressed. He showed little interest in the entire primping process, though he did sniff her shoes carefully. Made-up, hair done and dress on, Beck stood in front of her mirror and twirled.

The dress didn't twirl with her. It poufed. "Well," she said to Seamus, "it's not like I'm going to twirl for him on a date, anyway. Does it look cute?"

Seamus, dog that he was, didn't answer. He probably just wanted to go out. Still not certain what the rest of the night would hold, there was welcome knowledge in the ability to at least make a dog happy with a trip to the backyard and a treat, which she did promptly. A few minutes later, the satisfied dog climbed into his dog bed and took several turns while Beck sat on her couch and tried to pretend she wasn't ready early while she waited for the doorbell to ring.

Of course, she was enough on edge that, when it did ring, she and her dog both jumped. Her heart leaped, too, and it stayed lodged in her throat as she crossed over her hardwood floors to the front door and opened it. That she was going on a date with the gorgeous man standing on her front stoop didn't dislodge her heart from creeping its way to her tongue, either.

She had barely enough presence of mind to turn and command Seamus to sit and wait, hoping that some of their doggy school lessons would stick enough that he wouldn't bolt for new territories while she enjoyed looking at the sea-green eyes of the man she was going to have dinner with.

Dinner, with the best kind of dessert.

"You look amazing," he said as he reached for her hands. She smiled as he lifted her arms up and raked his eyes over her. His hands shifted, her weight shifted and suddenly she was spinning in the front doorway, in full view of her neighbors and with her dog's confused eyes looking on.

"It doesn't twirl so well," she said when she was stopped and facing him again.

"I don't care about the dress so much. That was a nice excuse to look at all of you, though." He leaned over and kissed her full and hard on the mouth. It was a welcoming kiss, one that said hello, and how are you. Wanting a kiss that invited more than greetings and promised intimacies, she pressed against him, opening her mouth and tempting him to explore further.

Caleb knew his stuff, she thought as a strong arm wrapped around her, holding her tightly against him and giving him room to deepen the kiss.

He tasted good. Like breath mints and something she couldn't name, other than to say it tasted like Caleb because he'd tasted like that the last time his lips had been against hers. A familiar taste and one that her body recognized as promising pleasure—and the deep parts of her belly responded accordingly.

Seamus barked once, clearly done with this

sit-and-wait business when there was a door open and a fun guest to greet.

Caleb was first to break the kiss. He pulled away slowly, a naughty smile on his face and heat in his eyes that matched the warmth spreading from her belly to all the good parts of her body. "Well," he said, then gave his lips a quick lick. "I'm sorry that I made dinner reservations instead of ordering pizza."

She patted the soft blue of his dress shirt. "You look too nice to stay in for pizza. How about this? I'll take off my panties before we go out for dinner and you can think about that all night."

Caleb raised his eyebrows. "I can get behind that."

"Come in, then, and I'll get my underwear off and we can get going."

She stepped back over the threshold and he stepped forward, still holding on to one of her hands. He kept a hold of her hand as he stopped to greet Seamus. He only let go when she tugged and reminded him that she needed both hands to make good on her promise.

"Do I get to see what you had been wearing?" he called out to her back as she disappeared into the powder room.

In answer, she opened the bathroom door a smidge and tossed the lacy black panties out into the open, hoping Caleb got to them before her dog did. Of course, after she adjusted the skirt of her dress and stepped out, both her date and her dog were looking at her with equal amounts of satisfaction. Her dog's mouth was open and his tongue was hanging out, and Caleb looked particularly smug, so she assumed that the panties had gone to the right animal. Asking felt like it intruded on her fantasy of being a sexy girl about town—so she didn't.

Reality got in the way of her fantasy as soon as she sat in the passenger seat of Caleb's car—enough so that she must have grimaced.

"Anything wrong?" he asked, shifting the car into Reverse.

"The dress is itchy," she replied, the shock of it jolting her into honesty.

He barked out a laugh, stopping longer at the stop sign than needed until he recovered. His humor didn't dull the dress's scratchiness, but it did prompt her to laugh with him—which made the rough texture a little more bearable.

He patted his suit jacket. "I've got your underwear in my pocket. Want to put them back on?"

Horrified, she looked at him. "They're in your pocket?"

"Yeah," he said, the same good humor lacing his tone. "Where was I supposed to put them?"

"I guess I don't know. I've never tossed a pair of panties at a man before."

"Well, I'm not certain there are rules regarding how a man takes care of a woman's panties. No fear, though. I've seen *Sixteen Candles* and learned it's wrong to show them to my friends in a bathroom."

She giggled at the reference, amazed that he could make the idea of him in a restaurant bathroom showing her underwear to his friends funny. But he'd thrown out the words like they didn't even matter, which made the lightness in them matter more. He was teasing, of course, and poking a little humor at her inexperience with dating, but the joke seemed aimed more inward.

Layers were part of his attraction. An orange with a tough skin that took work to get away, but revealed sweet fruit underneath. Fruit with a bite. The pucker was part of the enjoyment.

"But," he said as he hit the turn signal and pulled onto the main road that would take them to the freeway, "coming from my own experience, a gentleman only gives them back at the end of the night or when a lady requests them."

"How many pairs of women's underwear have been in that suit pocket?"

He tsked. "I don't kiss and tell. And it's not about how many have been there in the past. It's about you and me and your underwear in my pocket. And," his voice got a little louder as he warmed to his subject. She smiled with amusement, sinking as far back into the seat as was comfortable, given the lace torture happening on her.

"And," he said again, "I think keeping your underwear in my pocket makes me a regular Boy Scout. I am *so* prepared for anything that might happen tonight that I have your underwear in my pocket. You know, in case your dress gets itchy." He sounded so pleased with himself that she couldn't help but be pleased with him, too.

"Well, I appreciate your preparedness. And I will take my panties back. Not sure where I'll keep them on my way to the restaurant's bathroom. It's not like this dress has pockets." Since her clutch didn't fit much either, she'd have to shove them between her breasts.

Caleb didn't say anything as he merged onto the highway, but as soon as they were speeding toward downtown, he turned his attention back to her. "I could give them back to you now and you can shimmy them on in the car in the parking lot. I promise to look."

She must have made some noise because

he shrugged and said, "Or not look. That's up to you."

"I could dig them out of your pocket now, then shimmy—was that the word you used?—into them while you're driving," she offered, still highly amused with this entire conversation.

"Not fair," he protested, changing lanes. "If you don't want me to look, I promise I won't. Word of a Boy Scout."

She giggled and placed a hand on his knee. "I know you won't look if I say no."

"But just because I won't look, doesn't mean I won't *imagine*, and that would be distracted driving, for sure." That may have been the most sensible thing he'd said since she'd opened her front door. She was getting wet just thinking about him watching her put her panties back on. Thinking about him having fantasies about what it would look like didn't tone down the heat between her legs any.

"Parking lot it is."

"Can I look?" he asked, with such restrained interest that her smile—already pretty big—got larger. Boy Scout, indeed. He sounded as curious as a kid in a science museum.

"Yes," she answered, certain she wanted that as much as he did.

"Excellent."

"Where are we going?"

"Bida Manda," he said, referencing the Laotian restaurant in downtown Raleigh. "Maybe I should have asked if you like the place."

"I love it. I don't eat there often, but I love it."

They spent the rest of the drive to dinner talking more about restaurants in The Triangle, new ones, old favorites and ones that had closed. The force of Beck's thoughts, though, were on how she was going to make getting her underwear back on a sexy show, instead of a demonstration of her fumbling around in the car. She'd probably end up banging her head.

She need not have worried. Once they parked in the deck and Caleb turned off the car, he turned to her with such clear heat in his eyes that she knew that the idea was more important than the reality here. She didn't have to struggle to be sexy; she just had to be her and be here, which helped her with her resolve.

Emboldened by his attention, she moved the passenger seat of the car back. Then she took a deep breath and pulled the skirt of her dress up, reminding herself that they were in a big parking lot, the chances that someone would walk past them were slim and the chances that someone walking past would be interested enough to look in the windows slimmer still.

As that last bit of reassurance settled in her

brain, she let herself sink into the cocoon of safety that Caleb, with his dreamy hair and unearthly eyes and easy smile, seemed to create. They might be in downtown Raleigh and there might be thousands of people milling about, but it was just the two of them here in this car, and the two of them were all that mattered.

"Oh," he breathed out once her skirt was entirely hiked up. "That looks bad. I should kiss it better."

The red irritation covering the sensitive areas around her hips did look bad, but she couldn't feel them any longer. All she could feel was anticipation as Caleb unbuckled his seat belt and squirmed in his seat until he was able to lean over and kiss her pussy. He only kissed it once, and gently, no tongue—but that one kiss was so full of promise that Beck melted in her seat.

"Does it feel better?" he asked, once he was upright—though he managed to still feel close to her, like he was still in her space. Probably because she wanted him to be. Because she wanted his mouth back there and she wanted his cock there and she wanted him.

"Yes," she said, lost in the world of the two of them together, naked limbs entangled.

"Good." He gave a hard nod. "I'm going to be thinking about your pussy all through dinner and I'd hate to think about it feeling badly used."

"No worries there," she replied, still breathless and not sure when she'd get her breath back. She wasn't sure she even wanted to. Euphoria carried her through the awkwardness of wiggling around in her seat to get her panties on.

If she breathed, the clouds holding her up might disappear.

Caleb must have been keeping his eyes on her the entire time, because when she was done, he was looking at her, his face soft and—she glanced quickly—his cock hard. He smiled at her when their eyes met, like they shared a secret.

They did, she guessed, but the secret was deeper than the debacle with her panties. The secret was intimate and emotional—tinged with sex, sure, but weren't all good romantic relationships?

He held his hand out. She slipped her palm into his and he gave their joined fingers a squeeze. "Ready for dinner."

She smiled at him and nodded, unsure of her voice.

Good sex, he'd promised. Good company. Good conversation. Beck needed more of all three in her life.

CHAPTER ELEVEN

THEY HELD HANDS as they walked from the parking deck to the restaurant and while they waited in the restaurant's crowded lobby for their table. Caleb didn't let go of Beck's hand until forced to, as they had to take their seats. Or, maybe it was Beck who wouldn't let go of his hand. He wasn't sure. He only knew that he'd never held hands like that with any of his other dates and that it felt nice. The slight pressure, the warmth and the deep knowledge of a small part of her body. He understood why "holding her hand" had been a big step forward when he'd been a kid. There was more to it than he'd remembered.

Once seated, they made small talk about the restaurant, the menu and what they wanted to eat. They each ordered cocktails. To his amusement, Beck looked sheepish as she ordered a piña colada. "It feels like a silly drink to order, especially in such a nice restaurant, but I can't pass up the homemade coconut cream."

"And it's on the menu," he said to reassure

her—of what, he wasn't sure. With the way she smiled and chatted with the waitress, she could order whatever she wanted, and he'd be content to sit here and gaze at her while she did it.

"I'll ask Justin to put an extra umbrella in the drink for you," the waitress said, placing her hand on Beck's back. Beck had that effect on people. Not that people wanted to touch her, but that people were drawn to her.

Astonishingly, she didn't seem to notice. Or, she noticed the people—which is why they were drawn to her—but she didn't notice that they warmed to her differently than they warmed to him. She carried a bubble with her and she expanded that bubble to include everyone who wanted in.

It was that latter part that was unusual.

"Thanks," Beck said, looking up at the waitress. Not glancing, nothing so quick and dismissive. No, she looked and *saw* the waitress as a person, separate from her job and her role at the restaurant.

Beck saw things about people, past the roles they presented to the world. What did or would she see in him? And how much did he want her to see?

The questions vaulted around his head like Olympic gymnasts, some sticking their landing better than others. He and Beck had been having a light, joking conversation on the drive over. Nothing about the night had felt serious until he'd offered her his hand and she'd taken it and neither of them had seemed willing to let their hands part until a situation forced it.

He could navigate the conversation back to light and fun. Casual was his specialty. It helped him disarm sources at work and let him pass through the lives of so many women with minimal hurt feelings. But he liked having his hand held. He liked the way Beck looked at him as if the rest of the room—the rest of the world, even—had faded into the background of existence and he was the one person who mattered most of all.

Not that her look was personal. He knew that. The look was all part of Beck's singular attention on the person she was talking to.

But it sucked him in all the same and he didn't want to let it go. So, he held his hand out on the table in the hopes that she would slip hers back into it. When she did, all warm and soft, he abandoned casual to learn as much about the beautiful woman sitting across from him as was possible in the short time they'd be together before some great guy found her.

"Tell me something about yourself?" he asked, too swamped with questions in his own head to pick one. Some reporter he was, asking a stupid question like that.

But she was Beck, so her smile made her chin a little more pointed and her eyes a lot brighter when she asked, "Anything?" She bit her lip and he could see mischief in her eyes, as though she was trying to think of the silliest thing in the world to tell him.

The problem with thinking, of course, was that she looked stuck on all the seriousness of life. Sometimes, thinking was a foot in the mud. Getting unstuck might mean a ridiculous slurping noise and a face-plant.

He tossed her a rope. "Tell me about your childhood. What are your parents like? Did you have a family pet? Siblings?"

His questions weren't as innocuous as he'd hoped them to be. Beck looked like…well, she looked like a space heater trying to warm a freezing gymnasium. Cold seemed to descend upon her and she held tightly to herself, trying to warm it. He'd never seen anything like it and he wouldn't have said it was possible, until now and Beck.

"You don't have to answer that," he said, closing his hand tighter on hers, offering what support and comfort he had.

"It's okay." She cocked her head, the small space heater of her heart winning the battle against the room. "My parents are important people. They've worked in DC politics for so long that they've forgotten that some people go home, eat dinner, maybe play a family board game and tuck their kids in bed with a kiss. It's hard to know how to describe them, because their lives are so foreign to me and mine to them."

She was battling the anguish at the edge of her heart, he'd give her that. He understood her particular angst, though. "Are you a disappointment to them? I understand that."

A little of the pressure in her eyes lifted. "You would, that's right. They would prefer me to have your job. Political reporter for the newspaper of record in a state. They would at least know what to talk with you about. And you'd understand their passion over policy and bills and..." She shook her head.

"And you don't?" His dad didn't like his job—he thought Caleb was crooked for even being a reporter—but Caleb could talk to a salesman like his father and know their job, their concerns and their wins. It was the world he had grown up in.

She shook her head harder. "They weren't interested in me as a kid. I'm not sure why they had a child, except maybe that they were expected to and it was good for their career to have a child to talk about."

Her eyes pleaded with him to make sure he knew that whatever she said next was important. "I wasn't neglected. Don't get me wrong. I had a nanny and she read me stories and she made sure I ate a good dinner, and she listened to my stories of kids and school. I think my parents thought I would be so impressed by their example—their singular importance in the world they moved through—that I would follow in their footsteps."

"But you didn't." He tried to imagine the childhood she described and failed at the moment her parents would come through the front door after a day at work. His dad had often been angry and often had too much to drink— to take the edge off, he'd said, though it always seemed to sharpen that edge. But his dad had been there and around and talking to him and his sister. Of course, Caleb had always assumed that their dad talked to them because their mother was dead and there wasn't anyone else to talk with, but maybe it had been because they were his kids and he thought it was part of his misguided role as a parent.

Buried under Beck's words was the hint that she had almost never seen her parents. "I didn't," she confirmed, with an almost imperceptible shake of her head.

The waitress came by with their drinks. Beck paused to thank the woman and share a laugh about the plethora of drink umbrellas the bartender had included, like he had shared their joke. The waitress also brought by their shrimp chips—little fried pink puffs that vaguely tasted of shrimp. Those came to every table. To Caleb's surprise, the waitress also placed the order of summer rolls on her tray on their table.

"On the house," the woman said. "One of the line cook's grandparents had their anniversary party at your restaurant. They raved about how well you took care of them."

Beck appeared lost in thought for a moment, but then she exclaimed, "Of course. The couple who'd honeymooned in Tuscany. They brought in a particular Brunello they had wanted to drink with their dinner."

The waitress cocked her head and then laughed. "That sounds like them. They come in here often for dinner and are *very particular* about their order. They're nice enough about it that none of us fuss."

Beck laughed, too. "That sounds like them. A sweet couple. Fifty years later, they were still madly in love, even if they argued about the town where they first tried a Brunello."

"Enjoy your drinks," the waitress said with a pat on her leg. "I'll be back in a few minutes to get your dinner orders. Unless you have questions now."

"To be honest," Caleb said, "we've not even looked at the menu."

The waitress smiled indulgently at them, almost like they were the old married couple arguing, with love, about where they first tried a wine. "No worries. You're one of those couples so into each other that you'll be here awhile." She patted her leg again. "It's cute."

Huh.

As the waitress turned away from them, Caleb tried to catch Beck's eyes and share a look. *Wasn't the waitress silly,* is what the look was supposed to say. *We're not serious at all. Just here for a good time. No biggie.*

Only Beck didn't share the look with him. Watching the waitress walking away, her face was placidly pensive. When she did finally turn to look at him, her cheeks were smooth and her eyes were bright and, as far as Caleb could tell, the waitress's comments hadn't fazed Beck at all.

"That was a nice evening, with that couple. Normally I don't attend the parties we have at the restaurant, but I made sure to come to this one. I wanted to celebrate with them. Everyone liked them. They tipped well, too."

"I'm impressed you remember them."

"Don't be too impressed." She took a summer roll between her elegant fingers with their unpainted nails and examined it for a moment before dipping it in the sauce. "I don't remember everyone who has an event with me, but they were particularly memorable and were restaurant people. So it means something special."

Restaurant people. Her comment reminded him that she'd been talking about her childhood, which sounded both so different from his and, yet, ended with the same result. Disappointed parents. "You didn't learn at your parents' knee," he prompted softly, wanting to know more about the situation that had created the soft and intensely kind person sitting across the table from him.

She looked at him sideways for a moment, her mouth closed and jaw open, caught midchew and her eyes all wide and curious. Then she swallowed and said, "Oh, right. No, I didn't learn politics—my parents' trade—from them. I tried. But whenever I asked questions, they told me I didn't know enough to understand the answer. By the time I knew enough, or they thought I did, I'd stopped asking."

She lifted one shoulder and rolled her eyes.

For a moment, he saw the rebellion of a teenager who wanted to talk to her parents, but no longer wanted to feel like a bother. It was a quieter rebellion than his teen years had been, but Beck was a quieter person. And all the more effective for it.

"Also by that time, they thought I was…" She paused to take a sip of her drink. It was clearly good, because her face brightened through her unpleasant memories. "*Insolent* is too strong a term. I never talked back. I said please and thank you. I got decent grades. But they read my coldness as effectively as I'd read theirs and they didn't like it."

"Were they…" He didn't quite know how to ask what he wanted to know, so he took his own summer roll to buy himself some time. "Happy together?" was as close as he could come, though *happy* didn't seem a word that could ever be applied to people who found Beck to be cold.

She shook her head. "I don't know. Maybe. They share the same ambitions. They like to debate policy and economics and societal woes and their solutions. I think that makes them happy together. They could get a divorce. It's not like it would hurt their careers. But they don't, so I assume they get something out of each other."

Caleb was relieved when the waitress came by again. He needed time to collect his thoughts and a moment to watch Beck pulse with warmth at the near stranger and time to wonder quietly how she came out of the iceberg she called her childhood.

They each ordered their entrees. He wasn't even sure what he picked out. He almost always ordered the same thing when he came to Bida Manda, but this time he was caught up enough in her story to just point. Whatever it was he ordered would be good. Beck had a lively conversation with the waitress about the woman's favorite dishes here before settling on the beef larb.

When Beck turned back to him, lips pursed and looking as pleased as he'd ever seen a woman look, the question that had been lingering around him for the whole night sprang out of his mouth. "How did you get to be you?"

His question seemed to startle her. "Become me?"

"Warm. Kind. Interested in people. *You*."

Beck had a light flush, enough to tinge the apples of her cheeks. "Oh. That's nice."

"Also true. But you describe your childhood like it was the Arctic. And you're a tropical bloom who doesn't seem to belong."

"I glossed over my nanny because…because

everything with her was different. She took me to the grocery store and joked and laughed with the cashier. With me holding her hand, she walked down the street and smiled at people. In DC," Beck said, shaking her head. "She read me stories. Stories of women marrying a stranger in the Midwest and a girl who played with dolphins. And also tales of princesses and sisters who fight and love each other. Some women read *Pride and Prejudice* and wanted Mr. Darcy."

She smiled, playing with one of the umbrellas from her drink. "I wanted Lizzy's sisters. Her raucous family who spoke too loudly, said the wrong things, fought and loved each other."

"No siblings at all?" he asked, taking a sip of his own drink, a nicely tart and spicy drink with tequila, lime and jalapeño. He didn't think of himself and his sister as the daughters from *Pride and Prejudice*, but Beck sounded almost like little Jane Eyre, hiding behind a curtain with a book to offset her loneliness.

Except for the bright spot of her nanny.

"No. Just me."

"And the nanny."

"And the nanny," she said with a smile.

"Do you know what happened to her?"

She shook her head. "My parents decided I was too old for a nanny when I was twelve, I think. And I guess they were right, but I wasn't old enough to know how to stay in touch with her. I asked my mom about her once, probably a year or so after. She said Carolyn was working with another family and I shouldn't worry about her. So I just continued coming home alone and reading my books on my own."

Beck pulled her drink close, clearly thinking about drinking it, but she finished the thought that was on her mind first. "The way she said it made it sound like Carolyn had replaced me. It probably wasn't true. I probably could have written her a note or something, and I'll bet she would have liked it, but at the time, I didn't know that."

"Your parents don't sound like very nice people." Caleb really wanted to know who they could be. An important Washington insider couple—or at least a couple who wanted to be important—who seemed more concerned about official federal policy as it affected children rather than their own child.

"Nice isn't the point." She said those words with such matter-of-factness that Caleb had to wonder when she'd begun to make choices based on the opposite of what her parents would have done and if Beck even knew that was how she operated.

"I don't understand."

"Don't understand what?"

"You grew up with cold, unfeeling parents who share a cold, probably unfeeling relationship. You're divorced. And you want to get married again. I don't understand it." He shook his head. "And I'm not trying to be obtuse. I really don't understand it. My dad's a hard-ass, but I know he loves me, even if he doesn't understand me. And he and my mom seemed to be happily married. I mean, I remember them being affectionate with each other."

Beck shifted around in her chair, pushed her cocktail to the side and grabbed one of the shrimp puffs. "I want the Bennet family. I want the fights and the love and the frustration. I married a man who grew up with that and didn't want it. *That* was our mistake with each other. But if I want it, then there must be a man out there who wants it, too. And wants it with me."

Caleb thought back to his relationship with his sister, to the fights they'd had in the back seat of the car and over their first video game system. But there had also been nights when the only person he thought could understand him was his sister and he'd spent hours sitting in her desk chair while she'd sat on her bed and listened to him. Removing her from his childhood left him cold.

And when he'd watched those kids in the park and wondered about his life with children, at soccer games and dance recitals, he'd thought about having more than one. He hadn't thought about the fights he would have to break up, but he thought about how they would always have a best friend and how great that would be for them as they were growing up.

Beck wanted that for her life. *That* he understood as surely as his sister had understood him.

"Here are your dinners," a perky voice said from behind him. He shifted a little to the left so that the woman could place his food in front of him. Apparently, he'd ordered salmon and it looked delicious.

For the rest of their dinner and through dessert, he and Beck talked about lighter subjects than unhappy childhoods and failed marriages. She talked about the books she was reading and told a funny story about Seamus. He mentioned that a General Assembly member had seen them together out on their first date.

He didn't mention that Bernetta had said he'd looked into his date and teased him about dating around. But he thought about it, same as he thought about how he'd wanted the same things Beck had once.

BACK AT BECK'S HOUSE, with Seamus walked and fed and looking up the stairs like it was past time for everyone to go to bed, Beck poured them both a glass of wine to take upstairs while Caleb looked at her pictures.

"Are these your parents?" he asked, pointing to a picture of two older adults looking serious while sitting on an uncomfortable looking couch.

"Them?" Beck came over to him. "Yup. I think I took that last time I went up for Thanksgiving."

"How long ago was that?" Given what she'd said about her parents, he didn't imagine her spending the holidays with them.

"A year or so before Neil moved out. He liked to spend holidays with them. Their house gets professionally decorated and they have fabulous parties. He always enjoyed mingling with their guests."

"You?" She had her father's square jaw, but her eyes were all her mother. They were an attractive couple, no doubt about that, and even in the picture, he could tell that their clothes were expensive.

"I wasn't included in their parties when I was a kid or teenager, and I wanted to be. Now I'm not interested." She shook her head and sighed. "That's not quite true. I'd love to have a better relationship with them. I'd love to have kids with doting grandparents and a mother to call when I need advice. But we can't seem to get over our disappointment in each other. Neil was a patent lawyer. They liked him and his work. They think my job is little better than the people they hire for their parties."

She laughed, but there was no humor in it. "Of course, they're right."

He put his hand on the small of her back, steering her away from the picture and sour memories. "Let's sit naked in bed with our wine. We can rub each other's backs and tell goofy stories until we're ready for sex or to brush our teeth. Whichever comes first."

Caleb found himself in the role of comforter instead of clown, which was strange, but not a bad change. Especially when Beck stilled on her way to the stairs and pressed into him, as though she was trying to remind herself that he was there.

The woman's face in the picture needled at the back of his memory, but he dismissed her in favor of watching Beck's ass swing as she walked up the stairs in front of him. Feeling needed felt great. Feeling needed by this woman felt even better.

CHAPTER TWELVE

SUNDAY NIGHT AFTER recovering from a languid morning with Beck, Caleb was in his office, shoving a stack of papers away from his keyboard to be able to use his computer. Since he often worked at home and always needed his computer to work, he didn't understand how the damn thing managed to get under stacks of paper. If asked, he would say that he worked, stood up and came back to a buried computer. Since he lived alone, there was no one else to come around, detritus in their wake.

But the papers were always on his keyboard and he added this new set to the growing pile. Given the size of the pile, the papers would topple over in about a month. That would be his sign to organize everything and start the process again.

Reporters were a disastrously messy set of people, but Caleb tried not to slide too far into the pack-rat habits of his coworkers. He kept the rest of his house neat at least.

All the better to have women over.

All the better to have Beck over, which hadn't happened yet and should soon. He wanted to share his space with her *and* he wanted the memories of her stretching in his bed, naked and satisfied.

He was staring at a blank search bar, trying to think of how to search for Beck's mother's face when he couldn't quite remember why it was familiar or why he even cared when his phone rang.

"Yeah," he answered without paying attention to the face on the screen.

"Why haven't you been online dating recently?" his sister's voice said on the other end of the phone.

"Can't we pretend we don't see each other on dating sites?" To his horror and her amusement, Caleb and his sister showed up as options to each other on a regular basis on dating sites—it didn't matter which one and it didn't seem to matter how many times he hit whatever *hell no* option was available on the site.

Candice claimed seeing him was relief—one less creepy comment she was going to get. Sure, the matches were via some questionable algorithm and it didn't mean anything, but seeing his sister offered to him as a potential romantic partner set his teeth on edge.

"You're such a prude."

"I don't see how…" He stopped himself before stepping any deeper into the argument she was looking for. He hated to be called a prude and she knew it. Which, of course, was why she did it. "Anyway, I'm not a prude."

"I know," she said, perky as could be. "My friends tell me all the time."

He rolled his eyes. He'd been on a date with *two* of her coworkers and he hadn't realized they knew his sister when he'd met them. Neither had he realized they were coworkers of each other, of course. The latter probably wouldn't have mattered, except he'd been on dates with both of them on the same day and they'd talked at work later. With his sister, who still laughed about it.

Frankly, her friends had all been warned off him, which he didn't think was fair. He did his best to leave women better off than he found them and it's not like he could control who the dating algorithms presented to him. If he could, he sure as hell wouldn't have to reject his sister once a month.

When he didn't rise to this bait to argue with her, she sighed. "You didn't answer my question. I was scouting around for any new meat and there was your face. Only the site said you'd last been active online a week ago.

I didn't *know* you could go that long without looking for a new date."

Meat. It was an odd clue, but enough of one for him to start typing in the search box.

"I've been seeing someone," he said, paying too much attention to whom he was searching for and not enough to the fact that he was on the phone with his sister and she was a shark.

"Seeing someone, huh? Has the great rake of the twenty-first century met his match?"

"What?" He looked up from the search results list he was scanning to realize his mistake. "Rake. That's a stupid word. What's up with you tonight?"

"What?" she said, probably looking all innocent even though there was no one around to see and argue that she knew exactly what she was doing.

"I've been on a couple of dates with a woman. She knows the score. And I haven't had time to look for more company." Hadn't needed it, really. Just the memory of his date with Beck last night would be enough to keep him occupied for the week. And they would see each other again this weekend. They'd made tentative arrangements before he'd left her house and were trading ideas via text.

He should invite her over. They could watch a stupid movie and have sex on his couch. Seamus could even come with her. Domestic as it was, it still sounded like one of the best evenings he could imagine.

There she is, he thought as he switched to scanning image results instead of a series of links—only after he clicked from the picture of Beck's mom to the article about the lawsuit a bunch of meat packing companies brought against some laws regulating slaughterhouses.

Washington insiders, indeed. Beck's mom at least was as inside as they come. She worked for a firm that tried cases in front of the Supreme Court with such regularity that only the justices could claim more familiarity with the proceedings.

He'd had an image in his head about her childhood, with a nanny and parties and wealth. He added a couple million dollars to the price of the house that he'd pictured in his mind and an onion farm of pungent layers to her parents' disappointment at her life. There was almost no way that *kindest person ever* would be a moniker they would be proud of. Beck had grown up in rarefied circles, but the people she'd most wanted to love her hadn't invited her to participate. And so, she'd neatly stepped out of that world to make her own life as she saw fit.

Figuring out at least who her mother was filled him with a million questions for Beck—

most notably, how had she done it. He vaguely understood *why*, but couldn't imagine resisting the pressure her parents must have put on her to transform into their image.

Only, they hadn't, he realized. Put pressure, that is. They expected she would do and be who they wanted without bothering to look and see if she was. Probably she got good grades and so they didn't ask what else was happening in her life, what she was thinking, what goals she had. By the time they thought to ask, she'd already decided that their world wasn't for her and gone looking elsewhere.

He closed his hand on his new insight. Then he realized that his sister hadn't said anything in a couple of minutes. Or, worse, she'd said something and he hadn't been paying attention so she was creating a story about his relationship with Beck that fit her dreams for her brother rather than the reality.

"Are you still there?" he asked reluctantly.

"Are you?" Her smirk rang loud and clear.

"I was looking something up online when you called. Didn't see a reason to stop just because the phone rang."

"You're not paying attention to your only sister?"

"You're doing dishes." His sister couldn't stay still. She was probably still the same kicker in her sleep that she'd been when they were kids.

No wonder, between the two of them, they were the king and queen of one-night stands.

"Not true," she huffed. "I was cleaning out cat boxes. Now I'm sitting on the couch and trying to recover from the grossness of it all."

"You could *not* have cats." He briefly contemplated looking for information on Beck's dad, but then decided he'd find out who the man was if she decided to tell him. Otherwise, he didn't need to know.

"I'm not the one who's afraid of commitment at every turn."

"Hey. I've been married."

"Yeah. And now you're afraid of the word."

"Once bitten, twice shy," he said, and then winced. He was a better writer than that.

"So, this woman you're dating who's left you too busy to look for more dates…"

"I'm not talking about this with you."

To his surprise, Candice didn't grumble at being told no. It probably should have made him suspicious, but she distracted him from his misgivings by saying, "I saw Dad yesterday. He wants to know if you're coming home for Thanksgiving."

"It's not even June."

"I know. Would you believe he's got a girlfriend?"

"What? Really?" Caleb thought his dad would

be in mourning for their mom until the day he died, if only because it gave him the excuse to say there had only ever been one good woman in this world—ignoring the fact that he has a daughter.

"Yeah. She visits her son over Thanksgiving and Dad's already planning to go with her."

"Huh."

"That's about what I said when he told me. But you know, when he talked about Mom, his eyes got all soft. I've never seen that before. I guess I knew that her death probably hurt him, but it didn't occur to me how much."

"Because he never cried." To Caleb's memory, his father had blinked at the death of his wife and then gone on yelling at his kids over how they didn't do enough chores. If the man had mourned, he'd done it privately.

"Seeing his face light up when he talked about his girlfriend and hearing the sadness in his voice when he talked about Mom made me think that maybe he didn't show how sad he was back then because he had kids to raise. No time to be sad. But I think it hurt him enough that he wasn't willing to look for anyone else. Didn't want to risk being hurt again."

"That's a lot of Psych 101 to apply to a man after one lunch."

"Dad and I talk. You can't judge our relationship by the one you have with him."

Caleb considered how Beck described her own childhood and how the warmest woman he'd ever met turned into an ice pop at the mention of her parents. The fact that he and his dad seemed to do nothing other than rub each other wrong and then fight about it didn't seem so bad anymore. At least Caleb knew his dad cared about him. The man wouldn't yell so much if he didn't.

"Yeah. Maybe I should call him for lunch. See if I can meet the girlfriend."

Again, his sister was silent long enough that Caleb said, "What are you thinking?"

"Nothing," she said, her feigned innocence back with the force of Napoleon's army. "But if you do that, let me know how it goes. I'll be *fascinated* to hear."

He rolled his eyes and closed down the windows on his phone. "Whatever. I'm glad you called."

"Me, too. This was an enlightening conversation."

"Don't get any ideas about…anything," he said, finally deciding that being specific would only come back to haunt him.

"I don't get ideas. But I will be tracking your

online-dating profile to see when you sign on next."

"Don't you have anything better to do?" he asked, considering and then dismissing signing into the website she was talking about to throw her off. Not only was he not interested in seeing who else was on there, but the ploy wouldn't work anyway. She'd know.

"Than spying on my older brother? Nope."

"Bye, Candice."

"Bye, dear bro. Stay out of trouble."

"That's my line," he said, but the phone was already dead.

Candice was a pain in the ass. Little sisters never grew up.

ON MONDAY MORNING, as Caleb was scrolling through his newsfeeds on his phone, he saw a brief article about mountain bike riding. Remembering that Beck had been interested in learning to ride a mountain bike, he texted the article to her.

She didn't respond for an hour. Then he got a nice text saying thank you. She didn't leave the conversation there, though. In a long series of texts, she told him about a wedding that had been at her restaurant on Saturday night. The ring bearer had bolted as they waited to process. Apparently he was hot in his suit. The restaurant next door had been watering their plants. The water coming out of the hose must have seemed like a good idea.

The kid had walked down the aisle near sopping wet. His parents hadn't brought a change of clothes for him and the restaurant didn't have anything in lost and found. The kid had dripped all over the aisle. The staff had tried to interrupt and wipe the puddles off the floor. The bride had balked. Wiping up puddles didn't go with how she had imagined her wedding. Then the bride had slipped, landing in a heap of white and lace.

She wasn't hurt, Beck assured him, though no one had been sure for several long seconds while her shoulders shook. She was crying, but more with laughter than anything else. As the bride had explained to the staff later, it served her right for insisting that taking a small measure to assure her safety would get in the way of the perfection of the day.

The rest of the wedding went off without a hitch and was apparently one of the most fun weddings that the staff had ever worked. The bride had *owned* the dance floor—Beck had put asterisks around *owned* so Caleb knew where the emphasis should be. No worry of ruining her dress, and the fall meant she'd ripped enough of a seam that she could move a lot easier.

After that story, he and Beck slipped into a week of easy conversation through texting. They didn't make plans to see each other sooner than the weekend—neither broached that topic at all, but they also didn't go more than a couple hours without sending each other a message.

It was nice. Nothing Caleb had ever experienced before with a woman he was dating, but nice.

Do it! There's no one here to judge, Caleb's text said. She'd been telling him about the couple that had come into the restaurant earlier and how frustrating they had been. Then she'd pulled back before unloading on him about how terrible they had been. Not like Jennifer and Tanner—or any number of other couples that she met with—but truly awful. They'd talked about how this friend hadn't given them a nice enough engagement present and so they were going to stick him with the elderly great-uncle who smelled like urine. Then there was the cousin with a disabled child whom they didn't want to invite because the kid would ruin their wedding pictures.

Beck had done her darnedest to discourage them from booking the restaurant without seeming too obvious, all the while thinking horrible things about the couple, how they deserved each other and how she hoped they would both burst out with boils.

Normally she could swallow her evil thoughts and replace them with the bland nice ones, just as she'd been raised to do—but not with this couple.

This was a new thing, needing somewhere for her distaste to go. Through their texts, Caleb had somehow been able to intuit that she had more she wanted to say and that what she wanted to say wasn't kind. Intuit and there, in text, was permission to be petty.

Wherever they book their wedding, I hope a waiter spits in their food.

There. She'd said it. And felt immediately better when she saw what came back.

:-D. Not so hard. Though I'm fascinated to know you have mean thoughts. You should share more of them with me.

Permission and an invitation. A safe place to share a piece of her she kept hidden from everyone else, even Marsie. And that she'd never shared with Neil. God, and getting the words out made her feel instantly better. She wasn't able to right her ship and think *nice* things about the couple, but at least she had mind-space enough to write polite emails responding to other couples.

I don't have many mean thoughts.

Liar. ;-) You can trust me.

Another freeing feeling. She could trust him. She could place the parts of herself she kept hidden from other people in his hands and he'd take care of them, keep them hidden.

It's possible I spit in their water.

That made me laugh loud enough to get nasty looks from the other people in the hallway. There might have been scowls directed at me from both the floors above me and the floors below me.

I didn't. Not really. But it had felt good to type.

New Beck, Beck who was dating someone for sex and company only—that Beck could say stuff like that. The strictures were gone from New Beck.

Your secret's safe with me. I still think you're one of the most gracious women of my acquaintance.

"You have a glow about you, dear," an older woman's voice said from the door to Beck's office/closet.

"I'm just amused," she responded, looking up from her phone to the owner's wife, Helena. Her text conversations with Caleb ranged from the serious to the silly. Right now, the silly seemed serious.

Helena was the type of older woman Beck strove to be in forty years' time. Poised and graceful, with pastel suits and bright scarves, no matter the season. "Amused is good. Relaxed is better. And, yes, I think that's what I see."

"Relaxed? That seems accurate enough." She'd come into her office a ball of nerves, angry at the couple and feeling sorry for their friends, even though she didn't know them. Outraged at the world for producing people like that and knowing that no matter what venue they booked, they would make the staff's lives horrible. Telling Caleb that she'd spit in their water had given all the upset a place to go.

And he'd enjoyed it. Not judged it. Not told her she wasn't being polite, that people expected better of her. He'd both known she was kidding and been amused that she was kidding like that.

"Leslie said you're dating someone." Wrinkles softened Helena's face, though her eyes stayed as sharp as ever.

"My rebound guy." No way was Beck going to use a term like *fuck buddy* around Helena.

"Do such things really exist? It seems like all the men in my granddaughter's life are rebound guys." Soft scarves, soft makeup and soft white hair couldn't hide the hard tone of disapproval.

"I think you get out of one relationship and are supposed to take the time to figure out who you are before getting into another serious one." She shrugged. "But it's still nice to be taken out."

"I don't know, dear. I think we are never the same people by ourselves as we are with someone else. Are rebound men just men we don't like ourselves with?"

Beck didn't have an answer for that. She *did* like who she was with Caleb, even the snidely parts she'd just shown him. Those parts had always been there, but she'd never *liked* them before. She'd never been able to be frustrated and gracious at the same time. It was nice.

"Helena, how long have you been married?"

"Fifty-six wonderful years."

"How did you know Jeremiah was the right man for you?"

The older woman's cheeks reddened. Or maybe it was a trick of light and too much blush. Whatever it was, Beck wasn't prepared for the answer. "I farted on a date and Jeremiah thought it was funny. He told me everyone does it and that I was still the most beautiful woman he knew. You think I look so nice at home?"

"Yes." Surely Helena's pajama sets matched her robes and her slippers and she knew how to sleep so that her hair looked as done in the morning as it had when she left the salon.

"When the grandkids aren't around, I wear a pair of slippers older than you. My point is, Jeremiah knows and loves all of me. And I all of him. No reason to like or dislike who I am around him. I'm Helena."

Was that the answer? Not to toss out Old Beck or embrace New Beck, but just to be Beck.

"The young are so easily confused," Helena said, a giggle she wasn't fully able to hide in the back of her throat. "Let life happen, dear. Don't try to fight it."

Helena's advice sounded oddly like Marsie's admonishment that Beck needed more joy in her life. Of course, trying to find the joy felt like not letting life happen, so the two pieces of advice jumbled together in her head, neither helping her understand the other.

With one light step, the older woman was in Beck's office, placing a warm hand on her shoulder. "My advice didn't help, did it, dear?"

"There's so much advice in my life right now. I'm not sure any of it's helping."

"You'll find a man you can fart in front of and it'll all be okay."

Now there was a practical piece of advice that didn't have a competing piece of advice floating around in Beck's head anywhere. Not that she was sure she could do anything with the advice, but Helena seemed to feel better as she walked off to check in on some of the regulars eating lunch in the dining room.

CHAPTER THIRTEEN

DRESSING FOR A movie at Caleb's house was certainly easier than figuring out what she was going to wear for a night out on the town, but the *packing* presented its own unique challenges. First off, did she pack? If so, how much did she assume? Bring a toothbrush and assume she can use his toothpaste? Bring pajamas? Fresh underwear?

Caleb hadn't expected to stay the night the first night and he hadn't brought anything with him. But last week he'd brought a toothbrush and used her toothpaste. No pajamas, but she hadn't worn any, either.

This had all been easier in college. Or, college had been long enough ago that she'd forgotten what it had been like to overthink under different circumstances.

Finally, she shoved a toothbrush in her purse and grabbed Seamus's leash for a trip outside. At least packing for the dog would be easy. His needs were simple and he wouldn't understand not wanting to feel like he was moving in.

A toothbrush wasn't moving in. It was dental hygiene. Nothing more.

After a quick trip to the backyard with Seamus, she grabbed her phone and noticed the text notification from Caleb. Call me.

In her recent calls, she also noticed there was a missed call from him. She was supposed to be at his house with the dog in twenty minutes. A text like this was not a good sign. But, as she caught a glimpse of her red lips and carefully casual eye makeup, it didn't matter. She liked Caleb, but they'd only been on two dates and exchanged a few text messages. Maybe more than a few text messages, but nothing serious. If this ended terrible...

Well, she'd be sad. But she'd be okay. She'd always be okay. And if he was calling to cancel a date, she was going out anyway. She could take herself to dinner. Maybe even see a movie. She could sit in a movie theater on her own. Bring a book to a restaurant.

Pep talk over, she called him.

"Hey," he said. "Um, I've got a problem."

"Oh," she said, trying to sound casual. He hadn't promised her forever. All he'd promised her was good sex and good conversation, and she'd already gotten two nights of that.

"Hah," he said. Even through the phone, she could tell he was trying to sound casual, and that she'd accidentally insulted him. "You thought I was calling to cancel our date."

Relief flooded her. "You told me what to expect, and that didn't include anything long-term."

"No. But I don't bail unexpectedly. I'm not interested in commitment, but I try not to be a jerk. If I'm the one who ends this, I'll do it cleanly, not twenty minutes before a date. Can you give me the benefit of the doubt?"

"Yes," she said, no question in her mind. Twice, Caleb had been up-front with her, almost to the point of it smarting. He wasn't the type to beat around the bush. She'd decided to trust him. She'd shared hidden parts of herself with him. She did trust him. "What's up?"

"There's a kitten on my back deck. It showed up five minutes ago."

"Oh." She clasped a hand to her chest. She was a dog person, but only someone with a heart of stone could resist a kitten. "Are you going to bring it in your house?"

"Yes, but it's got some blood on it. I caught it and it's in a box. I couldn't feel anything wrong with it, but I'm not a vet."

"Yeah. Okay. Blood isn't good. Are we canceling the date so you can take the kitten to the vet?" She would be disappointed about that, but in life there were excuses and there were reasons. This was a *reason*.

"I don't want to. I was looking forward to tonight."

Lust shot through her belly. *So was I*. She had wanted to see his eyes darken with desire again. Feel his hands on her. Arch her back and press her breasts against him. She shimmied in her jeans, stopping herself from getting herself riled up when her night would probably be spent at home, with the dog.

"I don't think this will take long. I doubt there's anything wrong with the kitten. So, I figure I'll be at the emergency vet for a half an hour or so. Stop by the pet store to get a litter box and some food. Be ready for our date in... an hour and a half at most."

"Have you ever had a pet?" She'd taken Seamus to one vet appointment since she'd gotten him. She'd been at the vet for forty minutes. He was a perfectly healthy dog *and* she'd had an appointment.

"No."

"You'll be at the vet longer than thirty minutes."

"Oh." He sounded so surprised and disappointed that Beck had to grin.

"Want me to meet you at the vet?"

"You would do that?" Relief echoed through his voice.

"Sure." She didn't need to be curled up on the couch with him to feel wanted and sexy. All she needed was for Caleb to look at her with those hot eyes. "We can do the movie after."

"I'll text you the address of the vet. Meet you there?"

"Absolutely." The line went dead and Beck smiled a little at the idea of Caleb carrying a yowling kitten in a box. He was sweet as can be. No wonder he was the most popular man online.

Hardening her heart against a man with a kitten was going to be hard. New Beck was up for it, though. New Beck was up for anything.

CHAPTER FOURTEEN

CALEB SAT IN the emergency vet waiting room with a screaming kitten in a box on his lap, feeling decidedly out of place. He had zero experience with pets. When he was a kid, his dad had considered them a waste of money and food. Then he'd gone to college and was too busy to even consider getting a furry friend. Then he'd gotten married and Leah had said a dog would be great practice for having kids, only she'd never found a dog she liked. They were all too small or too big or smelly or the wrong breed. Which was probably for the best, really. He didn't know that he could have stomached her complaints about the dog and how the walks it needed were ruining her life. Or hearing about how he never did his share.

Maybe he would have gotten out of the marriage sooner.

Maybe.

Getting out of his marriage, even though it was an unhappy one, was one of the hardest things he'd ever done. Wishing for ways that it could have been worse seemed like a fool's regret—and all regret was foolish.

Better to focus on the present. And Beck. And the kitten mewing on his lap.

The lobby was nice. The chairs, which had plastic arms and padded seats, were decently comfortable. They reminded him of the ones in his doctor's waiting room. There were magazines he liked and the paper he wrote for. The fish tank was amazing.

But being at the emergency vet was one of those times where he missed having someone else in his life. With Leah, this could be one of those situations they either excelled at as a couple or crashed and burned. But even with the risk of crashing and burning, she would have been a person to sit next to.

A vision in black and dark denim sliding in through the door caught his attention. Beck sailed over to him in heels that made her legs look a million miles long and jeans that hugged her legs, making him wish for a better angle. Beck had great thighs. He could spend hours between them.

"Hey," he said, holding on to his box and making to stand up when she waved the movement away and bent down to kiss his check. The top of her button-down was just an enticement. Without a cat on his lap, he would be able to see straight down to her navel. Tonight, he'd kiss that navel.

Then she sat down next to him and reached for his hand and gave it a squeeze and he stopped thinking about sex and started thinking about how nice it was that she was here for him. *Reliable.* This is what was meant by the word, showing up for the important things. Being present. He'd bet Beck was *awesome* at showing up.

She was here now.

"You okay?" she asked, not letting go of his hand.

"Hmm? Oh, yeah. I think the cat's okay. And it's not really my cat. I just found it. If it's not okay, it's not like I'll have lost a pet."

"Do you believe that at all?" she asked, her voice soft. Her hand was warm and steady and present and forgiving. Her fingers were there for him.

She was there for him, which made it easier to say, "No. I feel responsible for the screaming thing. It didn't make this much noise at my house, which makes me worry that the blood does mean something."

She laid her head on his shoulder. God, she smelled good. Like musk and patchouli. Before she'd taken his hand, he would have said she smelled like a woman expecting a hot date. Now, he thought she smelled comforting.

"How'd you find the kitten?"

Her head was on his shoulder. Her hand was in his. Their arms were touching. If the kitten was out of the box, settled and purring, he could sit in these chairs and stare at the fish forever.

"I went outside to check how clean my patio furniture was. You know, in case we sat out there and ate dinner. I can be…" He paused. "Messy. And I wanted the house to look nice." He felt a little silly confessing that he'd had to clean for their date, but he could feel her smile and then her nod against his shirt.

"I did that before our last date. I didn't have a chance the first time."

He thought back to that first date, which wasn't that long ago but felt both like yesterday and as if he'd known Beck for years. Everything he remembered about that night was focused on Beck. If her house had been dirty, he hadn't noticed. "It looked clean enough to me the first time. Of course, with you in my view, there was no reason for me to check for dust."

"So, you were outside, making sure everything was comfortable for our dinner," she prompted after a pause—and he would swear she blushed.

"Right." He shifted a little in his seat so that he could lay his head on hers. "And I heard the mewing. You can't see the kitten through the holes, but it's black-and-white and tiny. The white is how I noticed the blood."

"Caleb Taggert," someone called from another room. A woman in scrubs stepped through the doorway and said his name again.

"Here," he said, hopping up, box in his arms. Beck was standing next to him. She came into the exam room with him. Though she didn't say much, he knew she was there. And that was all that mattered to him.

AFTER THE VET had examined the cat, Caleb stood at the counter, credit card in hand. The kitten was in the nicer cardboard box the vet had provided. He was afraid to look at the bill and see how much the nicer box was costing him. At least the airholes were nicer. And the kitten was quieter. Probably scared shitless and wondering why he—the kitten was male—had picked that porch to yowl on.

But the good news for both Caleb and his new pet was that the blood hadn't been from the kitten. When the vet had confirmed that the kitten was perfectly healthy and the blood had come from another animal, Beck had sucked in her breath. It had taken longer for Caleb to realize what that blood might mean. There may be other kittens. There may be a dead mama cat.

Tomorrow morning, he would get out and explore his town house, looking and listening for signs of other kittens. And, honestly, he didn't know if he hoped he would find them or not. Hoping they were either okay or out of pain seemed the only reasonable thing he could wish for right now.

The bad news for the kitten and Caleb's bottom line was the next trip to the vet in their future. The kitten was just shy of two pounds and he had to be neutered, plus all the vaccinations the kitten would need.

A black-and-white paw ventured out of one of the airholes, followed by a sad mew. Caleb reached out to place a finger to the paw. The kitten stilled for a moment, but didn't take his paw away. He smiled down at the sight. Holding hands with a kitten. He had a pet. A tiny thing that was reliant on him to keep him alive. It was the most commitment he'd allowed in his life since entering a lawyer's office and asking how to get a divorce.

He hoped he'd be the owner the kitten needed. He didn't travel for work and he believed it was okay to leave food out for cats during the day. Plus, there were pet sitters. And he had neighbors if he was going to be late getting home every now and then.

A slight hand touched his back and he relaxed into the reassurance. "This took longer than I thought," he said, by way of apology.

"Yeah," Beck said. "But he's a cutie. And I think he'll be a handful."

"Aren't all kittens?" the receptionist said as she handed Caleb back his card. "It's part of what makes them so much fun. Just make sure you've got a safe place for him to be when you're not home and he's looking for trouble."

"Remember that, Caleb, when you find the kitten climbing your curtains. Fun." Beck's voice was light. He hoped his mood would be when her prediction came to pass. 'Cause he didn't know much about cats other than the videos that passed through his social media feeds, but those were enough to tell him that they were attracted to places they shouldn't go—and often destroyed expensive items in the process.

He tucked his credit card back in his wallet and picked up the box, which weighed nothing, considering there was a life inside.

The streetlights out in the parking lot reminded Caleb of the time. "It's late."

Beck smiled a half smile that crinkled the corners of her eyes. Adorable. And she was

here with him. "That took about as long as I
expected it to."

"And I still have to get supplies. I'm sorry
about our date."

"Don't be," she said with a shake of her head.
"The kitten is cute and more important than
you cooking me dinner. Is there good Chinese
food around here?"

"Sure."

"Why don't you call for Chinese food and
pick it up on your way home. I'll stop at the
pet store and get supplies."

"That sounds great," he said, relieved. More
than relieved. He was grateful for her steady
presence, for her easygoing nature that wasn't
at all bothered about their change of plans even
though her heels weren't designed to carry bags
of cat litter, and for her levelheadedness.

Dinner and the needs of a small animal
should be an easy problem to solve, but the
longer Caleb carried the box with the kitten
the more weight the tiny thing had. Needs. The
kitten had needs that were his responsibility to
meet. And he had the ability to disappoint the
kitten, which was heavier than forgetting to buy
cat food on the way home and never remembering to clean out the litter box.

Which was stupid, because of course the kitten would be disappointed in him. It was a kit-

ten. It was going to turn into a cat. And cats were, from everything he knew, superior beings, at least in their own minds. He was letting the weight of the commitment—and the possibility of failing—get to him.

And it was a cat, not a marriage or a child.

"You okay?" Beck asked and Caleb realized that he'd been quiet.

"Yeah. I was thinking a puppy might have been easier. Don't dogs love you unconditionally?" Maybe the cat judging him was at the heart of his problems. God, he was going home with a kitten and a beautiful woman. Any problems he was having were being created in his own mind.

She laughed. "That's what they say, but Seamus often seems all judge-y. He doesn't like to cuddle. He's not interested in making me feel better when I'm sad. And I'm pretty certain that half the time he thinks I'm stupid."

"Really? He seems like a good dog." Wagging tail, tongue hanging over his jaw, and a cocked head like he expected perfection out of the humans standing in front of him and knew he would get it.

"He is a good dog. But he's his own dog. And your kitten will be his own cat. And he probably won't be the cat you expect, but he might be the cat you need."

"The cat I need?" he asked with a disbelieving laugh.

"Yeah." She chuckled. "Someone said that to me about Seamus when I was complaining that he hid in my bedroom when I cried. No comforting head on my knee out of that dog."

"Did you believe them?"

"About as much as you're believing me now," she said with a knowing, mischievous smile.

He nodded, feeling better about the small life he was taking home. "Thank you."

"You're welcome." The world seemed to move in slow motion as she rose up and kissed his cheek. And she was coming home with him.

THE KITTEN MEOWED in its cardboard box from the middle of his living room floor. Embarrassing as it was to admit, even to himself, he was hesitant to let it out without the supplies Beck was getting. Especially after all that talk about kittens being a handful. Handfuls needed at least a litter box.

So, he had waited, browsing articles on cat and kitten care on his phone while the kitten sat in the center of the room and whined. Poor thing was probably hungry. Caleb was, too, and the smell of Chinese food permeated the entire house.

As soon as the doorbell rang, Caleb was on his feet and at the door before the chimes stopped.

Beck swept into his townhome in a cloud of energy and purpose. Plastic bags rustled as they banged against the door, and then he felt something hard hit his shin. "Sorry about that," she said, bouncing off him. "Where do you want the litter box?"

He peeked out the door to her car. "Is there more?"

"Nope." Her voice sounded far away, so he turned. Beck, and all her bags, had made it to his kitchen. "I hate making more than one trip, so I always grab more than I can reasonably carry. Hence my attack on your shins."

He shrugged, shut the door and followed her to the kitchen. The sight of her standing at his kitchen island stopped him dead. "You look amazing," he stammered out.

Her smile was wide, honest and full of beautiful teeth as she looked down at her smashing jeans. "This? I was wearing this at the vet's."

"I know. You looked great there, too. But my kitchen has more light. And fewer injured animals. So I get to see you a little better." And he wanted to see her from every perspective. To watch the fabric of her shirt bunch a little at the curve of her breast as she moved. To watch her walk in her sky-high heels.

This hot woman was in his kitchen. Even better, she was in his kitchen unpacking cat food dishes onto his counter.

"Where is the little monster?" she asked.

"You know, I've never had a pet before. And you calling it a little monster doesn't make me any less nervous about caring for him."

The easy way she waved away his concern helped him confess. "He's still in the box. I didn't know what to do with him. No litter box."

She looked up from the supplies she was arranging and he braced himself, though he wasn't sure what he was steadying his feet against.

Her lips had a slight purse to them and her eyes were soft. Sympathy, not pity. The two were very different. Caleb had seen both, directly aimed at him, more than once. "Kittens are easy. They're hell on wheels, but easy. Most of the trouble they get themselves into is trouble they can get themselves out of, so long as you don't kill them for ruining your furniture. And they come litter-box trained." She patted the large plastic tub on his counter. "So where do you want it? Someplace you'll remember to clean it out, but not where you have to smell it all the time."

"Um, guest bathroom, I suppose."

"Let's get that kitten out of the box," she said, coming around the island and putting a hand on his shoulder.

Then she swept him and the litter box and the toys and the food dishes up in her energy. When the thought passed through his head that he never wanted her to let him go, he held on to it for a moment before the import of such a radical idea smacked him and he dropped it like a grenade.

"YOU WEREN'T KIDDING about hell on wheels," Caleb said as he pulled the now-cold Chinese takeout food out of bags and laid it on his counter while his kitten seemed to toddle across every surface in his house all at one time.

His kitten. What a novel thought. It was such a little thing and yet seemed to carry so much weight.

"I know," she said, her voice as bubbly as her smile. "Kittens are the best. What are you going to name him?"

"Kitten?" She smiled in response, which is what he had been hoping for. "Honestly, I haven't thought that far ahead. When he showed up on my back deck, the only thought I had was to make sure he wasn't hurt. Naming him right now seems so permanent."

She stopped scooping chicken and vegetables onto her plate and looked up at him, her brows crossed. "But you're keeping him?"

"Of course," he looked up from dishing out his food so that she could see from his face that he was sincere. "I guess I meant that a name should reflect his personality and I don't know what that will be yet."

As if on cue, the kitten tried to leap onto his kitchen table and missed. They both turned toward the noise of him falling back to the floor and watched as his butt wiggled and he tried again. "What about Evel, like Evel Knievel?" Beck asked. "If nothing else, he seems like he'll be a daredevil kitty rather than a cuddle kitty."

He rolled the idea around in his head for a moment, thinking about how it would feel to call out "Evel" when hollering at the cat because it was climbing his drapes. "That sounds too prophetic. What about Robbie?"

"Robbie?" There was another thump, this time because the kitten was trying to jump from the floor to the chair. "Poor little thing," Beck said with a shake of her head. "Too small to get into everything he wants to right now."

"All the more reason not to call him Evel," Caleb said as he picked up his plate and moved to the very table the kitten was attempting to scale. "Robbie is Evel's son. Evel's real name was Robert. Robbie's nice and neutral."

She cocked her head at him as she set her plate on the table. "Does a neutral name matter that much?"

For a moment, he had a flashback to Leah questioning his readiness to be a father, but then he remembered the baby was a kitten and that the woman in his kitchen was Beck. This was their third date and already he could tell that she didn't pack negative layers into her words. For better or worse, she was able to casually lean against a kitchen counter, drink her coffee and tell him to get out of her house.

No need for layers, so he turned his mind to her question, rather than what she might mean by it. "I guess it doesn't. You and the vet called him a tuxedo cat, so…I'm going to name him Bond, James Bond."

"James Bond's a cute name."

He shook his head. "Not James Bond. Bond, James Bond. Best said with Sean Connery's slurred Scottish accent."

Her eyes widened, which looked extra cute with the piece of chicken suspended in front of her face by chopsticks. "That will be a long name to call out," she said with a giggle. "But I'll bet you'll laugh every time you have to say his name. Or when you feed him and say his food is shaken, not stirred."

He laughed along with her. "I hadn't thought about that. I wonder if they make little martini glasses for cats. Wasn't there a series of advertising for a cat food that had a cat living in luxury? That's how I imagine Bond, James Bond's life to be. If I had the skills, I'd make him a cat bed that looks like an Aston Martin DB5."

"Oh!" Then she held her hand up to her lips while she finished chewing, whatever she was thinking dancing in her eyes. "My friend Marsie's boyfriend could probably do that. I should ask him. He's handy and that would be cute."

"Let's hold off on that," Caleb said with a wave of his hand, a laugh and a tinge of reluctance. He liked having offered up a silly cat name and the laughing and teasing that was coming out of it, yet he was bringing it to a close when what he really wanted to do was to push Beck further. To make her laugh harder.

Not that he hadn't laughed and teased with other women. Jokes, smiles and alcohol were part of the reason he liked dating so much. That, and women smelled so damn good. All of them. And had cute laughs.

But as soon as the specter of commitment appeared, he ran like the cowardly lion. Which made Beck different. He knew she wanted

happily-ever-after and he was still here—
by choice. Then he'd had that thought at the
vet's office of never wanting her to let him go.
Thoughts like that couldn't be fully dropped.
The memory of them lingered and the residue
made him want to see how far Beck would go.
Would she call her friend's boyfriend to make
his new kitten a bed?

He wasn't stupid enough to not realize that
that was him looking for commitment from
her. Commitment that he didn't want, and so
it wasn't fair to ask for it.

Casual relationships only worked if both parties kept them casual—and that meant not asking your friend for favors, especially ones that
took time. He and Beck had tonight, maybe
tomorrow morning. He couldn't ask for more.

Those were his rules, not hers.

They ate a couple of bites in silence, the rain
he'd let fall slowing their parade of laughter.
The easy camaraderie wasn't coming back immediately, which strangely was okay. Departing
laughter had left an opening for deeper conversation and he was going to take it.

"So, have you thought about what I said
that first morning? About taking time to get
to know who Beck is when she's single and
trying new things out?" Caleb asked.

"Some," she said after swallowing a bite of her food. "It's not that exciting, though."

He pushed a mushroom off to the side of his plate. They weren't good cold. "I have a hard time believing that. And shouldn't you be the one who gets to decide if it's exciting or not?"

She blinked, slowly and a bit like an owl. It was cute. "It's hard to get used to not having the other person around as a foil or to comment on what you're up to, you know. Good or bad, there's a person who's there to support you, to tell you that your idea is cool, that you'll have fun and that you'll be awesome at whatever it is you're trying. I have trouble providing that level of energy for myself."

"Was that what marriage was for you?" Enjoyable conversation and good sex were all he was capable of right now, but that didn't mean he didn't remember the better parts about being married. Being intimate wasn't about taking your clothes off. It was about sharing a bathroom and hearing the other person talk about how they were too old for pimples or loved the way they'd grown into their teeth.

Intimacy was loving the small things, both the good and the bad. He missed that more than he missed the support.

A flash of light broke the burden of those

thoughts. He didn't miss the support because, likely, it hadn't been there.

A nice dinner with a woman and a quick roll in the hay—maybe repeated twice, but never more than three times—were not the same as encouragement to try something new, but they were closer to support than he'd had in years. To hear Beck talk about the real thing made the shallowness he'd been chasing feel...

Nope. He was worried about being able to care for a kitten. He wasn't so unaware of himself that he knew part of staying out of relationships was fear on his part, but Leah had been right that his job made for a hard relationship. And that babies took money he didn't have. Not that marriage meant babies, but he still wanted them. And he didn't want to hear again how he wasn't reliable enough to have them. Better to own that from the beginning.

And better not to let his mind linger on such thoughts for long. Right now, he had a kitten to take care of, a hot woman to romance and a light, pleasing attitude to maintain.

Besides, she was considering both his question and her answer and he wanted to know what she had to say, without distractions from his own thoughts.

"Marriage wasn't always like that for me." She was pushing her mushrooms to the side of her plate, too, which felt prophetic given their current conversation. "To be fair, I don't think I was always like that for Neil. I'm sure I fell short of supportive many times during our marriage. But that's the goal, right? To lift the other person up and to let them lift you up, too?"

Two thoughts struck Caleb at the same time. One, that Beck was easily admitting where she had failed her partner and expressing that failure as hope for a better future. And, two, that they seemed to regularly veer far from casual— further than Caleb ever let himself stray, and he hadn't fessed up to his own shortcomings yet.

"So, what would you like me to lift you up to?"

She pushed her rice around her plate and then set her chopsticks down. "It's been nice to have someone to share my snide thoughts with."

"That's all," he said, unable to hide his surprise.

She shrugged. "I'm nice all the time. It gets tiring."

"What about with Neil?"

"I was a royal bitch when we were getting a divorce, but while we were married, he told me once that my job wasn't hard, and I never complained about my customers again."

"Complain all you want to me. I'll still think you're the nicest person I know. And everyone needs a place to let off steam." So far, this was easy. "What else can I support New Beck with?"

"I've been taking a drawing class. It's pretty fun. I'm terrible, but Seamus doesn't sit well for portraits, so I'm going to blame my model."

He could imagine them in her house, her dog looking off to the side, wishing to be somewhere else and someplace more comfortable than seated on the hard kitchen floor while she drew him. But, because he was a dog, he would sit there politely until she told him to go. Politely including heavy dog sighs, though. The image made him laugh. "Absolutely. Anything you draw that's less than perfect is the dog's fault."

Beck caught his eye and smiled, as though she knew the picture he'd drawn in his mind and it fit reality exactly. "I'm still thinking of signing up for that mountain bike class. That sounds badass. And much more like something pre-divorce Beck would never do. Too risky."

"Do you have a bike?" He snagged a couple of extra pieces of broccoli from the take-out containers and added them to the chicken on his plate.

"No. That makes learning to mountain bike harder." She giggled. "But I've had drawing pencils and charcoal for years. So that doesn't make drawing very post-divorce."

"I can help you get a bike. I used to bike every chance I got and know a lot about them. We could go pick something out together."

She eyed him suspiciously. "How far ahead are we making a date? Does this violate our agreement to be casual?"

He waved away her concern. "Nah. No matter how long we keep each other company, I hope we'll stay friends. And friends can help lift each other up into expensive mountain bikes as easily as lovers and husbands can, yeah?"

"Yeah, okay," she agreed. "When?"

He didn't have a date tomorrow, so in theory they could go bike shopping then—assuming she didn't have a date, either. But spending almost twenty-four hours with one woman, even one as great as Beck, seemed too far from fun for comfort. So much time together slid into commitment, and he didn't want her to get any ideas.

"How about next weekend? We can make that our date. Maybe get lunch before. Or dinner after?"

"I'd like that. Should I do some research to see what I want?"

"You can and I can, too, if you like. You'll be

looking for an entry-level mountain bike and not looking to spend too much money. That will limit our choices and you can simply pick the bike you find most comfortable from the ones you ride when we're out."

"What," she exclaimed, with faked horror. "You mean you're not going to take me out to buy the fanciest, most expensive bike we can find?"

"I can if you want," he said with a chuckle. "I'll lift you up as you're wasting your money as easily as I will when you're making a good decision."

"It's settled, then. Next Saturday. We can work out the details later." There was a crash in his living room and they both leaped up to find Bond, James Bond strolling across the floor like nothing amiss had happened.

"Nothing looks broken," Beck said.

"Not even that cat," Caleb agreed, surprised, especially given the noise of the thump and the size of the kitten. Bond, James Bond butted a nose against his ankle and Caleb reached down to pick the tiny thing up. The kitten was so small and light, barely resisting in his hands at all. And this creature was relying on Caleb to keep him alive.

That thought was almost as stunning as the

fact that he'd made a date with Beck for next week before checking his other options. She was the first woman he'd made a date with a week in advance. And now he'd done it twice. Not that he was committing himself to anything other than helping a great girl find the perfect bike. Next Saturday was only something more if *he* decided it was.

He didn't. And he wouldn't.

"You didn't bring Seamus. Are you able to stay the night?" he asked, steering his mind back to less weighty topics.

"I called my neighbor to let Seamus out later tonight and early tomorrow morning. I shouldn't be too late because he'll want his walk by then, but I can stay over."

"Good," Caleb said, shifting the kitten to one arm and reaching out to Beck with the other. "Come upstairs with me."

"But the dishes?" she asked as she slid her hand into his.

"Will keep until tomorrow."

"And the cat?" she asked as soon as his foot hit the first stair.

"What about the cat?"

"Is Bond, James Bond sleeping in the same bed with us?"

"Where else would he sleep?"

"This should be fun," she said, giggling.

Sex while a kitten was attacking his feet turned out to be a challenge, but Beck's happy sighs as she tucked herself against his arm suggested he had been up to it.

[faint text from previous page showing through]

CHAPTER FIFTEEN

Hey. THE TEXT had been waiting on her phone as soon as she got home. By the timestamp, it looked like Caleb had sent it almost as soon as they'd kissed goodbye at his door.

Thanks again for coming over. And bringing all the kitten stuff. I had a good time.

You're welcome :-) she typed out before setting down her phone and grabbing Seamus's leash. I love kittens.

She got the leash on her excited dog, and then typed out the rest of her message while Seamus struggled to sit at the door.

I had fun, too. I'm looking forward to Saturday and bike shopping. I'll need a helmet.

Phone in her pocket, keys in her hand and dog sitting—barely—Beck opened the door and stepped out into the cool spring morning.

As with last week, when they'd texted back

and forth, the phone was too tempting to ignore, though she tried. When Seamus stopped to sniff a cluster of bushes, Beck pulled out her phone and read his message.

And gloves. And a pair of bike shorts. I'll bet you'd look hot in the bike shorts.

She snorted, letting Seamus linger, sniff and pee for longer than usual while she typed out an answer.

Thank you! Though don't bike shorts have the padding around the butt? I'll look like I'm wearing tights over a diaper.

Seamus was ready to go, so they strolled on to the next interesting clump of plants. Beck said hi to a couple of neighbors who were also walking their dogs, and Seamus got a chance to sniff some butts, his tail wagging. By the time he stopped to do his business, there was another text waiting for her.

Hmm... I wouldn't call it tights over a diaper. I'd say you'd look like a woman ready to bounce down a mountain like you own it. And that would look hot. No question.

You've never seen me ride a bike. It's been several years since I've even been on one. I think you'll be less than impressed.

She pulled a bag out of her pocket and tried not to smile as she picked up the pile Seamus had left. Smiling seemed to open up her nose and the pile stank without her inhaling more of it. But she couldn't help herself. Caleb made her smile. And it was worth the extra cough as she tied up the bag and the smell, and she and Seamus continued on their way.

She didn't get a chance to check her texts until she got home and fed Seamus. As she'd hoped, there was another message waiting for her.

You're Q, bringer of the tools Bond, James Bond needed. Of course I'll be impressed.

After the text was a picture of Bond, James Bond curled up around his water dish, asleep in what looked to be a pool of water. Kittens, man. They sure were cute. Bond, James Bond *almost* gave Caleb a patina of reliability and stalwartness. A man for the future.

A man for the kitten's future, not for hers.

Casual, she reminded herself as she read the message a second time. This was a casual relationship. All Caleb would ever be was a handsome, charming stop on her way to happily-ever-after. She couldn't read more into the message than that.

Even if she wanted to.

Time to cut her hopes and giggles off.

I've got some things to take care of at work. See you on Saturday!

On her way up the stairs to shower, she tossed her phone in her purse so she wouldn't be tempted to look at it again.

ON A SUNDAY? Caleb typed out. Throughout the rest of his morning, he checked his phone, but there wasn't a responding text from Beck.

Just as well. The small empty spot in his heart felt a lot like missing her and missing her would mean that their relationship couldn't stay casual. If he felt like their relationship wasn't staying shallow and fun, he would want it to end. Any other time when he'd felt like his time with a woman might not stay casual, he would want to end the relationship—and did. But he didn't want this relationship to end.

Backward logic applied, his relationship with Beck was still casual. And if their relationship was casual, he couldn't miss her.

Luckily, before Caleb could question the soundness of his logic, Bond, James Bond dashed into the room after a toy mouse that was almost as big as he was. Caleb set aside his phone and grabbed the feather toy. Playing with a kitten was a good distraction against waiting by the phone.

"LESLIE, WHAT DO you think defines a casual relationship?" Beck asked her banquet captain as they went over the menu for a wedding.

"What makes you think I would know?" they asked, running their finger down the paper and checking it across the setup instructions Beck had typed out a couple of days ago.

"Youth. And you know Caleb. Or know of him. It sounds like at least two of your friends have been on dates with him. What were those relationships like?"

Her coworker looked up with a raised brow. "Do you *want* your relationship with Caleb— or any man—to be like every other woman's relationship?"

Beck considered Leslie's excellent question. "I guess not. No," she said firmly. "But I want to know what's *normal*, so that I can know if I'm doing better or worse."

"Again, what makes you think I know?"

Beck shrugged. "Again, youth. You haven't

been married for ten years. You have more friends who are the right age to be dating. And you've met Marsie. She's the last friend I had who dates. Nothing Marsie does or thinks can be considered normal."

Leslie laughed. Marsie was intense to the point of occasionally being overwhelming, and she was smart enough that she got lost in her own weeds sometimes. But she was kind, treated everyone with the same courtesy and tipped well. Beck's coworkers loved her. Still, Leslie agreed. "Don't ever judge yourself against Marsie. She marches to the beat of a different drummer, for sure.

"And I don't think youth is helpful, either. Shouldn't what's *normal* change as you age and your needs and wants change? Right now, I want a good time, but I'm twenty-six and my parents have finally stopped wondering when I'm going to be like my older siblings. My brother's married with a couple kids and my sister's married and pregnant. Settling down is the least I can do, as far as my mom's concerned. Though more grandkids would be good, too."

"I want a good time," Beck said, though she could hear the hesitation in her voice.

She rested her chin in her palm and looked at Leslie, who looked back in silence. Finally,

Beck said, "Okay. I want to get married again. But do I want to do it *now*, first relationship out of the gate? Probably not. Caleb's right, there. I'd like to try the field out a little. See who's out there. Have some fun."

"From what I know, you'll get that with Caleb, though I'm still not sure how you would know what defines better or worse for a casual relationship, beyond that you're having a good time and he's not hurting you or playing mind games."

Helping Caleb rescue a kitten had been a good time and the desperation in his eyes when she'd shown up at the vet's had given Beck confidence that he wasn't playing with her. But the night hadn't felt casual. It also hadn't felt as though they were two friends who were having sex. It felt as though they were on the verge of sharing intimate pieces of themselves and hoping the other person responded with acceptance—and maybe even love.

It had been a long time since Beck had gone through this process, but she remembered it from Neil. Nothing about Beck's relationship with Neil had ever been casual.

"We're having a good time," Beck said slowly.

"You don't sound sure."

"I'm not sure I'm cut out for a *good time*. I

think I'm hunting for more. I mean, I know I want to get married sooner rather than eventually, and I think I'm going to poke around the corners of every relationship with a man to see if the possibility is there. I know it's not with Caleb, but I'm looking in closets and under couches for it anyway."

It was Leslie's turn to consider what Beck was saying before responding. "Well, from what I know of Caleb—which is limited to the experiences of two of my friends, and I don't think that's a good number from which to judge—he'll end your relationship before you find anything."

Beck laughed. "Are you telling me that I should look to my heart's content?"

Leslie smiled in response. "I guess. So long as you know that finding anything means a kick out the door."

"That's probably for the best," she said with a nod. "I'm not sure I'd be good about ending this thing without help. I'm afraid I'd stay in it, hoping for potential, and that would be bad."

Leslie looked at the menu for a moment, but then seemed to remember something and looked back up quickly. "Are you going on dates with anyone else? Your relationship with Caleb isn't monogamous and he's probably seeing other women. You should see other men."

"Ugh. Yeah, I should." Beck hadn't opened the dating website since setting up her date with Caleb. Bird in the hand and all that...

Which was stupid, because Caleb wasn't a bird and he wasn't in her hand and he'd promised that he wouldn't even stay in her sight line.

Leslie's eyes went soft with concern and they reached a hand across the table. "Beck, I've worked with you for a while and I watched you hold yourself together while getting a divorce and saw the longing in your eyes when there's a couple who seemed particularly well-suited for each other. If you don't date other men, you're going to want that with Caleb and it'll be like trying to catch a rainbow while running down stairs."

"You're right. You're right. I know you're right."

"So you'll do it?"

"I'll do it."

"Will I need to double-check your work?" Leslie asked, excellent boss that they were.

"No," Beck said with a laugh. "But you can anyway."

WHEN BECK GOT home from work, she made herself a cup of chamomile tea and sat at her desk as if she was working, back straight, distractions hidden and Seamus asleep in the corner of the room. She was *working on* something, so there was that at least. Looking at dating profiles felt a lot less like fun catalog shopping since meeting Caleb, and she couldn't pretend there weren't flesh-and-blood people behind those pictures anymore.

Leslie was right, of course. Beck's goal was getting married, and if she only spent time with Caleb, she'd make marriage to him her goal. She wouldn't mean for it to happen; he would be there, convenient and attractive. The switch from generic husband to specific husband would happen even if he wasn't the right person for her—and even though he wasn't interested in getting married.

She agreed to this casual deal knowing full well that the breakup would hurt. But if she allowed herself to get her hopes up, the breakup could send her to the floor in a flood of tears and she didn't know when she'd get up again.

So, men. If Caleb was her rebound guy and what Leslie said was true—she needed to be looking for the man she was going to marry. She didn't spend much time looking at each dude she came across, just a quick glance at the man's photos—attractive enough—and what he said about himself—no red flags. If she could think of something to say, she sent the dude a message. If she didn't know what to say, she winked. She'd recommended the scattershot method to Marsie when her friend had been using online dating. Marsie hadn't taken her advice, but Beck was going to try it and see how it worked.

The scattershot method had the added bonus that there probably wouldn't be enough new dudes added to the website to make signing back in and browsing the men again worth it anytime soon. She'd only need to sign in again if she had a message or needed to arrange a date.

She could live with that.

Leslie's advice had been to not put all her eggs in one basket. Caleb's advice had been to discover who she was when she wasn't married. Taking his advice, she opened a new window and entered the name of a local outdoor store and browsed their classes. They listed an entry-level mountain biking course, so she signed up and—feeling positive—marked that she had her own bike. After Saturday, she would have her own bike.

Signing up for the class didn't feel weird until she got the confirmation email. When she was married, she would have considered Neil before signing up. Not just to tell him that she was going to do the class and to ask him if he wanted to do it with her, but she would have also considered if *he* would want her to do the class and adjusted her life accordingly.

Her parents had loved Neil. They thought his ambition and work ethic would push Beck to do bigger and better things with her life. Since Beck had both wanted to please them and to get married and start a family of her own, she had gone along with it. She and Neil had seemed compatible, after all. They had used the same shampoo and conditioner, which in college had felt like a sign from God. Neil was ambitious and, though he hadn't wanted kids, he wanted to get married. "Married men do better in business," he'd said.

Her parents had told her he would want kids once he was settled down and not to pressure him, so she stupidly told him that she didn't want kids, either. No pressure! She'd learned all about the things he was interested in and kept the things only she was interested in to herself, so she wouldn't bother him. Looking back, the surprise was that they'd stayed married as long as they had.

But Neil wasn't around now. She hadn't a need to check anyone's schedule before she signed up for the class. If she didn't have anyone around the house to share her excitement about learning how to mountain bike, well, she didn't have anyone around to dampen her enthusiasm, either.

Feeling pretty good about herself, she printed off the confirmation email and the liability release. Then she circled the date on her calendar and, for good measure, drew a woman riding a bike. Before she could think too much about why she'd let marriage shrink her life so that it didn't include things like learning to ride a mountain bike without permission, she grabbed Seamus's leash and took him for a walk.

CHAPTER SIXTEEN

ON MONDAY MORNING, Caleb texted Beck a good morning. He'd tried to tell himself on Sunday that he didn't miss her, but didn't pretend to be so blind after his Monday meeting. He wanted to hear from her, even if hearing from her was arranging the time of their bike shopping date.

It took a couple hours for him to get a good morning response. The committee meeting he was sitting in was discussing pork water retention waste ponds and current regulations and...

And, frankly, it wasn't that interesting. He was here because he had to be, because he was pretty sure the rep who had introduced the bill under discussion was dealing in regulations and elected judgeships and voting districts, and when one back started to be scratched in a way that would interest the readers of his paper, he wanted to be the first to know. Caleb was recording the meeting and tweeting out any interesting tidbits, but really was building a foundation for further reporting work to come later.

"My pa is a humble farmer" was about as true an origin story for the rep and his bill as Caleb saying he would have to go home and take care of his child—by which he would mean his new cat—but the words would get him what he wanted, and so it wouldn't matter that they were a lie.

Getting the text back that said "Good afternoon! Seamus says hi," with a goofy picture of her dog was going to be the highlight of his day. With his phone out and the goofing off already underway, he swiped down the screen to see the notifications in his dating apps.

Normally he would at least click to look at the women's profiles or messages and send something in return. Not that he wasn't picky, but you never knew who might be interesting to spend a night with. And messaging a love—or sexual—interest was hard. He respected the effort and risk—which pretty much applied to anyone doing online dating right.

He smiled a little at the thought of being the arbiter of online-dating rights and wrongs. Of course, he'd probably been on a couple hundred dates. Some had turned into nothing more than coffee or drinks or dinner. Some had turned into a relationship that lasted a week, or two maybe. Never a month. He wasn't interested in a month.

But the man he was interested in started speaking again, so Caleb simply cleared all his notifications and went back to slightly listening and occasionally tweeting about the committee meeting.

I'M SUPPOSED TO kiss a lot of frogs, Beck thought as the man across from her wrapped his hands around his cup of coffee and brought it up to his mouth for a sip.

Sammy, her date, wasn't as good-looking in person as he had been in his picture and he had an annoying laugh. She tried to be generous and tell herself that he laughed easily. She wanted a man who had a sense of humor, and so she wanted to find joy in the sound of his laughter.

But the noise grated. In the end, the man's laughter versus having a sense of humor evened out in the wash and she decided not to think about it.

Sammy laughed again as he told his story. Okay, so she couldn't not think about his laugh, but it was still a neutral trait. And she didn't have to *actually kiss* all the frogs. She just had to go out on dates with them and see what the world of men looked like now that she was single.

"Oh," she interrupted as he started talking about his dog, "I have a dog, too. He's in some of my online-dating pictures."

"Right. I remember seeing him. Cute dog," he acknowledged before launching back into the story of his dog chasing his cat.

She'd arranged this date with Sammy quickly. He'd been in the set of men that she'd chosen at the beginning of the week, and here it was Thursday afternoon for coffee. Maybe, if they'd had the chance to email back and forth a little, she would have noticed that he talked a lot about himself and didn't seem so interested in her.

She smiled and nodded at what seemed like an appropriate point in the story. Maybe he didn't talk only about himself. Maybe this was a story he liked and, once he finished telling this story, he would pause and get to know her. She picked up her cup of coffee, sipped her decaf latte and waited.

Her coffee was empty and the last of the froth at the bottom was cold by the time he asked about her. By that point, she wasn't willing to be forgiving or find excuses in her head why he talked so much or why his laugh was horrible. No, she was simply sick of his stories and how much he laughed at them.

She didn't answer his question, saying instead, "I don't think this is going to work out between us, Sammy. But it was nice to meet you." Her chair squeaked against the floor as she slid it back and stood up. "Best of luck with online dating."

Then she picked up her cup and walked over to the busing bin, giving him as much chance to talk as he'd given her.

On the walk back to the restaurant, she called Marsie, who answered on the first ring. "Is this the world of men, now?" she asked as soon as her friend said hello.

"Not a good date?"

"No. He talked only about himself. By the time he asked a question about me, I was ready to leave. And so I did."

Marsie laughed. "Did you say anything before you got up and bailed?"

"Sure. I'm not a jerk. I told him that we weren't going to work out and I wished him luck with the rest of his dating. If he's not going to ask his date anything about themselves, he's going to need luck. And he had this annoying laugh. Like a donkey."

"Ooohhh. If you've stooped to petty comments, it must have been really bad. Both his laugh and the date."

Beck sighed. "It was boring more than anything else. His stories weren't even that interesting. Caleb tells a lot of stories, but Caleb is a reporter and his stories are interesting."

Marsie tsked. "Mr. Donkey could have interesting experiences and still tell boring stories. Caleb probably tells interesting stories because he's an interesting guy."

"Sure. He is an interesting guy." And funny and charming. And he was interested in her and her life. All things poor Sammy didn't seem to be. And, in this case, Beck was pretty sure she could judge Sammy on that one date.

"Do I get to meet Caleb?"

Beck stopped at the crosswalk to wait for the light to turn in her favor and stared at everything and nothing while she considered her answer. "I'd love for you to meet Caleb. I think you'd like him. But that seems to skirt too closely to a real relationship. I mean, you don't double-date in casual relationships, do you?"

"I don't know. I've never had one. I think you can chart your own territory here and do what you want."

There was the crux of the problem, as far as Beck understood it. She wanted to get married. She agreed with everyone that she needed to survey all the goods before picking. She also wanted to keep dating Caleb. It was hard for her to manage both wants at the same time.

The light changed and Beck kept on to the

restaurant and the rest of her workday. "I'm working on setting up other dates. Maybe one of them will develop into a man who you can meet."

Beck knew her friend well enough to know that, on the other end of the line, Marsie's lips were twitching. But her friend didn't sigh. All she said was, "You're walking a hard path. But I suppose if you walk it right, having Caleb in your life will help you keep your head on straight about the other men you date. He could keep you from feeling lonely and falling for the first guy who makes googly eyes at you."

Beck giggled at the phrase "googly eyes," as Marsie had meant her to.

"On the other hand," her friend continued as if she hadn't set her friend up for a laugh, "you could compare every man you meet to this paragon of attractiveness, and that's not fair to anyone."

"He's not just attractive," Beck said. "He's also charming and smart and interesting and has a job he's passionate about. That's all pretty cool."

Now Marsie sighed. Stopping in front of the restaurant, Beck giggled again. Making Marsie sigh was part of the fun.

"You shouldn't compare any of the men to each other. You need to take each one as a whole person, complete in their self and evaluate whether that whole self is the whole self for you."

"Oh, I know that. And, really, any man who is interested in a long-term relationship already has one *big* advantage over Caleb. Bigger than his romantic good looks and being good in bed."

"Well…" On the other end of the line, Marsie hedged. If Beck had had any doubt that Marsie was happy with Jason in bed, they were eradicated in that one prevarication. "You'll want to make sure you get 'commitment-oriented' and 'good-in-bed' in the same guy."

"Seriously, Marsie, do you think I can do this?"

"Do I think you can date a guy you clearly like while trying to see other men and not get your heart broken? No. Do I think you can find your way through this period of your life to a relationship that fulfills you? Yes."

Trust Marsie to get right to the heart of the question. And not to beat around the bush with her answer. "Thank you," Beck said. "I needed to hear that."

"And, Beck," Marsie said as Beck was about to say goodbye, "I know from hard experience that the first step to happiness is knowing that you are whole and complete within yourself.

That you don't need a partner to have a good life. They make life better, no doubt about that, but you don't need one, especially if needing one makes you think you should hide yourself. Take care of you, first."

"I know. I know. I know." Beck repeated the words to herself because she needed to remind herself of them. "Thank you."

"Any time."

Feeling a core of steel she hadn't fully been able to say she had and knew she needed to nurture, Beck slipped her phone back in her purse and opened the door to the restaurant.

CHAPTER SEVENTEEN

BECK OPENED THE DOOR, looking amazing in a pair of jeans that fit her just right and a loose purple top. The color somehow made her brown hair look more luxurious. She looked good enough to eat, though he limited himself to sweeping her up in his arms and giving her a long kiss as soon as he was through the door.

"Ready to go bike shopping?" he asked as soon as he was ready to pull away, though he kept one hand on her waist because he liked touching her.

He was surprised to hear her answer, "Not really."

"No?" Seamus bumped his leg with his nose, so Caleb reached out with the other hand to pet the dog, who pressed a warm dog torso against his leg. "You still want to go, right?"

"Oh, I still want to go. I had a long week of work and…" She paused, seemingly nervous about what she was going to say next—which made him nervous about what she was going to say next.

"I had a date."

"Oh." Suddenly, he could feel every long inch of where his hand was resting on her hip and he knew he had to tread carefully. Snapping his hand away would make it seem like he was angry, and he wasn't. But keeping his hand on her hip right now felt…awkward. A claim that wasn't his to make.

Whose fault is that?

"It's okay that I tell you, right?" Clearly, neither of them knew what to say in a moment like this. And why would they? Talking with your current date about your other dates was probably in the neighborhood of unprecedented, if not in the actual house, in the living room, sitting on the couch and drinking a beer.

"Yeah, yeah, yeah." He pulled his hand away and crouched to pet the dog. Dogs were good in situations like this. Seamus seemed able to sense that something strange was happening in the emotions of the people above him, though his fix was for Caleb to pet him more.

From his position on the floor, Caleb craned his head so that he could see Beck while he spoke. They'd gotten themselves into this strange position—correction, *he'd* gotten them into this strange position—and open communication was the only way for it to work. "We made an agreement. I'm glad you went on a date."

He was, wasn't he?

Sure, of course he was. He wanted Beck to be happy, and finding the right man and getting married is one of the things she thought would make her happy. If she wanted that for herself, then he wanted that for her, too. *He* didn't have the ability to commit, but there were men in the world who did, and he wanted her to find them. He also wanted to keep hanging out with her—and keep having sex with her.

And they'd agreed he would give her advice. He was the man of a thousand dates, after all. So, he turned his head quickly to the loving eyes of the dog, took a deep breath and asked, "How'd it go?"

"Not well." She seemed more annoyed than disappointed, which didn't speak well for the guy she'd been on the date with—though it was a toss-up if Caleb would prefer a date being disappointed in him than annoyed. Both had probably happened.

"He talked about himself too much. Not just too much, but *only* about himself. He didn't ask a single question about me."

A trail of shame tagged along behind the wave of relief that tumbled over him. "So," he said, looking down at the dog so she wouldn't see the relief in his eyes, "not the man for you?"

"No, not the man for me. So this week when

I wasn't working, I was talking with my friends about what the man for me might be like and trying to decipher all the things I read in online-dating profiles."

The pit in his stomach thudded as he laughed. "I said I would help you untangle men and pick the good ones from the bad ones, but I'm not sure I can help you figure out online profiles. I don't even know what I mean by a lot of the crap in my online-dating profiles. I mean, I know what I say in them—but mostly I'm trying to sound charming and easy to get along with. Nothing that I would read too much into."

She laughed, as he'd hoped she would, and he mustered up enough bravery to look at her, letting the dog nuzzle closer in for pets. "I guess I wouldn't read too much into mine, either. I was hoping, you know, that I could avoid another date with a man who only ever talks about himself by reading something in their profile, but I guess that's a false hope."

"Okay, buddy," Caleb said as he patted Seamus on the head. "My knees hurt, so I can't be down here any longer." Not only did the crouching hurt, but the damn joints creaked as he stood up. He should probably exercise more. Or figure out how to not get old.

"If you figure out how to read into a profile, let me know. But it's good you're looking for more dates. Really, really good." Stupid thing to say, and it sounded stupid coming out of his mouth. But, really, what did a man say in situations like this? He'd agreed that she could come to him with information about her dates and he'd give her advice, from a guy's perspective. All he had to do was keep up his end of the bargain. No problem. Not committing was exactly the kind of thing he could be relied on for.

"So," he said with a clap of his now dog-grime-covered hands. "Let me wash my hands and we'll get going. We can talk about what bikes you might want to look at on the way over. Or you can be surprised by whatever the bike store has to offer."

"Let's be surprised," she responded, a sense of mischief in her voice. "I want to hear how your past week has been. And entertain me with cute stories of how Bond, James Bond has wrecked your life." To his surprise, she lifted up on her toes and kissed his cheek.

As if the situation they'd found each other in wasn't confusing enough.

THE STORE WAS packed when Beck and Caleb walked through the door. Wall-to-wall people, bicycles, bicycle *stuff* and seemingly only one poor soul to help everyone.

"We can look at some of the bikes while we

wait for the guy to be free to help us," Caleb said as he guided her to the wall of bikes on the right. "We'll need someone from the shop to help us get a bike off the wall so you can ride it around, but looking at them should give you a feel for what you can afford and we can talk about what the different features mean. I think you'll probably want a women's bike in medium or a men's bike in small, but you should always ride it to get a feel for it."

"Is there a difference?" She remembered there being a difference when she was a kid and the girls' bikes were pink or purple with the swoop between the handle and the seat. Together with her friends, she'd come up with a million different reasons why the boys' bikes had a spoke-thing that went straight across and the girls' ones went down. As an adult, she was certain they hadn't come up with the right answer.

And the question of the difference between the two styles of bikes still felt stupid. It was something she could have easily looked up online.

But Caleb shrugged, as though asking the question wasn't any big deal, which made her feel better. All part of his magic, rebound-guy charm. "Between the men's and women's bikes? The geometry is a little different—the angle of the top tube, for example." By which he must mean the spoke-thing that went straight across on boys' bikes and sloped down on girls' bikes.

"But you should buy whichever one you like to ride. How comfortable you feel on the bike is more important than whether it's called a men's bike or a women's bike. Or size, for that matter. And there are other bike stores in the area we can visit. They'll all have different brands. We can visit them today, too, if you're up for it," he said, smiling.

When Caleb smiled, his face changed completely. No longer was he her romantic Byronic hero, needing a voluminous white shirt and tight pair of breeches to complete the look. Suddenly, he was just a guy, like any other guy. Only not quite like *any other* guy. He turned from a romantic lead designed by nature to turn heads of all the women they passed to a guy who caused tingles down her back, and her back specifically.

Some of it was the attention he gave her when he was with her. People and all their associated noise milled around them in the shop. But she was the only person here, for all Caleb seemed to notice the other people. For all his warning that there might be other women he was dating and that he wasn't interested in anything long-term and that this relationship wouldn't go further than fun, when she was with him, she felt like she was the only woman in the world who mattered.

Frankly, it was intoxicating. Like all addictive substances on earth, she could get used to feeling like the center of Caleb's world and never want to give it up. Also like all addictive substances, the feeling was dangerous. She had to be on her guard.

"Do you have time for all that?" she asked, reminding herself that they had only made plans for bike shopping and lunch. He might have different dinner plans with a different woman.

God, thinking that sucked. She *liked* Caleb. He was interesting and fun. And then there was the difference between how he looked when he was smiling versus when he wasn't, hinting at a depth to him that most women—most people, she corrected—probably never got near. Not only did he play his cards close to his chest, but only the careful noticed that he was holding cards to begin with.

"I've got all day," he said. "And all night, if you can find a twenty-four-hour bicycle store. Tomorrow, even, if you need."

And *whoop*, suddenly the metaphorical rug was pulled out from under her and she was flat on her back. She could steel herself against him having a dinner date tonight or another coffee date tomorrow, but she couldn't do that and not be surprised when he was ready to spend the weekend with her. She didn't know how to hold both truths in her hand at the same time.

"For my sake, I hope shopping for bikes doesn't take that long," she said, steadying herself in his smile. "Though more than lunch would be fun."

Trying something new, Beck. You're trying something new. And, really, learning to draw and taking a mountain biking class and figuring out how to casually date a man like Caleb were all the same kind of new thing. No difference. No difference at all. If she could do one, then she could do the others.

Do Caleb, she thought and then giggled at her own adolescent joke before she could stop herself. At least the inane joke took her mind off how unsteady she felt.

But this *would* be like learning to ride a bike. She may have been a child when she'd learned, but she'd felt unsteady then, too. The feeling had passed and this one would, as well.

"What was the giggle for?" Caleb asked.

"A stupid joke. Not even one worth repeating, and I'm embarrassed that I even thought it. Let's think more about what to do after bike shopping. I promise it's more interesting than my jokes."

"Okay," he said slowly, clearly not quite believing her, but also not wanting to push it. "Dinner after bike shopping? We could cook together and watch the movie we didn't get to last weekend. That would be fun. Maybe after we give your new bike a spin."

"Sure. But at whose house?"

"Does Seamus like cats?" he asked.

She thought back to their walks and any other possible cat interactions he may have had over the short time she'd had him. "I think he's okay with them. He's never chased them when we're walking. I'm not sure he's really interacted with them. Does Bond, James Bond like dogs?"

She laughed again and continued, "That laugh was for Bond, James Bond's name. It's silly."

"I know," he sounded so pleased with himself that the smile stayed plastered to her face. "That's why it's such an awesome name. He's going to grow up into a staid, fat and lazy older cat and be stuck with his ridiculous name and a reminder of his kittenhood. If he ever starts bringing other cats home for dates, I'm going to get out pictures and tell funny stories about him." He raised one dark, elegant eyebrow. "As for whether he likes dogs… I don't know. But Bond, James Bond is up for tackling anything."

"Sorry for the wait, folks." Beck jumped at the sound of the unknown male voice and then turned to see the one poor employee standing behind them. She and Caleb were standing by the same rack of biking jerseys that they had stopped by when they'd walked in the door. They'd fallen into conversation and hadn't moved.

So much for looking at bikes while waiting for the guy to come help them.

"I've got a couple more people to help before I get to you, but I wanted to see if I could point you in any direction while you're waiting."

The man looked at Caleb, only glancing over when Beck said, "I'm looking for an entry-level mountain bike."

"Well," the guy said, his odious tone puffing up his chest and making Beck brace herself against whatever he was going to say, "bikes for *you* are going to be over there, with all the women's stuff. Check them out, find one you like the paint job on. I'll pull it off the shelf so that you can ride it." Then, without seeming to realize that he'd been insulting, the man walked off, presumably to insult another woman.

They stood in silence for a moment, staring

after the dude. Caleb broke the silence. "Want to try another store?"

"Yes," she replied, relieved that she didn't have to explain why she didn't want to spend her money in this store.

In tandem, they spun on their heels and walked through the sliding glass doors. Once in the car, Beck turned in her seat and asked, "Is there really no difference between men's and women's bikes?"

"No more difference than the geometry, like I said. And I'll guess that they paint women's bikes different colors than they do men's bikes, too. For whatever reason. That guy was a dick. You can buy any bike you please and certainly aren't going to be picking one out based on paint colors."

She didn't say anything as she processed both how dismissed she'd felt by the guy in the store and Caleb's reaction to such treatment of her.

Caleb noticed her silence and was clearly wondering about it, because he cleared his throat and said, "Unless you want to. If you want to pick a bike out based on paint colors, I won't stop you. Everyone gets their own reason for picking."

She laughed and then laughed some more at how relieved he looked by her laughter. "I've picked out many an expensive thing based on paint colors, but in this case, I'd like to know more about the features of each bike. And then I'll pick the one in my favorite color."

His laugh was closer to a bark and he hit the steering wheel with his hand. "You're great. That guy is a jerk and we're going to have a good time tonight. These are the truths of my day."

THEY DID HAVE FUN. Any time Beck began to feel self-conscious about her bike-riding ability—it had been *years* since she'd been on a bike—Caleb would make a joke and she felt better. After she had tried out her fifth bike and was choosing between the two that had felt the best, Caleb chatted with the man who'd been helping her pick out bikes. Of the two, she ended up picking the red-and-black one—a men's bike, no less—though she liked the look of the blue bike better. The guy had said it would be a bike that would grow with her and she liked the idea of growing into a better bike as she became a better rider.

"Hey," Caleb said, nudging her arm a little with his elbow while they stood at the service desk and the technicians looked her bike over. "That was good. It's hard to do something you're not comfortable with in front of an audience. I'm not very good at it."

"Feeling like an idiot at anything is hard. But I've decided that it's the only way to be better. However, you might notice that I've not shown you any of my artwork."

"I have noticed," he said, with one of his cheeky smiles. Caleb was a man who could express himself through a million smiles, and she could come to love them all.

No, you can't.

Well, she thought in response, *I can certainly like them all.* That's allowed. Her inner better sense didn't respond, which was good. She wasn't in the mood to argue with herself, anyway. She wanted to have a good time tonight. All sex and fun and laughter and no thinking about the future.

Learning.

"You could practice by drawing a portrait of me."

"Hah," she said, loudly enough that the man working on her bike looked up. "I'll make you a deal. I'll draw a portrait of you if you draw a portrait of me. We can trade."

"How do you know that I'm not some secret artist? Or that I didn't spend my high school years doodling the portraits of pretty girls in my notebook."

The image was both so ridiculous and so perfect that she had to shake her head. "I don't, but it would fit with my idea of you as some kind of Byronic romantic hero. Watercolors. Poetry."

"Being exiled to France…"

"You'd look nice in a beret, red scarf and a black-and-white-striped shirt. Very romantic."

"I'm not sure any Frenchman would wear that in real life."

It was her turn to nudge him. "You're ruining the fantasy."

"Ma'am, your bike's ready," the store's employee said, interrupting them. "Do you want me to help you get it to the car?"

"I'll take care of it," Caleb said from her side. "We can load the bike on the rack together. It's not hard."

The man pushed the bike through the swinging gate and Beck took it by the handlebars to push it out of the store.

"Happy with your purchases?" Caleb asked as soon as they were out of the building. She'd also bought a helmet, water bottle and holder, gloves, and bike shorts.

"Yes. It'll be good. I hope I like mountain biking."

"That'll be a fine enough bike for tooling around the neighborhood, too, if that's all you decide to use it for."

They stopped at his car, Beck holding her bike and Caleb reaching up to undo the latches on his bike rack. As he reached, Beck got to admire how long and tall and lean he was. "You know what I'm happier about than the bike I'm taking home?"

"What's that?" he asked, turning around and reaching for her bike.

"The man I'm going home with. I like the fantasy of a strong man lifting heavy things for me. It's better than the beret and red kerchief."

He flexed, though any bulging muscles were lost in his long-sleeved shirt. Which was okay. She'd take the shirt off him tonight and enjoy the muscles then. They both laughed, and then she helped him lift her bike onto the car and got in the passenger seat.

CHAPTER EIGHTEEN

ON MONDAY MORNING, Caleb had so much energy he was bouncing around the legislative building. Not just taking the stairs—hell, he hopped up and down flights of stairs like a hyper five-year-old. He wasn't even breathing hard when he got to the top.

Well…that wasn't entirely true. He was thirty-five years old and he'd bet even navy SEALs panted a little after popping up a flight of stairs. *But* he felt good enough to run back down and spring up the flight again if someone dared him. And that was almost as good as not being out of breath.

Once in the office, he signed into his computer and headed for his regular cup of coffee while the computer ran through all its regular morning nonsense. The mix of community coffee cups looked the same as any other morning, but instead of grabbing for the boring black mug with the newspaper logo on the side, he reached for the kitten mug left by some intern long past. A kitten mug to match his jumpy, excited Monday morning.

"Whoa." Bernetta's voice was easily audible over the noises of the staff room, the pouring coffee, the buzzing snack machine and the fridge that had sounded like a car running with no oil in the engine for the past three years. Even the amusement in her voice was loud enough to carry over the clank you could set your watch by.

Cup full of mediocre coffee—*but free!* the chipper voice narrating his morning sang out—Caleb turned to face the smirking politician.

"God, you even look like the cat who got into the cream. I could hear you whistling as I came down the hall," she said.

"I wasn't whistling." He hadn't been, had he? Humming, maybe, but whistling—no way.

"Yeah, and I'm not black."

Caleb laughed. "Okay, so I was whistling. Was I at least whistling a good song?"

"You were whistling an 'I had a great weekend' song. From the peppiness of the tune, I'm guessing there was a woman involved."

He held up one hand in mock innocence and drank a sip of his coffee before he answered. "You caught me. I had a great weekend." Saturday. Saturday night. Sunday morning. Sunday morning *again*. And then going out for brunch and bringing the dog, who looked around like someone had brought him to a candy factory but wouldn't let him sample the goods.

"Yeah?" Bernetta softened, which made Caleb a little suspicious of what she was thinking—especially since she'd been so hot to tell him how *into* Beck he had been at the bar. She was probably thinking things that weren't going to happen.

"Same woman?" the representative asked.

Yup. She was definitely getting ideas about things that weren't going to happen. "Same woman. But it's nothing."

"You were whistling."

"She's a great woman. Funny. Smart. Hot. Really nice." Like really nice. Thoughtful and kind and genuine. She had this way of looking at you like she could see your humanity deep in your eyes. Like there was something of value in each and every person she came across and like it wasn't even hidden that deep down. When she looked at him like that, he wanted her to look closer and longer. To have her know his personness intimately enough that she would be able to explain it to him.

With that thought came the lingering fear that she would discover something inside him that wasn't worthy of the future she had planned for herself. That he wasn't made for quiet evenings laughing in the kitchen while a kid dropped Cheerios on the floor.

"But she and I have talked about this. I'm not the kind of guy you stay with for anything long-term. Since she wants to get married, she's dating other people. We even talk about it."

He hated that they'd talked about it, but they had. Once. So that was a true statement.

"Are *you* dating other people?" Bernetta asked with an arched brow.

"Like now? Or like in general?"

"Don't be obtuse." Her voice was amused, but her face had folded into a scowl. He decided Bernetta was simply as confused as he was about the fact that they now talked about their personal lives and ignored both the scowl and the fact that she seemed to think this was funny.

"Beck and I have been on four dates in a total of four weeks." When he put it that way, it seemed like a long time. But when he looked back on it, that month with Beck seemed like no time at all and like there should be more time. Dinners on Wednesday nights, for example, not just weekends.

But that would make what he shared with her a relationship, instead of two people sharing a good time together—and maybe sharing a good time with other people. "*Right now*, during those weeks, I've not gone on a date with anyone else."

"Do you have a date with anyone else lined up?"

"What's with the twenty questions about my personal life?" He took another drink of his coffee. In the time they'd been talking, it had cooled enough he could take a gulp of the horrid stuff rather than a careful sip. So, at least one good thing was coming out of this conversation.

"Beck, you said her name was?"

He nodded.

"I just saw her at a glance, but she seemed like a nice lady. I have a sense about these things." *That* Caleb didn't doubt. Bernetta was the person whose nose itched right before something big broke.

But then she ruined his trust in her intuition by saying, "I think you need to settle down. You were a better reporter when you were married."

"What?" His coffee cup banged against the side of the counter when he opened his arms in surprise. "That doesn't seem possible. I've got more free time now to follow up on stories. No one is at home to be angry that I'm not going to be in time for dinner."

She inclined her head in agreement, but

her eyes corrected his assumption. "Also, less focus. Less sympathy for the emotions of the people in your stories."

"I write about politics, which often means I write about corruption or abuse of power or the forgotten common man. Where's the room for sympathy?"

She shrugged. "I don't know. I only know that I've read all your stories for years, and you were better when you were married. Even when you were going through the divorce. I guess you seemed to understand that people have layers of motivation for the things they do—and that came through in your writing. Now, you're a playboy and so are the villains in your stories. No depth."

"Maybe it's not me who's changed. Maybe it's the villains." He needed to sit down for this conversation.

Bernetta joined him at one of the small tables in the middle of the staff room. He must have looked something awful, because she patted his arm. "You look dazed."

Dazed was better than awful. "I have a hard time believing you. Everything about being single should make me a better reporter. My job is all I have. I give it everything I've got."

She nodded. "Yeah, and I think you resent the job for it. Which, really, Caleb, isn't fair to the job. It's not the one that's asking for everything from you. *You're* giving everything to it and then you are mad when it takes all that you give it."

"Not asking for everything?" *That* was a ridiculous statement if he'd ever heard one. Reporting, especially political reporting, was a 24/7 job. It could suck out every last moment of your life into the crapulence—because rarely was anything about politics pretty. He knew more than just how the sausage was made. He *lived* how the sausage was made and it was enough to make him never want to eat again.

It meant he couldn't joke on Twitter or Facebook. It meant his friends asked him who they should vote for, which was one of the last questions he ever wanted to answer for people.

He *loved* his job. He loved that his role in this world was to take the complicated world of governance and tell people like his father both how it worked and how it influenced his life.

But nothing about that was *nice*. Not like Beck was nice. There was almost too much humanity in it. Humanity enough that it could blind the people involved to the world outside the legislative building's doors.

Suddenly, before he realized it was happening and could squash it, his hand twitched to grasp Beck's. He needed a lodestone to point him to true north.

"Of course the job asks for everything," he replied. "It wants all of my time. It wants all of my energy. It wants all of my thoughts. And it doesn't pay me shit for any of it." There was the crux of his divorce. He couldn't be there for his ex and he didn't make enough money for her to be comfortable being there for herself.

"Oh, and the lack of job security," he tacked on, remembering the other objective that had been lobbied against him when he and his ex had discussed kids.

"Uh, I have less job security than you. The citizens of Durham could choose to let me go on a regular schedule and there's always someone itching to get my job. Not to mention that this isn't a full-time job and it also doesn't pay much, so I still have to work."

"I can't remember right now—do you have kids?" He *should* remember. He'd worked with her long enough that he should know the kids' ages and where they were working right now. But his mind was full of Beck and can'ts and won'ts and unable-tos that he couldn't think of what was.

She must have understood, because her smile was indulgent without being insulting. "Yes. Two. And two grandbabies, one in sixth grade and one in fourth. I have pictures of them on my desk."

"Right. God, I'm an idiot." He rubbed his hand though his hair and then regretted the action immediately. The goop he put in his hair every morning was still fresh enough to be sticky. He wiped his hand on his pants.

"Anyway, I think I knew that. I'm just…"

"Self-absorbed," she finished for him, one black eyebrow raised high. But her voice was still kind, so he decided to agree rather than take offense.

"I've added some pictures since your divorce. You've been in my office and looked right at them, but I don't think you see them. When you were married, you paid attention to those pictures."

He'd stopped looking at pictures of other people's kids when he'd decided he couldn't have any of his own. No reason to rub salt in the wound.

"I date," he said, knowing the justification was poor even as it came out of his mouth. He pushed his coffee cup away. It was probably cold by now and the sludge was disgusting enough when it was warm.

Bernetta tapped her nails against the table. They were a bright electric-blue today. At least he paid attention to *that*. He wasn't completely lost in his own world.

"I think the dating makes you even more self-centered."

"You know, this is a harsh conversation. Especially for early on a Monday morning." He didn't feel like whistling anymore—that was for damn sure.

She shrugged again, her nails still doing their dance on the table. "I know."

"And you're not concerned about it."

"Nope," she said with a slow shake of her head. "I'm not."

"Why do you care? Why are we even having this conversation in the first place?" He and Bernetta were work buddies, but they weren't friends in the sense that they should be having this conversation at all. And Bernetta was a private person—because she liked her own privacy. She was an elected official, for Pete's sake. He wasn't in the habit of having intimate conversations about personal lives with elected officials, much less about his own personal life. He was here for work and to talk about work.

Maybe he was as self-absorbed as she accused him of being. For many of the people walking in and out of this building every day, work and their personal lives were intimately acquainted. From the interns to the Speaker of the House, each and every person had a story about when they decided politics was important and that they should have a bigger role in it.

Where they could affect change.

He didn't know Bernetta's. He wasn't sure he knew anyone's.

And wasn't that a horrible thought.

She was opening her mouth to tell him *why* they were here talking about his dating life, when he said, "Wait. Don't answer that. I've got another question I want you to answer first."

She stopped, mouth half open, and looked at him, amused. Then she made a big show of closing her mouth, crossing her arms and leaning back in her chair. To complete her look of exaggerated curiosity and patience, she raised her eyebrow again, this time nearly up to her hairline.

He ignored it. She was the one who'd interrupted him to comment on his personal life. She came *here*. He hadn't gone looking for her. So she could handle a little interruption.

"Why do you paint your nails?"

"Honestly?" she asked with a bark of laughter. "You're going to ask me that?"

"Yes. I'm working on a theory. This is a hard place to be an African-American woman." She raised an eyebrow in a *you're telling me* gesture, but he soldiered on. "You're a traditional dresser as fits both your role and your uphill battle for a seat at the table, but your nails are never traditional. If they are pink or red, they also have flowers painted on them. Sometimes they're all the colors of the rainbow at once."

She side-eyed him. "Is this theory about me, or about you?"

"About me."

"Do I get to know your theory yet?" She shrugged when he shook his head. "Okay. Well, I paint my nails because my husband likes it. Because it makes a huge difference in his quality of life and it makes very little difference in mine—other than that I've made my husband happy and that makes me happy."

"Oh." He sat back in his chair and regarded her, though—self-absorbed creature that he was—he was thinking about himself. He wasn't sure what he'd expected, but it wasn't such an open, honest answer and it certainly wasn't an answer that came with relationship advice or that spoke so much to how a happy couple behaved.

"Did that help your theory?"

"I'm more of an idiot than I thought."

She shook her head and he noticed that she had a small dimple above her lip when she was trying not to laugh. He was noticing a whole lot of things now that she'd given him a shake and opened his eyes. "Isn't that the case for all of us?" Then she pointed one of her long blue nails at him and asked, "What was your theory?"

"I told myself that I didn't know personal details of your life beyond the bio on the General Assembly webpage because you were a private person. It couldn't have been because I was an egocentric asshole. But you told me why and you told me so easily that I'll bet you would have told me if I'd asked anytime in the past couple years. And I'll bet you would have told me about your grandbabies and your hobbies and anything else I cared to ask about."

She nodded, looking at him as though he was the stupidest person to ever walk the face of the planet. Which, right now, he might be.

"And this is why you told me I was a better reporter when I was married. Because, I think, when I was married, I asked those personal questions of people."

He even dimly remembered asking Bernetta similar questions when they were both in local politics in Durham. *Not* about her nails—he wasn't stupid enough to ask women about their beauty routines on a regular basis—but he remembered asking about her daughter's pregnancy.

He couldn't remember the last time he'd asked her how her family was doing.

Like he knew that Patrice, who wrote for the paper about the food scene in The Triangle, had a grandmother who owned a Gullah restaurant outside of Charleston. But he'd known that a couple years ago, and Caleb had no idea how well Patrice's grandmother was doing now. Because he hadn't asked.

He was a reporter and he hadn't asked.

"I didn't work closely with you when your marriage fell apart, but even I could tell when you stopped asking people about their lives. Like you were afraid to hear about someone's happy news. To hear that someone was succeeding where you failed."

She was right about being afraid, but wrong about why. He'd been afraid of hearing about the things he wanted, but couldn't have. Hearing about happiness and family and hopes and dreams.

He had politics. They had politics. There were elections to talk about and shifting alliances and protests and backroom deals—that had seemed like enough for everyone to talk about without any of the other crap.

"So, why are we having this conversation?" he asked.

This time, she didn't hesitate to answer. "Because you were a better reporter when you were married and asked people about their lives. Because, right now, we need good reporting almost as much as we need air. If we don't have reporters and people who read what they have to say to keep our politicians accountable, then we have nothing.

"When you were married, your interviews included questions about people's personal lives. Sometimes it made it into your articles and sometimes it didn't, but the roundness of the person's life and how politics affected the person was there. That captured readers' attention. It made what is happening in this building more real for the average Joe on the street."

"Huh."

"That's all you've got to say? Huh?" For the first time since they'd been talking this morning, Bernetta seemed irritated.

"The reason my ex gave me for why we couldn't have kids—my job got in the way. I didn't make enough money. I wasn't reliable enough." He waved his hand. "You get the idea."

"I do," she said with a nod.

"It's a pretty nasty catch-22 for my job to need me to have the family that I can't have because of the job."

"Who says you can't have a family because of your job? My husband and I were dirt-poor when we had our kids. My daughter is an ER nurse. Her husband is a high school teacher. They make it work. You *make* it work if you want to make it work. And if you don't, then you won't."

The fact that Bernetta was echoing the same thing he'd finally understood about his ex-wife—that she would have only ever had objections to having kids, because she didn't want to have them—didn't mean that he liked hearing it from someone else.

Especially when that someone else was implying that *he* was off base.

"This job kills relationships," he said, one last grasp at being right.

"Eh," she said with a shrug. "Reporters are adrenaline junkies and they don't know how to turn off their work, even to sleep. But that doesn't have to kill relationships. You just have to find the right person."

"What if I don't want to get married? No settling down to have my two-point-five kids and the dog." Is that what he wanted? Did he even know what he wanted anymore? Beck knew what she wanted and—while he didn't like the idea of her having coffee dates with other men—she was trying to find it. And she was trying to find it without losing herself. He admired the art and mountain bike classes, too.

Beck had much to admire about her.

"No one says that you have to. I'm just saying that you looked happy with that woman—happy enough that you didn't notice me. And there's got to be value there, too."

She pushed herself away from the table. "Anyway, as I recall, the committee meeting you're assigned to starts in an hour. You probably have email to check before then. I know I sent you something."

"Are you going to tell me what your email says?"

"No. That would spoil the fun," she said, her eyes alight with amusement. Then her lips sobered, though her eyes were still bright as she asked, "You going to at least think about what I've said?"

"Sure. Thinking I can do."

Bernetta scowled at him. Of course, her eyes didn't change their humor, so he chalked this conversation up to a success and considered himself the winner.

Though he wasn't sure what he'd won.

CHAPTER NINETEEN

BECK STOOD AT the party run by one of The Triangle's bigger wedding dress salons, holding a drink and trying to look friendly to the women milling about. Be approachable. Look helpful. These kinds of events didn't result in a massive number of bookings—brides were usually looking at dresses and giggling with their friends—but she handed out a lot of business cards and brides often told their friends or stopped by the restaurant for dinner to check the place out.

Plus, it was important to be seen and for her to chat up the other bridal vendors. Photographers, DJs, bakers, florists—they were all a close-knit community who referred to their own network of friends and vendors they thought did a good job. One could never tell how someone would hear about the restaurant being a good wedding venue.

"Hey," a woman said as she came up to Beck, a glass of champagne in her hand. "It's nice to see you."

"Oh, hi." It took Beck a moment to put the face to the person. It was Jennifer, the bride who'd come into the restaurant and wanted her to paint the walls. "Did you find a venue you liked?"

"Yeah. Yours."

The news was unexpected enough that Beck cocked her head and furrowed her brows. "But you didn't like the restaurant. You wanted to repaint the walls a more exciting color."

"I know." The woman waved her off. "I still want to paint the walls a different color and it's still not my perfect venue, but I've thought a lot about what you said."

"Oh," Beck said, racking her brain to remember what she'd told the bride.

The woman waited, brow raised, for a moment before she took pity on Beck. "You know, that we should each think about what we want, separately, then talk about where we overlap and where we can compromise and where we can't."

"Right," she replied, nodding as she remembered. "And what about that made you decide to book my restaurant for your wedding?"

"At the top of both of our lists was buying a house. A wedding at Buono Come Il Pane gets us closer to that. It's not like I'm even compromising *that* much. I've talked with other people who've had a wedding at your restaurant. They said it was awesome, that you took care of everything. *Easy*, was their word. No one else has described using any other venue as easy."

"Well, okay. That's good," Beck said, unsure of how else to respond to the woman's statement that the restaurant wasn't what they wanted, but it was what they would take. An underhanded compliment if Beck had ever heard one.

"If you're settling, though, I don't want you to be unhappy with your wedding. I can understand that we're not your first choice, but we shouldn't be a reluctant one."

"Oh, you're not!" Jennifer said, her eyes wide in surprise. Her fiancé probably liked that look. It made the woman seem innocent and… untouched, almost. Bow-shaped mouth, big, round eyes. She almost looked like a 1920s' movie star.

"We started looking at houses the other day, you know. To see what we could afford. And I got so excited about our plans, and I realized that Buono Come Il Pane fits right into that plan." As the woman talked, she got more and more excited, which helped Beck relax. When the wedding was over, the restaurant would have a happy bride and a happy bride was a good bride, a bride who would help them get more business.

"That's good to hear. Have you picked a date?"

"I wanted to see what dates you had available for November. I want a fall wedding. Dark reds. Deep oranges." Her drink sloshed in its glass as she rubbed her hands together, caught up in her dreams for the future. "Anyway, I should wait until Tanner and I can come in together to meet with you."

Beck nodded. "Yes, that's a good plan. Better to do that as a couple."

"I'll email you and we'll get this ball rolling." The woman's face was bright with excitement.

This was why Beck liked working with brides. She liked working with older couples planning a silver anniversary and parents planning a graduation, but brides were the best—especially the ones who were leaning into their future with a smile on their faces. It was the lean Beck liked so much.

"Have you thought about *my* advice?" the woman asked, tilting her head closer to Beck, her voice lowered like they were sharing intimate secrets. "You know, that the handsome ones are trouble."

Caleb. Trouble indeed. Sunday morning, they'd lain in bed, sharing coffee and conversation, dog on the floor and cat at their feet. It had been enough to make Beck *believe* and believing was dangerous.

She wouldn't tell this woman that, though. "I've been on a couple dates. And you were right that some men are interested in long-term and others aren't."

The woman seemed perceptive enough to tell that Beck didn't want to talk further, because she nodded knowingly. "Sometimes, you have to get your heart broken."

"I *am* divorced," Beck said, indignant at the implication that she didn't know what it was like to have her heart broken.

The woman shrugged, too excited by her future and her wedding and her true love to notice or care much about Beck's indignation. "Breakups when you're dating are different. Divorce is probably worse, but it's not the same thing. It's losing your dream while it's still a dream and not when it's reality. Or that's what I imagine, anyway," the woman finished breezily.

"I'll consider that piece of advice, too," Beck said, not including that she'd give it the consideration it deserved—which was probably only half a minute's thought and no more.

"Do. And I'll call you about an appointment. Toodles." The woman waved as she glided off to find the next puzzle piece of her dream.

Caleb, Beck was still thinking as she watched the woman walk off. He was a problem. A handsome, funny, charming problem who encouraged her in all her ventures and supported her dreams, except the one that was most important to her.

CHAPTER TWENTY

BECK PLOPPED ONTO a chair across the table from Marsie and asked, "What's up?" Her friend had called and asked to meet as soon as they could. From anyone else, that wouldn't be surprising, but from Marsie it was almost unheard of. Marsie was the woman who at one time had scheduled which days—and for what—she would be open for first dates. She had even considered that she was being flexible when she had Sunday morning coffee and drinks after work on Wednesday.

Marsie shook out her napkin and arranged it on her lap. While her friend was busy getting herself ready to say something, Beck studied her. She looked...*glow-y* was the first word that came to mind, but Marsie had been shiny happy since her romance with her coworker had come about. This glow-y had a harder edge to it. Almost like Marsie was hungover, which seemed completely out of character for her, especially at lunch on a weekday.

"I have news," Marsie said and then took

a delicate sip of water. She looked around. "I didn't expect to tell you here."

Here was Beck's work, with her coworkers watching them. Beck didn't usually eat lunch or dinner here. Not that the food wasn't good—it was—but because it was work. "You said we should talk immediately. I had lunch free, but only if we ate here. If you like, we can talk about something else and meet someplace more private later."

"No," Marsie said, shaking her head. "I want to get this over with."

"Is it bad news?" Beck asked, suddenly worried. She hadn't felt like she'd needed to worry about her friend for a while. Marsie and Jason were happy together. God, they were even cute to watch. Uptight Marsie couldn't help herself around Jason, offering up little bits of affection when she didn't think anyone was watching, and he was supportive of her demanding career and equally demanding perfectionist personality. They felt like one of those couples that was meant to be.

What if, horror of horrors, it was worse than Marsie and Jason breaking up? Beck didn't even want to *think* about what might be worse. The fear was enough to make her snatch a piece of bread out of the basket the food runner was bringing out before he could set it on the table. She'd apologize later—after the carbs hit.

But Marsie only smiled, shook her head and said, "No. Not bad news. Just unexpected." She paused and the silence between them got heavy before Marsie lightened it by blurting out, "I'm pregnant."

"Oh!" Beck clasped her hand over her mouth. "That's great news. Really great news." She just barely stopped herself from saying "Really great news" a third time. Too much repetition would make it sound like she wasn't happy for her friend, and she was.

It's just that she was jealous, too.

Now, though, was time to be supportive and happy for Marsie. Beck could wallow in her jealously later. "How long have you known?"

Marsie swallowed her own piece of bread before answering. "I'm three months along and have known for about a month. Once we learned and decided to keep the baby, we figured we might as well follow protocol and wait the rest of the month before telling anyone. You're the first person I'm sharing this with and I wanted to tell you in person."

Beck smiled the biggest smile in her arsenal. "I'm glad you did. This is the kind of news that's best shared in person so I can hug you."

She pushed herself out of her chair and

leaned over to her friend for a big hug. "I'm so excited for you. I know how much you wanted this." She meant every word. Even if she never had children, she could be happy for her friend, who had wanted them, too.

And she could be happy for herself, too. That part was harder, but Caleb had helped her feel...not loved, because he'd warned her about that. But that she was fine the way she was with the things and person she wanted to be—even if she didn't get to be all of them.

Settling into that feeling, she focused all her attention on her friend. "So, what happened?"

Marsie giggled, which was always cute because it was unexpected out of her serious friend. "I don't kiss and tell."

Beck waved the silliness away. "This seems rushed, for you. And you never rush things."

Her friend pursed her lips and looked sideways for a moment, suddenly sheepish looking. "You know me. I follow all the rules."

"Yes," Beck answered, encouraging her friend to go on.

But their waiter interrupted them to take their order before Marsie could answer, and then it took a while for Marsie to answer. Like she was waiting for as much privacy at a crowded restaurant as was possible. Only when Marsie answered did Beck realize *why* she didn't want anyone to overhear.

"Well, we were good. We talked about not using condoms and me getting on the pill and we both went to the doctor and got our STD tests done. And I got on the pill and you're supposed to use protection for a month and… well…we didn't."

Beck had to take another piece of bread to process what Marsie was saying. "Like you didn't at all for a month or like you got carried away?"

Her friend flushed from her hairline down to the V-neck of her blouse. "Like we got carried away once. Maybe twice. It was great not to worry about where the condoms were, only I should have kept worrying."

Beck didn't have to dig for her smile this time. She could feel the corners of her lips pushing her cheeks out wide in a big, honest, pleased grin. "Things must be going well if you could get carried away."

"Hey now," Marsie said, with a scowl that bordered on being downright pleased with herself. "I was distressed that I'd been irresponsible. I'm never irresponsible."

Only Marsie could think that one—two!—nights of unprotected sex with a man she was in a committed relationship with, knew was clean and wanted to have a baby with was irresponsible. Maybe it wasn't *smart* or *careful*, but it seemed too mild a crime for a word like *irresponsible*. Still, it was Marsie and everyone had their own expectations of themselves. Marsie's were sky-high, which was one of the most important things to know about being her friend.

Which also meant that Beck had to swallow another giggle of happiness for her.

She reached her hand across the table and grabbed her friend's and gave it a squeeze. "This is such wonderful news. Even if it's earlier than you planned. You both want the baby and you want to be together."

Marsie beamed. "I know. That's what I eventually came around to. I hate unplanned things, but Jason wasn't planned and that worked out. This baby is a part of Jason, so it will work out, too."

Beck had pulled herself back to reality long enough to thank the food runner who set their plates in front of them. Then she turned her attention back to her friend and asked, "What do you need from me?"

"Well, Jason and I need to get married. Can you help?"

"Absolutely. How quickly do you want to do this?"

"As soon as we can. I'd like to not look visibly pregnant in my wedding pictures. It's not that I'm ashamed or think I did anything wrong, but…"

But even if Marsie was pleased with the result, she still understood herself to have slipped from her high standards. "Of course. Let me see what we have here coming up. If we're all booked, I'll help you find another place. I know all the vendors. We'll get you set up."

"Thank you." Marsie's smile flittered away and she looked nervous again. "I have to tell my parents."

"They'll be too excited to be grandparents to think about the fact that you're not married."

"And they've not met Jason yet."

"Really?"

"I've asked them both to come several times, but they're always busy and for different reasons."

"Yeah, okay." Beck supposed she would have remembered if Marsie's parents were in town, but she thought they would want to meet the man their daughter was over-the-moon about. Beck's parents weren't the most loving or involved, either, but they kept up pretenses.

Now, now, her inner voice said. She was probably selling her parents short. They had done the best they knew how. She would like to do differently than they did, but that was not the same thing as saying they had done poorly. They had done what they believed was important.

She picked up her glass to wash the wistfulness in her heart away and said, "Tell me what kind of wedding you want. Let's get planning." Better to think about what she could do than to think about what might never happen.

She and Marsie spent the rest of their lunch giggling and planning and brainstorming. Her best friend's wedding might be planned in a rush, but it would be everything her friend had ever wanted, even if Beck had to rob a train to make it happen.

BECK'S HIGH LASTED through the rest of her workday and halfway through her drive home. But she wasn't able to escape her jealousy as she got closer to her overly large and overly empty home. She didn't not want Marsie to be happy—and she was happy for her friend. But she wanted what her friend had.

Pulling into her garage next to the empty space that used to hold Neil's car turned the jealously inward. She couldn't escape her own role in where she was now. Her parents had wanted her to get married and they had liked Neil. *She* had liked Neil. She had loved Neil— she hadn't been faking that. But she married a man she knew didn't want kids, and she'd said that she didn't want kids because she wanted to marry him and she thought she could change him.

She had lied to him. The fact that she'd also lied to herself didn't make her any more innocent of her crimes.

It just made her more culpable.

By the time Beck stepped into her house, she was in a full-on funk that even Seamus's joy at seeing her couldn't tamp down. In enough of a funk that she couldn't help herself from responding to Caleb's How are you? text with Not good.

They weren't supposed to have the kind of relationship where they shared intimacies like this with each other. It hadn't been part of the ground rules they'd established way back when, but Beck had come to understand it as a rule. At least, Caleb never shared those deep parts of himself, even though she sometimes did.

Both of which angered her.

What happened? he asked.

It's nothing, she responded, even though it was.

I got some good news from a friend and it's made me think about my own life. I'm in a funk is all. A glass of wine and dinner and I'll be fine.

Maybe a bottle of wine, but she wasn't going to admit to that. And she'd be sure to take the dog for a walk first. She was all messed up inside, but she wasn't stupid enough to drunk dog-walk.

Not more than once, anyway.

Want me to come over? I can bring wine or dinner or both.

Both, she texted back before she could think better of it. She wanted company and Caleb was good company.

No. That was a lie. She wanted company and she loved Caleb's company. He didn't always make her feel happier, but she always felt better when he was around.

Be right over. I'll text you when I'm headed your way with food in the passenger seat. What do you want?

You. She didn't type that, though. Her edges felt rough and vulnerable enough as it was without confessing that she might need his company. Besides, needing his company would probably scare him away—and she didn't feel done with him yet.

The end would hurt, no doubt about that.

Putting the end off would only make the hurt more intense. Right now, though, that didn't matter. A hug from Caleb did. A chance to rest her head on his chest and to feel his hands smoothing down her hair.

So she typed.

I'm easy. Surprise me.

And kept a little bit of herself to herself for now. Then she grabbed the leash and took the dog out.

Turning the steel to unwind with it like the bull's noose, maybe? Right now though is that didn't matter. At this house that had ... A chance to ... lay his hand at his chest and to feel ... hands.

Stood over it.

CHAPTER TWENTY-ONE

CALEB PAID FOR his dinner and then stepped to the side while he waited for the woman behind the counter of the Middle Eastern restaurant to pack up his hummus, pita, baba ghanoush and a couple of other delicious dishes. He had a bottle of white wine in the car and had picked up a bunch of flowers at the grocery store while he'd gotten the wine.

Grocery store flowers weren't the nicest, but he didn't want to drive around to find an open flower shop, not when Beck had sounded so distraught in her texts. It wasn't just that she had said she was in a funk—people get in funks and that's not a big deal. Everyone deserves a good funk once in a while. What had made him worry had been the fact that she'd said, "I'm easy." Beck was a woman who knew what she wanted. She had opinions. She had desires. She had wants. And she knew how to express them.

He'd never known her to not suggest something for dinner. Even if they then negotiated what they wanted to eat and came to an agreement on something different than what she had wanted, she'd always had something to suggest. He wasn't such a doof that he didn't notice something as simple as that.

Flowers—even grocery store carnations—would help.

The woman passed over a plastic bag with his dinner and he stuffed a couple bucks in the tip jar. He took a deep breath before starting his car and then headed to Beck. He wanted to make her smile and if she didn't want to smile, he wanted to be the pair of arms that held her.

At her house, he knocked once and then walked in. She was sitting at her kitchen table, staring off into her backyard. Seamus looked up from his position at her feet and barked, but stayed next to his beloved owner. Unless he was mistaken, there were tearstains down her cheeks. She must be feeling worse than he thought. He set his armful of stuff on the counter and went to her. She sniffed when he put his hand on her back.

"You okay?" he asked. "Stupid question, I know, because you were crying but…"

She sniffed. "When I tell you what I'm upset about, you're going to think I'm a horrible friend."

"Not true." He moved his hand to her

shoulder and pressed his palm into her. She responded to his nudge by resting her head against his torso.

Once she had settled against him, he gave her hair a couple of soft strokes and then kept talking. "I could never think you're a bad friend. You don't have it in you."

"Yeah?" she asked, her voice trembling. "I met my friend Marsie for lunch today. She told me she's pregnant."

He sensed where this was going and his hand stilled, but all he said was, "That's great news."

"It is. But when she told me, I got so jealous I practically spit green fire. I pulled myself together for the rest of lunch and we talked about her wedding, but I couldn't pretend anymore when I got home. I'm too sad to pretend."

"You had wanted a family," he said, knowing the answer.

"Yes. It's my fault for marrying a man who didn't." She shifted her head and he lifted his hand so she could pull away and look at him. "I know better now. You can't change someone and it's real damn hard to change yourself."

"Change yourself?"

She settled her head against him again. "I alternated between trying to change his mind about kids and trying to convince myself that I didn't want any. Probably felt like a roller coaster for him. God, no wonder we got a divorce."

His heart clenched at her last sentence. It didn't matter if she was over her ex-husband. He didn't plan to get married again. He wasn't the kind of man who had kids. But he had to know. "Do you regret your divorce?"

"What?" She sounded surprised and then grumbled as she seemed to realize what she'd implied. "No. I don't regret my divorce. And I don't wish I were still married to Neil. I wish I hadn't married a man who didn't want kids when I knew in my heart that I did."

They sat in silence for several seconds, Beck resting her head against his torso and Caleb stroking her soft hair. Then Beck spoke again, softly. "Actually, I don't think I regret marrying Neil, even. I did what I thought was the right thing at the time. I know it wasn't smart *now*, but I didn't know it then. And I don't want to blame the person I was then. I just want to do it differently now."

"Marry a man who wants kids?" Caleb asked, unable to help himself. He was setting himself up and leading her on. He could see the future and all that his words implied. But he also couldn't stop himself, any more than he had been able to stop himself from talking her out of kicking him out of her house the morning after their first date. Beck was the kind of woman you did right for, even if doing right set you up for trouble.

"Yes. Or at least be honest with myself about what is happening when I *do* marry someone. I want to get married again. I *liked* being married. But being honest with myself is more important. And being honest with him. That's more important than having kids."

She was quiet for a moment, though he kept his hand on her head, wanting to keep contact with her, to keep their connection. "Though it would be nice to have kids, too."

The night had quieted down around them. The last of the birds that had been singing outside were quiet and the crickets hadn't started up yet. Her kitchen was still and stillness was the perfect place to share one's secrets. So he opened his mouth and confessed. "I wanted to have kids."

For a moment, he wondered if she had stopped breathing. Not that he could *feel* her breathing through her scalp, but there had been life in her. Movement. And it went away with his confession. The world seemed to end.

Only it didn't, because her head turned against his shirt and she said, "You did?" with no judgment or ridicule. She didn't bring up that he had been solidly against marriage or any long-term relationship that might lead to children. She was simply asking for clarification.

And, because she was Beck and the rules didn't apply to Beck, he gave it. "Yeah. My ex and I had talked about it."

Only that wasn't the whole truth and Beck deserved the whole truth. "Not just talked about it. Before we got married, we had said we were going to have two kids. Hopefully a boy and a girl, but that we would be happy with whatever kids God blessed us with."

"What happened?" she asked, again with no judgment. She was just Beck, quietly asking for more information, but not demanding it and not condemning him if he didn't give it.

"I don't know. It was never the right time." Nope. That wasn't right again. Beck deserved right. She offered him nothing but complete honesty and she deserved the same in return.

"My ex never thought it was the right time. My job was never stable enough." He could understand that. Kids took money to raise. They took investment and time, and ballet lessons and soccer and preschool and daycare were all expensive. But Leah had had a better job than he had, with more flexible hours and better pay. He didn't mind earning less than his wife. He had minded not having kids.

"There's never a right time to have kids,"

Beck said softly. "It's like getting a dog or finding a better job or redoing the kitchen floors, only more so. You just have to do it and hope for the best."

"Yeah. Wanting them wasn't enough and..." He stopped for a moment, a realization only now hitting him.

"Your ex didn't want them," Beck finished for him.

"I guess not." He had, quite literally, never considered that she didn't want kids. Before announcing that they would ruin her life, she'd never said she didn't want them. She talked with him about what their names would be. They'd talked about how they would raise them and how their kids would be adventurous eaters and sleep through the night and not have potty-training problems.

In your head, your future kids were always perfect.

Never once had she said, "I don't want children" or "I changed my mind." Until that day at the soccer field, the closest she ever came was, "We're not ready yet." She hadn't even had the honesty to say, "*I'm* not ready yet," which might have given him an opening to ask when and if she would ever be ready.

Usually her response had been, "You're not ready yet," meaning he didn't make enough

money and his job might go away and he
wouldn't be there for her when she needed him.
When the child needed him.

The realization that his ex probably hadn't
ever wanted kids made him sad. Maybe they'd
had too many problems to work through, but
if they couldn't be honest with each other,
then they would have never been able to work
through a single problem, much less a whole
pile of them. And, poof, a relationship that had
been born on the wings of hope crashed and
burned.

"Do you still want them?" Beck asked, pulling him and his thoughts into the future.

"I never considered it to be an option for me
now," he replied.

She pulled her head away with enough force
that he knew she wouldn't be resting her head
on his chest again. Not tonight. "Really? You
just got a divorce and didn't think that maybe
you could still have kids? It was that easy for
you to change your mind?"

When she put it like that, it sounded stupid,
but kids required a partner.

"I've not given it much thought. Not since I
signed those papers. My entire industry is in
flux. I never know if I'll have a job tomorrow."
Those were his ex's words, but that didn't mean
they weren't true. His paper struggled. *All* pa-

pers struggled. It didn't matter that the capital was non-stop, interesting news. At some point, no matter how important it was to their lives, people stopped paying attention to the political infighting and backstabbing. They tuned out.

And people who tuned out didn't buy papers. They also didn't pay for online access to newspaper websites. They didn't click ads on the paper's website. All things he needed people to do to pay his salary.

Maybe Leah hadn't been ready to have kids. Maybe she hadn't even *wanted* them, but that hadn't made her words untrue. His job wasn't stable. Kids took money to raise and he hadn't had it. He didn't have it now. He would probably never have it. Enough for him to get by, but no more.

He sat in the chair opposite her and then stretched out his hands across the table to her, already missing her touch. She may not have even noticed that she slipped one hand into his, but he did. From their first outing for drinks, he'd felt that connection to Beck. Each time she touched him, she burned a memory into his skin.

He *craved* those memories.

"It seems so unfair," she said and he looked up at her, in her eyes, so that he could hear what she thought was unfair and really know it. He wanted to know everything about her.

"I mean," she continued, "I want kids. I lied to myself and to Neil for years, but I'm being honest with myself now. I want kids and the clock ticking in my head is as much of an impediment as finding the right man to have kids with."

"You're still young."

"Am I? I'm thirty-two, which isn't old. But getting pregnant will only get harder for me. That limits the amount of time I can spend just *being* with a guy before I get pregnant."

Sometimes Caleb felt like the world hadn't prepared him to think about what life was like if you weren't white and male and that that deficit in his education hurt him more than it helped him. Even though he felt like an idiot, he still asked, "Why is this unfair?"

"You're thirty-five. You could date around like you are now for another ten years, then remember you want to have kids, find a woman younger than you and settle down. That option isn't really open to me."

"You really think so?"

Beck barked out a laugh, so unexpected for her normally refined self that he blinked and sat back in his chair—though he didn't let go of her hand. "Yes. You're good-looking. You're interesting. You pay attention to the woman you're with—even now, when I know you see other women."

He didn't and he hadn't, but he didn't correct her on that point. Now didn't feel like the time.

"The cards are stacked in your favor. Right now, the only thing I can imagine working against you is that, in ten years, you'll have such a reputation as a player that no woman will be willing to trust that you want to settle down."

Thunder might as well have clapped through the sky for as much doom as her words seemed to portend. Not that he couldn't imagine a woman turning him down—he could and it had happened many times, but the idea that his past could and would be used against him was beyond his experience.

Then she pulled her hand out of his and pushed away from the table. "Of course, life is unfair enough that some woman will feel like she's accomplished something special because *you* decided that now was the time to settle down. She'll feel like she conquered the wild rake or some such nonsense."

"'Conquered the wild rake,'" he repeated with a laugh he couldn't contain, even though nothing else she said was funny. "If you said that with a British accent, it would sound like something out of a nature documentary. Like I'm a wild tiger or something."

Beck stared at him, openmouthed and disbelieving for a moment. Then she laughed along with him. "That might have been a little overwrought. Still, I think my point is valid."

"I'd hate to think that some woman only wanted to marry me so that she could prove that she could tame me."

"Tame you." Beck giggled. "You brought me food, wine and flowers. You've shown up each and every time I've needed you. The idea that you need to be tamed is ridiculous. Hell, the idea that anyone would need to be tamed is stupid. If I learned one thing in my divorce, it's that you take a person as they are or not at all. If you decide to get married, to have those kids, it won't be because some woman tamed you. It will be because you decided you wanted something different with your life. She may be the woman for you, but she may also just be the woman for you who came into your life at the right time. Lightning can only strike if there's something there to hit."

"I'm not sure if I should be insulted or relieved."

She waved his concerns away. "Be relieved. You'll get to change your mind and, if you're lucky, the woman of your dreams will be there waiting for it to happen. That's not a bad problem."

For a moment, Caleb wanted to be defensive, to say it wasn't as easy as she was making it sound. And, in one sense, he was right. It wasn't easy. If he wanted to get married, he would have to silence the voice in his head that told him that marriage and a family wasn't for him, that he didn't deserve them and that he didn't work hard enough for them. That he would never be a provider, and a man should be a provider for his family.

Pushing against the voice in his head that said, basically, "You don't deserve this," wouldn't be easy.

But it was his battle to wage, if he chose to. Right now, he didn't choose to.

He closed his eyes, realizing that that meant the negative voices in his head were winning and he wasn't even bothering to fight back. And that made him sound like a coward of the highest order.

"But enough about this conversation. You brought me dinner and wine and flowers because I was feeling bad." Beck pushed herself up and out of the chair. "I'm feeling better. I confessed my sins and nothing struck me down. Thank you for that."

He *was* enough of a coward that he practically clucked. But he didn't have to stay that way. "Wait," he said as Beck walked away from him. She turned, her face open with curiosity.

"I've felt that way," he said. "Jealous of a friend for having kids, I mean."

She eyed him cautiously and then sat back down.

The situation, wanting to repair things with Beck, had ripped the words out of his mouth. Now that they were out, though, they kept coming and the relief left an ache in his belly. "At least a couple times while I was married and my ex and I were talking about kids. I have two friends with kids and the oldest kid is eight. Cute kid. Boy. He likes snakes and musical theater. He can sing all the words to *Hamilton*, the edited version, of course."

Caleb could have stopped there and it would have been enough. But he wasn't going to offer Beck *enough*. Beck deserved more.

And he needed to say the words. The thing about Beck that he hadn't yet gotten used to— might never get used to—was that what was good for her was also good for him.

"When Kevin had Oscar, that was probably the first time I tried to get Leah to come up with a plan for when we would start having kids. She'd mentioned that money made her nervous before, so I wrote out a couple budgets, including one where I lost my job and stayed home with the kid while she worked. Maybe I overestimated my ability to get work writing articles for other publications, but she agreed they were both workable budgets."

Beck was the one who reached her hand across the table this time and took his hand in hers. She gave a squeeze of understanding, encouraging him to go on. His ache pulsed, no longer distinguishable from the old hurts in his heart.

"We came back to that budget several times over the next several years. I got a raise when I moved into the political gig. And I brought out that budget every time one of my friends got pregnant and whenever anyone at work got pregnant."

He laughed wryly. "So I guess I got it out more than several times. I practically posted the thing on the fridge and talked about it any night I was making dinner."

This time, when Beck squeezed his hand, Caleb squeezed back. "I'll bet she got sick of listening to me and probably me bringing kids up in every discussion didn't help. But if she'd only been honest with me about not wanting them…"

"Then you could have gotten a divorce sooner," Beck finished for him. "And maybe you would feel less broken, because there was less time for the marriage to break you."

"But it's the divorce that really breaks you," he said with a shake of his head, not certain if that was true. Maybe it was the marriage. Or the failing marriage. Or the constant sense that something is wrong, in your own home, where nothing should weigh wrong on you.

"Mostly I brought up that stupid budget every time someone got pregnant because I didn't know what else to do. I'll bet my skin was the color of split-pea soup. Talking about the budget and how we could make kids work if we were only willing to try seemed like a more productive response to my jealousy than raving about it."

"Did your friends ever know that you were jealous?"

"My close ones suspected. They knew that Leah and I were talking about kids, and they knew nothing was happening. But I always got them the best baby shower present possible— I've spent so much money on diapers in the past ten years that I should get some kind of frequent-buyers' card."

Beck giggled. "I've done that. I'm probably doing that now, with Marsie. Only I'm trying to overcome my jealousy by making sure she gets the best wedding ever."

"Nah," he said with a shake of his head. "You're not helping Marsie because you're jealous. You're helping her because she's your friend and she asked for your help. Probably like I would give a hundred dollars' worth of diapers as a present anyway."

Her smile was soft, but real. "Thank you. The jealousy hurts. And I feel like a terrible person because it exists in my heart."

"It makes you human. And it's not like you want to take her pregnancy away. You simply wish for the same joy she's gotten."

"I want Marsie to have all the happiness she deserves—and she deserves loads of it. She's one of the best people I know."

"Do you feel better?" he asked.

"Yes." She cocked her head at him. "Is that what you came over here for, with your flowers, to make me feel better?"

"Yes. Or, if you didn't want to feel better, to be a shoulder for you to cry on. That would work for me, too."

"I don't like to wallow. I'd rather be pulled into a good mood than granted the space to stay in a bad one."

"I know." It was his turn to push away from the table. "It's one of the things I like so much about you."

As she turned to stand up again, she gave

him a big smile, full of all her big teeth that showed off her square jaw and pointed chin. It was the smile that had attracted him to her online-dating profile to begin with.

"Thank you," she said as she stood. "Thank you for coming over here. I needed someone."

"It's nice to be needed," he replied. If someone had asked him a couple of months ago if he would feel comfortable being the one another person had relied on, he would have said no. But, with Beck, he was a different person.

Only, that wasn't right, either. It wasn't that Beck made him a different person, but that Beck allowed him to be the person he had wanted to be with Leah. And that was freeing.

"What'd you bring me for dinner?" she asked, peeking into the bag.

"Hummus and other delicious food. I don't know where you keep the vases. If you could find one, I'll set the food out and then we can eat."

"Eat first. Sex later."

He laughed again. She made him laugh. "We could have sex first, and eat later," he said, though the sex was beside the point. The comfort they would find in each other's bodies would be the cherry on the top of the evening; it wasn't the evening itself.

"No. I need food. And wine. And then I want

you to hold me like you never planned to let me go. I know it's not true, but I need that for tonight."

"I can do that," he said as regret that it wasn't going to be true filled his body. Of course, he could be the one to change his mind about forever. But changing his mind about never getting married wouldn't change that his job was tenuous and his salary meager. And it changed nothing about the risk that he wasn't enough.

But he could pretend for Beck. "I'd be happy to do that for you."

CALEB'S EYES WERE DARK, warm and deep as the back of his hand brushed over her chin. Gentle fingers skimmed over her lips and knuckles bumped into her nose. As Beck stood in her bedroom, she looked into his eyes, letting his touch and the love in his gaze fill her—letting them push away the bad thoughts.

Love. That's not the right word, she thought, but he leaned forward and pressed his lips to hers, and the world fell away, and the difference between true emotion and the put-on version she saw in his eyes didn't seem to matter.

Those distinctions didn't matter when he pulled her shirt over her head, either, or when she put her hands to his stomach.

Neither of them rushed their touches or their

kisses. They explored each other's bodies. Only, that wasn't the right word, either, Beck thought as Caleb bent over her bare stomach and kissed the skin around her belly button. It was a worshipful pose and, as his tongue worked its way down her skin through her pubic hair and to the sensitive spots hidden among her folds, she felt like a goddess. Like the kind of woman a man could never leave, because he could never get enough of her touch and her smell and her sounds.

The reverence was in the heat of his eyes. The light touches of his fingertips and the occasional nibble of his teeth. When she came, his eyes closed as if in prayer. Once he moved to his back, his eyes never left her face. Not while she was rolling the condom down his cock, not while she settled on top of him and not while he moved inside her.

From the intensity of his face, she was his entire world. She was all he could see and all he wanted to touch—and he held on to her as if loosening his grip would risk losing everything that mattered to him.

After he came, she tucked against him, his kneecaps touching the backs of her knees and his breath hot on her neck. As she closed her eyes for sleep, even the last rational parts of her that knew he would eventually let her go drifted off into dreamland, unable to hold on to the reality of the end.

CHAPTER TWENTY-TWO

LESLIE STOPPED BY Beck on their way to their
locker. "You look tired," the captain said.

"I haven't been sleeping well," Beck replied.

"Oooh," Leslie said with a wide grin, like
they were in the know on some joke. "Late
nights."

Beck's shoulders fell. "Yes, but not for that
reason. I've been doing a lot of thinking."

The captain looked down the hall and then
behind them before saying, "Let's sit down.
Something is on your mind and you need to
talk about it."

Beck had work to do. Leslie had work to do.
But they were also right. She needed to talk,
so she simply nodded and let the captain lead
her into the cramped storage room for a little
more privacy.

"Spill," Leslie said, as soon as they were hidden in the shadows.

"Caleb is great," Beck said, starting off with
the positive. She liked to keep her mind on
what was positive about her life, though in this

case, focusing on the positive seemed to pull her mind away from what she needed to do for herself and her own sanity. Caleb might say that her snide comments were the salt that heightened her sweetness, but that didn't mean she was willing to pull completely away from the sugar.

"That's what I hear. The couple friends who've been on dates with him said he was charming and fun. By the time their relationship—if you can call it that—fizzled, they were primed for the man they wanted to marry. Like he left some magic with them so that they could more easily see what they wanted in a relationship and find a man who could provide that for them."

Leslie shook their head. "I don't understand, but I've never dated anyone like that." Then they barked out a laugh. "Of course, I've never dated anyone who's made me feel good enough that I was riding that feeling for months after. Maybe that says more about the people I've dated than it does about Caleb."

"Caleb might be too great," Beck corrected.

"Oh," Leslie said, realization slowly dawning. "Like, you don't think you can stay light, fluffy and casual with him?"

"Like, I don't know that I ever could. I know

I said that I would date Caleb *and* I would date other people…"

"But you haven't," Leslie finished for her.

"Not really. I mean, I've been on a couple of dates, but nothing that I took seriously. I don't think I seriously looked, either. Perfunctory dating."

Beck wrinkled her nose. "At first because it was easier not to go back online, but now it's because I think we're perfect for each other. If only…" Beck took a deep breath. She had to say it or she wouldn't admit it to herself, and if she couldn't admit it to herself, then she couldn't fix it.

"If only he would change," she finished.

"Oh, that's bad," Leslie breathed out as they leaned against a locker. "That's real bad."

"I know." Beck closed her eyes. "I realized it last night, as we were lying in bed after…anyway, *after*, and I thought about how I'd asked him to pretend like this was forever for the night and that he pretended so well."

"Maybe he wasn't pretending."

"See, I wondered that, too. And I can't wonder that. *He* has to wonder that. And after he wonders that, he has to think that he should change his stance on marriage. And then he has to want to call me."

"That's quite a list."

Beck shook her head. "Too many checkboxes, especially for one month in *and* for that man."

"So, are you not going to see him anymore, perhaps to see if you can prod him to start crossing off items on that list? You know, as he works his way down to happily-ever-after."

Beck shook her head again. "No. That's playing a weird game and I'm not interested in that. I'm doing this for me. Because I've waited for a man to change before and it was a fool's errand. I'm falling in love with a man who doesn't want to love me. It's nothing personal—he just doesn't want to love anyone. He doesn't think he's capable of dealing with the consequences of loving someone."

She took a deep breath. Leslie was a good person to talk to, though almost anyone would be a good person to talk to right now. Beck needed to talk through this. She needed to say all of these things aloud so that she acted upon them, so that she heard how they sounded and if she wanted them to change.

"I'm not putting myself through that," she continued. "I'm too old to wait someone out, but more than that, I've waited someone out and it's stupid. It takes lying to yourself and lying to the other person, and that's lying to too many people at once."

Leslie nodded. "Maybe that's the difference between dating in your thirties and dating in your twenties. I think I'd try to wait him out."

Beck snorted. "Take it from someone who tried—don't."

"So, when are you going to do this? End the relationship?"

"I've got to do it soon. This isn't the sort of thing you can sit on and think too much about. That's not fair to the other person."

"No, it's not.

"Oh, God," Leslie said, leaning over to envelop Beck in a big hug. "I'm so sorry."

If it hadn't been for the hug, Beck wouldn't have cried. She hadn't wanted to cry. She was at work, for God's sake. But Leslie was right; ending her relationship with Caleb was a thing to be sorry about.

Still, she said, "I knew this was going to happen."

"Yeah, but that doesn't make it easier," her friend said, patting her a couple of times on the back before pulling away.

"No," she said with a sniff. At least she hadn't cried a lot, though she would probably bawl later. She'd go over to Marsie's house for that. Marsie's tea had gotten her through many crying jags during her divorce. She made the best tea.

"Hey," Leslie said, "I don't want to make this about me, but I want to know for the next time. I told you that you should keep dating Caleb—did I give you bad advice?"

Beck gave her friend a soft smile. "No. You gave me fine advice. I needed to feel a lot of things in my first relationship post-divorce and I got all of them. Even better, I feel like I'm capable of making smart decisions about my heart now. Before I got in this relationship, I didn't think I was."

There was a harder lesson in store for her, she knew. But it was in the pile of things she didn't want to admit to herself. Which meant she needed to. "I read somewhere that judging relationships by the fact that they aren't death-do-us-part means most relationships fail and that's not fair. Most relationships *end*, but sometimes a relationship ending is success, and sometimes the fact that the relationship existed at all is a success."

She straightened her shoulders and stood tall, certain that she was in the right here. That, too, was a nice feeling. "I would have liked me and Caleb to have turned out differently, but the fact that I dated him at all and that I'm strong enough to know that staying in a relationship where we want different things is not good for me is a success."

And she was going to cling to that.

CHAPTER TWENTY-THREE

Do you mind coming over to my house tonight?
We need to talk.

CALEB SAW THE text just as he finished typing up the last of his story for tomorrow, and the adrenaline high he had been riding as the clock ticked closer and closer to 7:00 p.m. popped in an explosion of trepidation that felt like shattered glass in his stomach.

We need to talk. He knew those words. He'd used them enough since his divorce and, if he were being honest with himself, had figured he'd be the one using them this go-round, too. Beck liked relationships. She wanted to get married. She was a woman who stuck. It simply hadn't occurred to him that she'd willingly *un*stick herself.

More the fool him.

He hit Send and watched as his copy went into cyberspace to show up tomorrow on thousands of doorsteps across The Triangle. The window on his computer closed and, like a blip, he realized what a jerk thinking those things about Beck had made him seem like.

No. Not seem like. Be. He'd been a jerk. A world-class jackass of the first order. Sitting in cozy comfort with an awesome woman, certain she wouldn't leave you and knowing you would leave her when things got too cozy was something an asshole did.

Which made him the asshole.

Okay, he texted back, not sure what else to say in this situation. Great? Awesome? *Thanks for making the decision to break us apart, because I wasn't going to be able to.*

There. That was closer to the truth and it wasn't any more complimentary. The truth was, he wasn't sure he would have been able to break up with her. He wasn't sure he wanted to. But he was sure he didn't want to get married and have kids, and that was what she wanted, so he'd be keeping her from her dreams.

His heart sank at that realization. Another asshole thing to do. To know that the woman you...*loved*? No, that couldn't be right. But the possibility of love was the only thing that explained the pain in his gut right now. But she wanted something he couldn't give her and sticking around made him a parasite. Parasite was no better than asshole.

It was worse actually. He was stealing her

radiance for his own pleasure and not giving anything back.

Fuck. Had he done this to other women? God, he hoped not. And he didn't think so. He'd never been with another woman and not seen the end coming. So, he was a stand-up, peach of a guy there, too. Surprise! Congratulations on being loved by a man like him. As a reward for being the chosen one, your emotions get treated more carelessly.

I think I have a pair of earrings on your night-stand. And there's a Seamus toy at your house, too. Could you bring those over?

"I'm going to dump you in twenty minutes," texted in flashing neon, complete with a mermaid waving her tail. In case he hadn't gotten the message in the earlier text.

Back when they'd first started dating, when they'd been testing each other out by sharing secrets, she had mentioned that she'd gone to therapy to help her get through her divorce. Several people had suggested that Caleb see a therapist. All of them had been women, which had seemed like a sign that it wasn't something he should do. He could work his way through this on his own.

Like a real man. God, that was also an asshole thing to think. He was better than that. He was better than this…than this person he was being right now and had been with Beck. With Beck and all the other women he'd dated.

Even if they hadn't wanted more out of him than a good time, Beck did. And he'd been willing to string her along because he liked her too much to let her go.

Is that all? a voice in the back of his head asked as the base of his neck tingled.

Beck was texting him to dump him. He refused to pay any attention to that voice now.

Be right over, he texted back, having to stop himself from asking if she wanted him to bring dinner, like this was going to be a normal night where they laughed together. When he got home, he would see what kind of benefits the paper offered for mental-health care. Then he was going to call and make his appointment.

He could imagine how the first appointment would go. "What can I help you with?" the therapist would ask and Caleb would say, "I've been a massive asshole to this really awesome woman and I don't want to ever do that again. Can you help me?"

"Do you have any other goals for therapy?" he imagined the therapist asking as a follow-up.

"Yeah…" That voice at the back of his head started to supply the other futures Caleb had imagined for himself. The futures where he taught a kid to ride a bike and they did the Jumble together after reading the comics.

He shut down this train of thought before that voice began formulating an alternate future in any detail.

But, to make sure the therapy happened, he wrote a reminder on a sticky note. Everything that got written on a sticky note came true. Even if Bond, James Bond ate the sticky by the time he got home.

BECK POURED TWO glasses of wine and set them on the island in her kitchen. Horrible emotional moments were always better with wine, especially now that she felt emotionally stable enough not to be afraid of drinking too much of it and so was no longer stuck with tea or nothing at all.

Then she waited, with Seamus's head under her palm, scratching his ear, for the doorbell to ring.

Even though she was expecting the buzzer, she jumped about five feet when it actually sounded. She wasn't ready.

You will never be ready. It would be easy, so easy, to settle comfortably into a relationship with Caleb and wait for him to change. She even knew what it felt like to wait for a man to change. It wasn't a *good* feeling, but she knew it, and so it was comfortable.

This time would be different. This time, she was taking control over her life and making changes to get the life she wanted. Nothing wrong with that.

Even if she wanted to curl up with Caleb and never let him go.

Her feet dragged all the way to the front door, but—once there—she shook herself straight and tall. "Hey," she said to the man she'd let her hopes get up about. Seamus barked in greeting.

"Hey to you both," he said, Seamus's stuffed toy in his hand, hanging by his side. To her surprise, he looked sad. Not disappointed. Not bummed. Not any of the other words of minor inconvenience that she might have expected when dumping a man who had warned her that he couldn't be counted on for the long term—but sad.

Sad choked her up, too.

"Come in," she said, pulling the door open wide and stepping aside for him. "There are a couple glasses of wine in the kitchen."

He glanced sharply at her and it occurred to her that maybe she was supposed to just get it over with. Dump him, kick him out and be done with it. "If you want a glass, I mean. You might just want to leave. You know…"

"After you say the words?"

"Yeah." Words—that's all they were. Simple things, words. Simple, horrible things.

"You know what? I *would* like a glass of wine. I won't overstay my welcome, but if you're offering a glass, then I want one."

She nodded. "It's a red. One I remember you liking."

That got a small, sorrowful smile out of him. "Thank you. Thoughtful and caring, to the end," he said. There was no malice or sarcasm in the words, only the same heavy paint of despondency.

Caleb tossed the toy to the floor in the living room, and she followed him to the kitchen, Seamus bringing up the rear. She could hear uncertainty in the way her dog's nails scraped against the hard floor and she would bet his tail was low. He didn't like grief or heavy emotions. If she started crying, there was as much of a chance he would hightail it to the second floor of the house as he would stay around and try to comfort her. He might disappear from the conversation even if there wasn't crying. The low voices would be enough to send him running.

That thought boosted Beck's resolve. She only had enough room in her life for one emotional coward, and the dog was hogging the space.

Emotional coward. That's what Caleb was being. His confession a couple nights ago about wanting kids—about desperately wanting kids—and now he was afraid of the kind of emotional commitment that might lead to the family he'd once dreamed of.

One hurt and he was done. She wanted a braver man in her life.

Still, she appreciated his calm. Maybe he couldn't face what it meant to be vulnerable in a real relationship, but he was looking her right in the eye as he took a sip of his wine. Once he set the glass down, he dug in his pocket. "Here." He set a baggie with her earrings on the counter. "I don't want to forget and take them with me."

"Thank you." They shared a long silence as they stood, both staring at the earrings. Black drop earrings with a small pearl. One of her favorite pairs. She'd worn them to look for a bike with Caleb, and he'd seemed to really like them. They had watched Bond, James Bond bat at a toy and Caleb had turned to her and playfully batted at the drops. Silly, the things that couples do when no one is looking.

Not that they had really been a couple, but they had been close. So very close.

"You're going to have to say the words, you know. I'm not letting you off easy."

Saying them meant she was taking ownership of them. It meant she was ending this. It meant she couldn't take it back. Saying the words had been easy a month ago, when Caleb had been a one-night stand and she had only been guessing about what a great guy he was.

Knowing someone changes everything.

She took a deep breath. "Caleb, I don't think we should see each other anymore."

He nodded as he took a large gulp of his wine. She didn't think he would argue or disagree with her——he wasn't the type of guy who claimed he *owned* a woman's attention or that women *owed* him anything, but that didn't mean she expected him to nod, finish his wine and leave her life forever. Caleb was a fighter——for everything except those kids he'd once wanted.

She immediately chastised herself——that wasn't fair. He'd fought for those at one time, too. He just didn't have it in him to fight anymore, even if there was no battle. She could call him an emotional coward all she liked, but she hadn't lived his life and didn't know the path he'd walked. Only he could know that and only he could fix it.

"Do I get to know why?" he finally asked.

"For the same reason as before," she said, surprised by the question. "That I want to get married and have kids. That's all I've wanted since I started dating. And you're not going to be that man for me. You don't want to be that man for anyone."

"Why now, though?" he asked, before taking another drink of his wine. She picked up the bottle and offered to pour him more, but he shook his head. He wasn't going to draw this out any longer than necessary, for which she was grateful.

"Because I'm afraid to love you." She was going to be honest. Their relationship had burned short, but it had burned bright and it had been beautiful enough to deserve honesty. "Because I can think of a million reasons why I shouldn't end this. And because I considered waiting you out."

He closed his eyes, knowing what she had just admitted to.

"That's dangerous territory for me," she added, wincing at the pleading in her voice.

"For me, too," he said. "There's no way that could end with us sharing anything other than pain."

She moved her head, somewhere between a nod and a shake. Was she agreeing with him or shaking her head against the future he was predicting? She didn't know and it didn't really matter. "I don't want that. I want to look back on this month and think about how much stronger I am now, how much better off I am. And I want to give you some credit."

He set his wine on the counter with a shake of his head. "I won't take any credit for that. Beck, you were already strong when we started dating. Stronger than you knew. All you needed was time to realize it, and I was the man lucky enough to be with you when you did. Thank you for that."

She blinked. *Thank you?* Of all the things she had expected from Caleb, a thank you hadn't been one of them.

"Thank you," she said back. "For everything."

"Are we going to be friends?" he asked.

"I don't know," she replied honestly. "I'm afraid of what I might hope for if I agree to be friends with you."

"I'm not sure what you mean," he said, his head cocked and looking a lot like her dog when he was trying to figure out what she wanted out of him. He wasn't her Byronic hero anymore. Caleb was something else, something more normal and real. A person, with all the complexities, dark corners and bright lights that being a person brought with it.

She'd been attracted to the image of Caleb that she'd created in her mind, but she'd fallen in love with the person.

"Oh, Caleb. I'm breaking up with you because I love you. Because the thing I feared
most has happened. Staying friends with you
would always keep me hoping that you might
change. And that's a stagnant swamp that I
want no part of."

"You love me?" he said, still clearly confused.

"Yes, you doofus," she said with a laugh.

"But I'm..."

"Unavailable? Also charming and funny and
committed to your job and your community
and kind, and you've always been there for me
when I need you. As far as I can tell, the only
thing wrong with you is that you don't think
you're capable of anything more than dating
around. Hell, you even *want* more, I think. You
just don't think you can have it."

"I, uh..." For the first time since she had
known him, Caleb seemed at a loss for words,
as if all his charm and all his words had drained
out of him over the course of the past ten minutes and all that was left was the man.

Still handsome. Still a man she wanted to
take up to her bed. And a man who was going
to be leaving her house forever in five minutes.

"I think you should go," she said, when he
still didn't respond.

"Yeah. Yeah. I think so, too." His voice broke

and she realized he was trying not to cry. She hadn't expected him to cry.

He pushed away from the counter, startling Seamus, who had lain down nearby. When Caleb looked at her, his eyes were red and heavy with water. As if she had mattered to him in a way that she hadn't expected to. Not expected to at all.

"I'll miss you, Beck," he said, looking full at her. He seemed like he was no longer trying to hide his pain, and tears streamed down his face. "I'm sorry things worked out this way. I had hoped…"

Then he stopped, never saying what he had hoped for. Which was fine. Beck wasn't sure she wanted to hear it. She wasn't sure she'd believe it. What could he have hoped for, anyway? He'd been the one who'd laid out the rules when their relationship started. She was only following them.

"I'll see myself out," he said, pushing his half-full glass of wine farther across the counter and away from her. It felt like a rejection of her and everything she'd tried to give him, which was stupid, because it was a glass of wine. She was just sad and emotional and feeling vulnerable.

"Yeah. I think that's best," she said with a nod. She averted her eyes as he turned to the door, but as soon as his back was to her, she watched him walk out of her life. When the front door was shut, she scrambled to the front window and watched him get into his car and drive away.

Seamus peeked his head into the living room and she must have begun to cry, because he huffed and then disappeared. Over her sniffles, she heard him walking up the stairs, leaving her alone with her sadness.

CALEB MADE IT as far as the end of the block before he was crying too much to drive. He pulled into the parking lot of a small strip mall and let himself bawl, not able to remember the last time he'd cried so hard. He certainly hadn't cried like this when his marriage had ended. By the time he'd moved out of the house he'd shared with Leah, their relationship had run its course and had nowhere else to go.

But his relationship with Beck—that had had places it could go.

Except you were the one who put the rules on it, that she shouldn't expect anything, that obnoxious voice said again. *That there was no future in the relationship. That it would have to end and would probably end sooner rather than later.*

He'd set up the rules that ultimately cost him Beck. *He'd* done that. No one else. And he'd done that because another woman had hurt him. Because his ex-wife hadn't wanted kids and hadn't been honest enough with him just to say so. Because he hadn't been able to face how much that had hurt him, nor had he been willing to face that hurt again. The wall between him and a family had been built, mortared, and maintained by him and no one else.

Anger at himself dried the tears quickly. He didn't have it in him to cry when he wanted to punch something or have someone knock sense into him.

Not that either punching something or having someone punch him would help. He needed a different fix, one that didn't come with a bruise and went deeper than the surface. But the anger was enough for him to straighten his back, shift the car back into Drive and head home.

Bond, James Bond had found the sticky with the reminder for Caleb to look into his options for therapy. The pink scrap of paper was stuck in the corner of his dining room, tiny teeth marks in it. He snagged the paper from its final resting place and set it on top of the piles of other papers on his desk. Then he signed into the newspaper's HR website and looked for how to make himself better.

Beck had said she loved him, which meant

he had a chance. But he didn't have a chance if he didn't do the work to make him worth her risk. He wasn't so self-absorbed and idiotic not to know that, if she gave him another chance, she'd be risking far more heartbreak than he would be.

CHAPTER TWENTY-FOUR

"So, THERAPY," FLOYD, the sports reporter who covered the Atlantic Coast Conference beat, asked as they sat in a bar, each with a beer in their hands. "Man, the office would be all atwitter if it knew."

"So, maybe this could be *one* thing that we don't share around the office?"

Floyd shrugged. "Yeah, I guess. They're reporters, so they're curious and will probably figure it out, though."

"Really?" Caleb asked with a raise of his eyebrow. "They're going to be curious enough to...what? Follow me to my appointment? Tap my phones?"

"Hah!" Floyd turned his head to look over his shoulder as the waitress dropped a basket of fried pickles between them. "Thanks, miss."

The reporter turned back to face Caleb, though his attention was never far from the basket of pickle chips. A known cheapskate, the man was probably counting them and calculating how many he could have and still claim he only ate half and they should split the check. It wouldn't have been the first time.

"I'll bet that half of the office is in therapy or needs it. What'll happen is that you'll be in the therapist's office and someone else from the office will walk out of the office. You'll make eye contact, then silently agree not to mention that you saw the other person there. But you'll know. Every time you see the other person in the office, you'll know and you'll wonder if they told. Eventually, one of you will break."

"And maybe we'll start a trend for the office."

"Nah. Beer is too tasty." As if to punctuate his statement, Floyd drank almost half his beer in one gulp. "And it works almost as well. It's the therapy of reporters and cops, going back generations."

"It's not like I'm giving up beer," Caleb said, taking a sip of his own.

"Yeah, but it's not the same. You never did drink as much as the rest of us. And you go to the gym. You eat vegetables that aren't fried. And now therapy. Really, the only thing you had going for you was your unwillingness to settle down after your divorce. But I'll bet the therapy is supposed to stop that, too."

"It is." For all his joking, Floyd had been married for twenty years, supposedly happily.

For all his bluster, he didn't participate in any of the jokes about balls and chains. He and Bernetta and their spouses were supposedly friends, having all met in college. They played double tennis together. Like people who had a normal job and normal lives.

He should probably be talking to Bernetta, too, but she had to be home for a grandkid's soccer game. Which is fine. He wasn't sure that he was ready to face her honesty. He could come up with a plan while talking to Floyd and run it by Bernetta. By then it would be foolproof.

"Everyone is talking about how you haven't been out dating," Floyd said, signaling the waitress for another beer.

"Everyone, huh? How does everyone know I'm not out dating?"

"Because everyone knows someone who's been on dates with you."

Caleb sat back in his chair, not quite willing to believe that was true. "Everyone."

"Yeah. You went on a date with my niece. She said you were charming. That seems to be the consensus. Charming and honest about your unwillingness to commit. The honesty counts for a lot."

He hoped his history of honesty counted for something—anything—with Beck. When he eventually went back to her on his knees, with his apology, he hoped she would remember that he'd always been honest with her.

"Well, I've met a woman."

"And she made you change your ways?" Floyd asked, a brow raised with doubt. "'I'll change for you, honey,' seems like the first volley in a relationship that ends in unhappiness. You gotta want to change for you."

"Thanks, Freud."

"What? I listen to my wife talk with her friends. She's a smart lady, so I'm repeating what she has said about similar situations. Don't like it? Take it up with her."

"I'm changing for myself, thank you." He'd talked this over several times with the therapist, who'd explored his motivations from several different angles. It had been hard to be on the receiving end of so many questions—as opposed to being the man who asked them to begin with—but he was paying for the privilege, so he did it.

Two sessions in and the therapist had agreed with him. He wanted to change for himself, not for Beck. *And* that he'd be an idiot to let Beck go. The therapist was leaving it up to him to come up with ways to approach Beck and try to win her back.

"Be gentle," was his therapist's main advice.

Combined with, "Give her space and recognize ahead of time that she might not be willing to hear you out. And that's okay."

That Beck might not be willing to hear him out was okay, he guessed, but he wanted to fight for her. She was worth fighting for—as much worth fighting for as his dream of having a kid had been.

"Okay, so you're changing for you and not for her. And you're going to therapy, so you're braver than the rest of us in the office. And you're asking me for help, which I guess means you really need it. What do you want help with?"

"I need to show her that, like you said, I'm not changing for her. That I'm doing it for myself and I hope she'll come along for the journey." He took a deep breath and admitted to the hardest part. "And I need to do all of this while giving her enough space that she can easily say no."

Floyd eyed Caleb sharply and he wondered how much of that suspicious look was the man channeling his wife. "Can you give her that space to say no? 'Cause, if you can't, then you need to leave her alone."

Caleb pulled his beer closer to him. It had gotten warmish, which was fine. He didn't want to drink it anyway, but it gave him something to regard while he thought about Floyd's question. Again. "Yes. Yes. I think I can. I love Beck." There. He'd said it. Now he just needed to be able to say it to her. "But, if I really love her, then I have to want what's best for her and not what's best for me. Though I hope they overlap."

His coworker nodded. "Okay. Okay. So, what's your plan?"

Fortunately, Floyd kept nodding as Caleb explained what he was thinking. Even better, after Caleb explained his idea, Floyd said, "I think the wife would approve."

"I should have invited her, then."

"Nah," his fellow reporter said with a wave. "I like getting the chance to play the smart one with all the good relationship advice. Don't get to do that often."

Caleb laughed. "Yeah. I'll bet." Floyd was a nice guy and happily married, but he talked so much about sports and the local college teams that it was hard to remember he knew how to talk about anything else. Caleb had asked him here because the man was happily married and not shy about it. The man had to be doing something right. Caleb just needed to figure out what it was.

"My last piece of advice, before I head home to the wife and share the gossip with her..."

Floyd paused long enough to eat a couple of extra pickle chips. "I think the biggest thing for a happy marriage is picking the right person. The person whose flaws amuse you as much as they annoy you. Because those flaws aren't going away. And they only get more annoying as you live with them longer. So, if you don't think you can put up with them now... And don't tell me she doesn't have flaws. Everyone has flaws."

"She's got flaws," he said, though he couldn't think of any right now.

"Well," Floyd said with a laugh, "if you're willing to admit she has flaws so that you can tell me how perfect she is, I suppose you're pretty into her. If any plan is going to work, yours is."

"Thanks." Dating was easy. Dating never involved putting his heart in another person's hands and asking them to take care of it— which pretty much summarized what he was about to do.

"You going to eat any more of these pickles?"

"No," Caleb said. He didn't want pickles and he didn't want beer. He wanted Beck. He wanted kids with Beck. He wanted a family with Beck. He wanted the future that Beck wanted—and he wanted it with her.

"Dang. I guess I'll eat them all." Only Floyd could sound both eager and disappointed at the prospect of finishing off an entire basket of fried pickles. "Um, you still paying half?"

"Both your beers and the pickles are on me. Payment for advice and for keeping my secrets."

"Huh." Floyd dipped the last of the pickles into the ranch dressing and popped it into his mouth. "Should've ordered more."

"Are my secrets worth more than two beers and a basket of fried pickles?"

"Nah. But Dee is making tuna casserole for dinner tonight. I only pretend to like it."

Caleb laughed. "You poor guy."

"I know. I suffer. It's hard."

"Well, I'm going to head home and get started on my plan. If you want, I'll add another basket of something fried to the bill before I leave."

"Nah. I'm late enough getting home as it is. And the tuna casserole isn't so bad. There's just so much of it. That's the worst part. We're going to be eating it for days." For all his griping, Floyd didn't look too disappointed. And why would he? He loved his wife. She made him dinner. And he ate it to show how much he loved her.

Caleb was jealous, but at least now he could imagine a future where that was possible for him.

CHAPTER TWENTY-FIVE

BECK PULLED HER car into her garage and sat for a few moments before getting out. Today had been a hard day at work. To be honest, since she had broken up with Caleb, they had all been hard days at work. Wedding season was well underway, which meant brides checking in on their arrangements. Engagement season was also well underway, which meant prospective clients calling. It meant Beck was professionally obliged to ask, "Now, tell me how you got engaged? Who proposed to whom? Let me see your ring," and saying all of it with a smile and honest-to-goodness excitement.

No graduations to give Beck a break from all the lovebirds.

Not that she wasn't excited for their happiness. She was. She didn't begrudge the happy couples any of their happiness—though she had given herself another week to avoid Marsie before she stopped sulking and feeling sorry for herself and started planning her friend's baby shower. When she'd texted Marsie to say that she'd ended things with Caleb and needed some time to herself to recover, Marsie had understood. "Call me when you're ready," her friend had texted back.

In some ways, this breakup was harder than her divorce. At least during her divorce, she'd been angry. Flat-out pissed off at the world, at Neil and at herself. And she'd been able to rest in the knowledge that *she*—at least—had done everything she could to make the marriage work. They'd explored their options and were well and truly done.

She wasn't able to rest in the same comfort with Caleb. Possibilities still hung between them, but she was the only one who wanted them. And that felt like a waste of a connection. A sense of loss and missing out that hadn't been there during her divorce.

This was a flower cut down before it had a chance to bloom.

She sighed. One more week of wallowing, and then she was getting back online and back into dating and trying again. If she'd been able to find possibility with Caleb, then possibilities with other men had to exist—right? Life wasn't a one-strike-and-you're-out game.

In the meantime, she'd bought a bike rack for her car and was trying out what she'd learned in her mountain biking classes. She'd given up on drawing classes. Putting charcoal to paper hadn't been nearly as satisfying as bumping her way down the mountain.

She allowed herself one more deep sigh, and then she pulled her key out of the ignition and stepped out of her car to get the mail. Stuffed into the mailbox were a handful of coupon books and mailers about exciting deals for the people who'd owned this house before she and Neil had bought it years ago and who were interested in things like fishing and camping. Buried in the junk was a card with a return address she recognized, even though she tried to pretend that she didn't.

From inside the house, Seamus barked, reminding her that she was home and had business to take care of before she could open the envelope. She set it on the kitchen counter and took the dog out. Being a responsible dog owner came first, though she didn't take Seamus for the long walk he clearly wanted, judging by the pull he gave to the leash as they headed back home.

Back in the house, she got Seamus a rawhide to distract him from the missing walk and poured herself a small glass of wine. Then she picked up the envelope and curled up on the couch with it.

Hope had a weight. It lifted her heart, but it

also pushed down on her stomach, reminding her that hope was just that—hope. It was not reality, nor was it the future.

Hope had texture, too. Not the soft, bubbling texture she had expected it to have, either. As she turned the envelope over in her hand, examining the corners for clues, hope stabbed at her heart, reminding her that it flew into her life with pain, as well as with joy.

Once she had had a sip of wine and was convinced that the envelope was real and not a figment of her imagination, she opened it.

A postcard fell out, the back addressed to Caleb and already stamped. She turned the postcard over, saw checkboxes and decided it wasn't for her to look at yet. She needed to read the card first.

The card was cute. It had two martini olives on it, holding hands, and said, "Olive juice." Not quite the commitment she was looking for, but closer. And it made her smile, which was even better. She opened it. The original greeting that had come in the card had been scratched out with permanent marker and the rest of the white space was covered in Caleb's handwriting—big at the top and then smaller, as he'd started to run out of space, but not out of things to say.

Dear Beck,

I messed up. That's probably the bulk of what you need to hear, though it's not the bulk of what I need to say.

Once upon a time, I had dreams. And those dreams didn't work out. When faced with the harder choice to try at my dreams again or to give up and pretend they didn't matter to me, I chose to pretend. That was fine for a while. Then I met you and couldn't pretend anymore.

You are the stuff dreams are made of.

I'm seeing a therapist. If you're going to read any further, you need to know that, too. I want to be the kind of person you can commit to, and I want to believe that I'm the kind of person someone finds worthy of their time. It's the latter part that's hard for me. Especially because, in a desperate attempt to demonstrate that my divorce didn't hurt, I tried to prove that my ex-wife was right about me.

Stupid. Stupid. Stupid.

When you said that I never stopped wanting kids and I never stopped wanting someone to come home to and I never stopped *wanting*, you were more right than Leah could have ever been.

No matter what happens, I choose to believe you.

The next step is yours. Send me back the postcard or not, and I'll know what to do.

Olive juice means I love you,
Caleb.

Beck picked up the postcard and read the sentences next to the three checkboxes this time.

_ Never contact me again. (Or, don't mail the postcard back. I'll understand these are the same thing.)

_ Call me as soon as you get this postcard.

_ I need more time. But you can send me another card.

She didn't have to think about it to check the third option. And Seamus got his walk, because Beck wasn't going to wait for tomorrow's post. There was a mailbox at the end of her neighborhood and the last pickup was 5:00 p.m. If she didn't let Seamus stop to pee, they would make it. And she would float the entire way there.

CALEB CALCULATED THAT his letter would take three days to get to Beck. Sure, she was a fifteen-minute drive away, but the mail in this area could be…iffy. Three days to get to her. Three days for her to get back to him—if she answered right away.

She might not answer. There was *always* the possibility that she wouldn't answer. So, he was checking the mail when he got home from work every day, like he always did. No extra anxiety or worry. Not for another couple of days, at least.

Which meant he didn't even flip through the mail when he pulled it out of the box and only noticed the postcard peeking out from between the junk because everything slid across the wood when he tossed it on his kitchen table.

He snatched up the postcard immediately, and then held his breath while he flipped it over. She'd checked box three, he saw with a sigh of relief. Not as good as box two, but he could work with box three. Box three held possibilities. He had a newfound love of possibilities. He *clung* to possibilities.

Deadline first. He couldn't claim to be a dependable, family-oriented man if he didn't do the bare minimum required to keep his job.

Plus, he needed time to think about card number two.

BECK TRIED NOT to let her hopes get the better of her when she checked her mail over the next couple of days. Caleb needed time to write her back. If he even *wanted* to write her back. Except *of course* he wanted to write her back. He had written to her in the first place. He wouldn't write to her, say that he had messed up and then change his mind. Caleb had always been honest with her.

This back and forth wasn't about deciding if she could trust him, because she knew she could trust him. This was about deciding if she still *wanted* him.

Hell, who was she kidding? Of course she still wanted him. She was trying to figure out if she could trust herself and what she wanted. Faith—it was nearly as bad as hope and definitely as scary.

"You should make him work for it." She could practically hear Marsie's advice echoing through the house.

Today's mail held another letter. She bit her lip as she stood in her driveway, flipping the letter over and back and over and back, trying to figure out if there was another postcard in it or if he'd included something else for her. The envelope had two stamps, so there was more than a greeting card in there.

Like she had with the previous letter, she left

it on the table while she took care of Seamus. This time, she took Seamus for his full walk before sitting down with her letter and her glass of wine. She had plans to *savor* the letter.

She spent the entire walk thinking about the letter and what could be in it. She couldn't have predicted the first letter, so predicting what could be in a second seemed like a fool's errand. Seamus walked quickly, probably because Beck was eager to get home and he could sense her impatience. Of course, she rewarded him with a rawhide, so he had a pretty good incentive to be a good dog.

Once back at home, she curled up in her favorite spot on her couch and opened the letter. Again, a postcard fell out, which she put aside. Inside the card was also a letter.

Dear Beck,
Yippee!

That's the bulk of what I have to say. I messed up and I have another chance, so thank you. The problem with having such short check marks is that I don't know what you want from me.

I don't know what I want from you, she thought. Proof. But what did she need proof of? Proof that he loved her? Proof that he wasn't messing with her? Proof that she could trust him? Proof that they wanted the same things out of each other and that they were both willing to work for them?

She took a sip of her wine and set the letter down in her lap while she watched Seamus and thought about what she wanted. *Caleb.* She wanted Caleb. She wanted his smiles and his long, lean romantic looks. She wanted his sense of humor, his constant barrage of questions and his charm. His commitment to the things he cared about and the sacrifices he would make to get them.

No more complicated than wanting everything he had to offer.

I put the third check mark on there so that you could express interest, but also a need for more time. Since that's the one you chose, I guess I have to assume that's how you understood it, too. But what to tell you while you're taking that time?

I mentioned that I'm seeing a therapist. It's really helping. Going into a room once a week and telling someone your secrets and having that person's entire goal be to help you work through it—well, it's pretty awesome. I'm a great reporter. I do good in this world. But I never realized how afraid I was to have another person tell me that my *doing good* wasn't enough, because it didn't make money or because it wasn't stable. That I wasn't going to be enough for them.

Stupid me, confusing you with my ex-wife. Stupid me, confusing you with my father. Stupid me, confusing any woman with those people when I needed to take them at face value, especially since I wanted to be taken at face value.

The thing the therapist has taught me that really blows my mind is that it's not that you needed to trust me, but that I needed to trust you. See, for you to trust me, I needed to be trustworthy—and I think I was, as far as our agreement went. But you could be as honest as a summer day is long and unless I noticed and *relied on you*, I would always feel like I was coming up short.

Trust. It's a scary thing. And so strange. Blind, wobbly and solid as a rock—all at the same time.

I'm rambling. I don't know what you need from me and so I'm rambling, hoping that I'll find it.

Have I found it yet?

She smiled at that one. He paid so close attention to the world around him, always looking to see who was there, to see what expressions they were making and to understand how those expressions influenced what they were saying. And here he was, writing blind.

It wasn't like when he wrote for the paper—when his audience was this amorphous thing that he'd come to understand over the course of a decade. He was writing to her, and if they were in the same room, he would be searching her face for information, attending to every change in her tone of voice and backing off or going forward accordingly.

This letter, for all its remoteness, made him more vulnerable. He couldn't adjust what he wanted to say. He just had to say it.

As though he was leaping off a dark cliff and hoping she was there to catch him.

She turned the page over.

I guess I'm back—stuck—at needing to trust you. At taking my heart and my fears and putting them, quite literally, in your hand. The newsroom is a gossipy, judgmental place. We're all hardened reporters with no space in our lives for fear or vulnerability. The legislative building is worse. Anything that smacks of weakness needs to be swallowed.

It shouldn't surprise me that consuming so much bad emotion made me sick to my stomach.

I'm not hoping you'll make me well—that's my job. But I am hoping you'll stand next to me while I make myself well. I'm mostly there. The therapist says I'm not as broken as I think I am. She says—and this part is funny—that letting my fears get so big helped me cover up the fact that I wasn't trying to conquer them.

Does any of this help?

I'm a reporter and I would like to see confirmation before I believed something as radical as the political reporter went to the therapist. So, I'm including a printout of my visits. I trust you. Hopefully this will help you verify that you can trust me.

Love,

Caleb

She put the letter down and picked up the other piece of paper. Caleb hadn't been joking. While she hadn't needed to see it, he had included a printout of his visits to the therapist's office. Four weeks since they had broken up. Four visits.

She set the printout next to the letter on the table and picked up the postcard. Again, three options.

_ Don't contact me again.

_ Call me. <——In case it's not clear, this is the one I want you to pick. :-)

_ Send me another letter.

Knowing which to choose wasn't as easy this time. Like Caleb, she wanted door number two. But the *wanting* of it scared her. Everything seemed too perfect. She had wanted him to change. And he'd changed. She'd neither asked him to change, nor had she waited around for him to change. She'd taken care of herself and her own needs, like the world said she was supposed to and…

And the world was rewarding her for it. She should start doing other things the *theys* of the world told her to do, like meditate and eat more vegetables and volunteer. The latter was the most interesting of the sets of good advice. Take care of herself and take care of others. Those two went together like a matched set. Buy one and buy them both.

Believe in Caleb and believe in herself at the same time.

She could do this.

But she needed time to think about it and make sure Murphy or his law wasn't waiting in the sidelines somewhere, with a rock. She took a sip of her wine and read the letter again, paying special attention to the different twitches and the tightness in her belly. The wounds of the breakup were still fresh, but a long investigation showed that the trepidation tapping at her gut was more hope than fear.

Riding that hope and needing to talk to him in person, she checked the second box, and then she read the letter again while finishing her glass of wine and—having already missed the pickup at the mailbox at the end of her neighborhood—set the postcard by her purse to put in the mail tomorrow.

AFTER NEARLY MISSING the postcard in the mail the last time, Caleb had started flipping through each piece of mail as soon as he grabbed it from the box, so any neighbors watching saw him punch his fist into the air and hop when the postcard came back, box two checked. He didn't even wait until he was inside to call.

"Hello?" Beck asked from the other end of

the line. She sounded nervous. Of course she sounded nervous. He was nervous and she had as much reason to be nervous as he did. More, probably. After all, he was the one who'd insisted that *they* couldn't happen.

"Hello," he said and then cleared his throat. "I'm so glad you checked the second box. I've missed the sound of your voice."

"Oh." He could hear the smile in her voice. "I've missed the sound of your voice, too."

He sat on the step in front of his town house, not wanting to make any movements or sounds—even opening his front door—that might jinx the call. "We should talk."

"Yes. Talking would be good."

Caleb took his first risk that Beck understood his job, his work, and wouldn't punish him for it, trusting her. "My story deadline is seven. Can I come over after I turn the copy in? Maybe take me thirty minutes to finish. I'll text you when I'm on my way."

"Okay. I can make dinner. What do you want?"

"You," he said before he thought about how cheesy that sounded. "And to talk. I don't care what we eat. I just miss you, and I have a lot of explaining to do and apologies to make."

To his surprise, she replied, "Not so many. Your letters did fine."

"See you in an hour?"

"Yes."

"Beck," he said, before she could hang up. "I love you."

"Oh."

"I put it in the letters, I know, but…I wanted to say it out loud. I have hopes for coming over, but not expectations and, if the night doesn't go the way that I hope, I wanted to make sure I said it out loud to you, once."

"Thank you. I'll see you soon." Maybe he was reading too much into her voice—he was probably reading too much into her voice—but he thought she sounded *more* pleased as they were hanging up than she had when she had answered the phone.

Bond, James Bond attacked his feet as soon as he stepped through the door, batting at his laces and grabbing onto his ankles with all four claws, hitching a ride as Caleb walked through his house to his office. The poor cat—if life went the way Caleb hoped, he wouldn't be home again tonight and Bond, James Bond got lonely.

Hoping Beck would understand, Caleb gave himself ten minutes to play with his kitten. Then he rushed through finishing his copy, turned it in, grabbed his toothbrush, made sure the cat had food and headed out the door.

He held on to that toothbrush almost like it was hope itself.

CHAPTER TWENTY-SIX

BECK HAD OPENED her front door to Caleb many times over the course of their month together. She'd opened with him standing behind her, excited to have a man coming home with her, excited that it was this man and nervous about how things would go. She'd opened the door with a smile and joy in her heart, no rumbles of nerves in her belly, because it was Caleb and whatever happened on that date with Caleb would be good. And she'd opened this door with doom in her belly, because she'd known she was going to send him home and end their relationship and she'd known it was the right thing to do and she'd known she'd be okay.

And it had still felt awful.

Today, though, she opened the door and gave him the same lingering look that she'd given him on their first date. She took in the long, lean lines of his body and the dark shadow of scruff on his face. She examined his shockingly light eyes and considered how his hair would feel between her fingers. She was trying to memorize him, she realized. To have a version of Caleb she could keep with her always.

Fear wasn't behind her examination. No anxiety or nerves, either. Just the sharp twinge of hope that her future was standing on her front stoop and all she had to do was step aside.

"Like what you see?" he asked with a cheeky grin.

"I do." She stepped aside. "And I like you more when you're inside my house, instead of outside my house."

"Well, then." He took a giant leap inside, to be greeted by an overly excited dog who had just woken up to a surprise visitor.

Caleb had been happy to see her, Beck knew, but he practically beamed as he knelt on the floor and was adored by her dog.

"You know, he isn't usually that excited when *I* show up," she said wryly.

"Well, that's probably because I've been in the doghouse. I'm new and interesting." He looked up at her, grin overwhelmed by at least a couple of licks of dog slobber. Then he realized what he said and sobered up. "At least, I hope I'm interesting. And I hope that's good."

"It's good."

He took ahold of her outstretched hand and pulled himself up. "I should go get clean before we talk. I, uh, have hopes that I'll get better kisses before the night is over." She opened her mouth, not to object so much—because she had those hopes, too—but to caution against anything too solid happening tonight. A caution for herself, as much as for him.

Seeing him reminded her that the hurt was still tender.

But, before she could say anything, he wiped invisible dog hair off his jeans. "Not saying I expect anything, but hopes, you know…"

"They are killer," she finished for him.

"You can ride them like a wave and crash just as fast. It's everything I ever imagined surfing to be."

"Complete with sharks."

"Great white ones," he echoed. He was standing, but he hadn't yet dropped her hand and she wasn't about to drop his. Not until she had to.

She gestured her head to the kitchen, still not entirely sure how this night would play out, only that she wanted the action to get underway. "Dinner is broiled salmon, green beans and roasted potatoes."

"Sounds great."

They stood there for several long seconds, still holding hands and each of them clearly wondering how to move the night forward without letting go when Caleb shrugged. "Okay. Washing up for dinner."

"Yeah," she said, watching their hands as his fingers trailed out of hers and he disappeared into the powder room. Not quite willing to stare at the bathroom door like Seamus did to her—though the impulse to confirm that he was actually in there and would actually be coming out was high—she went to the kitchen to plate their dinner.

She was putting the last of the food on the plates when he stepped out of the bathroom, uncertainty clouding his face as surely as nerves were clouding her mind. "What now?" they said in unison.

"I guess we talk," she said. The problem was that she didn't want to talk. He was here. She wanted them to kiss and make up, even though she knew there was a middle step.

He closed the distance between the powder room and the kitchen with confident strides and grabbed the two plates. "We can talk while we eat. And we'll probably both need the glasses of wine."

"Yeah," she said, relaxing into his confidence. They would be okay. All her nerves and all his uncertainty and all their past mismatched wants and desires—they could work them all out. They both wanted to, and that put them halfway there.

Once were seated, food and wine in

front of them, Caleb snapped his napkin onto his lap and grabbed his fork before looking her directly in the eye. "What do you want to know?"

"Me?"

"I'm here to answer your questions, so that you know I'm on the up-and-up."

She pushed one of her green beans to the side, and then moved another to go alongside it. "Your letter said that none of this was about me trusting you, but about you trusting me. So, why am I asking the questions?"

"Because I've decided to trust you. No," he said as she sucked her breath in at the coldness of the word *decided.* "It's not like picking out a sandwich. You say what you mean, so I never have to wonder if you're telling me something you think I want to hear, but that—ultimately—you won't follow through on. I don't have to *decide* on that straightforwardness. I can see it with my own eyes like I can see the sky is blue and know that Bond, James Bond is a pain in the ass.

"But for a month, I told you how I wanted to live my life as a fancy-free man about town. And now I'm willing—no—*wanting* to get married. To have kids. I imagine that you need to know that I'm for real."

She stacked another green bean in the line.

God, she wanted to believe. She wanted to believe so badly. But she'd wanted to believe before. While those hurts had faded, the fear of them hadn't.

Then, in a flash, she knew she could believe. He, too, had been hurt. He, too, remembered what it was to feel like his dreams were out of reach. He, too, had a past that created divots in his confidence, and he, too, had fought to overcome them.

Only, he was braver than she was, because he was looking at her with confidence, his face open and easy, his shoulders back, and he wasn't pushing his food around his plate like a child. He was here and he wanted her to challenge him. He wanted to prove to her that he was worthy of her love and affection.

Even if she didn't think he needed to, *he* needed to. And she wanted to give him what he needed. So she stabbed a green bean and said, "You went from being married and wanting to have kids to being divorced and certain they weren't for you. What happened in the middle?" Then she shoved the green bean in her mouth. No more playing around. They were grown-ups and they were going to work this out.

She could see that she had been right to push him when he seemed to relax. "The past month has been…strange. Therapy, which still seems like an odd thing for me to do, even if it's nice to have someone else to talk to and to correct strange ways of thinking. Working. I don't know if you saw, but the General Assembly passed a law changing the way judges are voted for. There were protests. The Governor is going to veto it, but that was all anyone could talk about in the meantime."

Where is he going with this? She nodded, not wanting to press him. He had his own journey to take and she needed to let him take it.

"There was something about the mess of it all, the mess of the General Assembly and their grab to get everything they want that got me thinking about how we try to have everything. I had wanted Leah. And I had wanted kids. When I couldn't have Leah and kids, I confused that with not being able to have either."

She nodded, pushing a bit of salmon around her plate. "You said something similar in your letter."

"Did I?" He cocked his head at her, a slight smile on his face, looking like a mischievous child, and she had a flash of insight about what a son of his would look like. "I keep thinking that's a new revelation, but maybe it's been in the back of my head the entire time."

He speared a roasted potato and added a bit

of salmon to his fork, and then appeared to be deep in thought while he chewed. Once he swallowed, he started talking again. "Well, I don't know how much of all of this I said, but I'll finish my thought. Maybe I'll have a new idea and, if not, you'll be nice enough to pretend." He said the last bit with the same smile, so she knew there wasn't anything mean underlying his words.

"Of course," she said, inclining her head and smiling in response.

"So, I know I said I was stupid in my letters. Because I was. Here I was, thinking I couldn't have both kids and Leah and so I didn't want either. And I was flying through life on those thoughts and then you came along. A woman I wanted. A woman I wanted who was clear about wanting kids and a family and all the dreams I'd once had. And I was holding on to my fears so tightly that I almost missed the possibilities."

His smile faded from his face, replaced with something sad and almost fearful. "Beck, you're everything I ever wanted and I was too caught up in myself to see it. I almost let you go without a fight. Knowing you, being with you, then sinking back into the nights out with different women who are lovely distractions, but nothing more…"

He shook his head. "That would have been the tragedy of my life. And I was so close to letting that happen. To have held perfection in a bowl and been so afraid of it that I almost dumped it out."

"I'm not perfection," she said, worried about what his high hopes might mean for the reality of their relationship.

"You probably squeeze the toothpaste from the middle and I'm sure you'll complain about how late I work sometimes, because I do. But the goal will always be for us to be working toward something together."

His fork clinked against his plate as he set it on the table and then he reached his hand across, palm up, the way he had done on their first date. And as she had done back at the bar, she slipped her hand into his. How nicely her hand fit in his continued to surprise her.

"It's that working together that will be perfection, though I'm sure a bumpy sort of it." He squeezed her hand. "I love you, Beck."

"I love you, too."

"What do we do now?" he asked.

"I guess we finish eating. Then we date a little bit longer. Then we see about getting married and having those kids we talked about."

All the tension in him seemed to flow out

in a whoosh, all at once. "That's perfection, right there."

This time, Beck was the one to hold out her hand for Caleb to grab onto. And, when he slipped his fingers into hers, she wasn't worried about him letting go.

* * * * *

Get 4 FREE REWARDS!

We'll send you 2 FREE Books plus 2 FREE Mystery Gifts.

FREE
Value Over
$20

Both the **Romance** and **Suspense** collections feature compelling novels written by many of today's best-selling authors.

YES! Please send me 2 FREE novels from the Essential Romance or Essential Suspense Collection and my 2 FREE gifts (gifts are worth about $10 retail). After receiving them, if I don't wish to receive any more books, I can return the shipping statement marked "cancel." If I don't cancel, I will receive 4 brand-new novels every month and be billed just $6.74 each in the U.S. or $7.24 each in Canada. That's a savings of at least 16% off the cover price. It's quite a bargain! Shipping and handling is just 50¢ per book in the U.S. and 75¢ per book in Canada*. I understand that accepting the 2 free books and gifts places me under no obligation to buy anything. I can always return a shipment and cancel at any time. The free books and gifts are mine to keep no matter what I decide.

Choose one: ☐ **Essential Romance**
(194/394 MDN GMY7)

☐ **Essential Suspense**
(191/391 MDN GMY7)

Name (please print)

Address   Apt. #

City   State/Province   Zip/Postal Code

Mail to the **Reader Service:**
IN U.S.A.: P.O. Box 1341, Buffalo, NY 14240-8531
IN CANADA: P.O. Box 603, Fort Erie, Ontario L2A 5X3

Want to try two free books from another series! Call 1-800-873-8635 or visit www.ReaderService.com.

---

*Terms and prices subject to change without notice. Prices do not include applicable taxes. Sales tax applicable in NY. Canadian residents will be charged applicable taxes. Offer not valid in Quebec. This offer is limited to one order per household. Books received may not be as shown. Not valid for current subscribers to the Essential Romance or Essential Suspense Collection. All orders subject to approval. Credit or debit balances in a customer's account(s) may be offset by any other outstanding balance owed by or to the customer. Please allow 4 to 6 weeks for delivery. Offer available while quantities last.

Your Privacy—The Reader Service is committed to protecting your privacy. Our Privacy Policy is available online at www.ReaderService.com or upon request from the Reader Service. We make a portion of our mailing list available to reputable third parties that offer products we believe may interest you. If you prefer that we not exchange your name with third parties, or if you wish to clarify or modify your communication preferences, please visit us at www.ReaderService.com/consumerschoice or write to us at Reader Service Preference Service, P.O. Box 9062, Buffalo, NY 14240-9062. Include your complete name and address.

STRS18